RESCUE MAN

A Deadly Rescue

CHARLES M. DUPUY

Copyright © 2022 Charles M. DuPuy

This is a work of fiction. Names, characters, places, and incidents either are the product of the author's imagination or are used fictitiously. Any resemblance to actual persons, living or dead, events, or locales is entirely coincidental.

Cover Design: Teddi Black
Interior Design: Megan McCullough

This novel is dedicated to all the men and women who went willingly into battle and were rewarded with the horrors of post-traumatic stress disorder (PTSD). It has been called by many names in many wars. In our Civil War it was called 'insanity' and 'melancholia." In World War One it drew the label "shell shock." In World War Two it became known as "battle fatigue." Now the world knows the affliction as PTSD. There is no easy resolution from it. Many suffer miserably for the remainder of their lives.

Prologue

THE TEN-MAN TEAM I'd been part of for the past two years were all seasoned veterans. We worked well together. We had each other's backs every night we went out to search old Baghdad for arms caches and contraband, and all ten of us returned to base under our own steam, night after night.

We were a polyglot team, made up of Italian, Polack, Russian, Hispanic, Irish, and what I call Heinz 57 varieties. I fit that category. My mother is Japanese, and my dad is Heinz 57, so I guess I'm half Japanese. I ended up at six-foot four and two hundred and forty pounds, thanks to the genes from both sides. I towered over Mike, our leader, and everyone else on the team.

As part of the U. S. Army in occupied Iraq, our mission was to act on tips from intelligence and informants. Word would come down that there were weapons hidden in identified buildings throughout Baghdad, usually in personal residences. Armed with the information, my team would head out at dark thirty on foot to the building, smash down the door and rush inside, catching the unsuspecting occupants flat-footed. Two-thirds of the intel tips were valid and a third were bogus. If we hit a bogus one, our leader had a bagful of Iraqi dinar to give the unhappy owner to pay for a new door, and then we moved on to the next one.

Maybe we'd become too casual, too confident in our breaches of the buildings we entered. I don't know. I do know that everything changed on November thirteenth. It was a mission like hundreds we'd gone on before, so we may have been on autopilot. When we blew open the door and rushed inside, we were met with a fusillade of AK47 fire that changed my life forever.

One

THREE YEARS EARLIER

I WAS HANDED my bachelor's degree in Life Studies from the University of Southern Aurora in May of 2003 and struck out to find my niche, charged by four years of academic promises. After three months of searching, I'd struck out. Nobody was hiring a college grad with a degree in Life Studies. What was I to do? The news channels filled my forebrain with the incredible military successes in Iraq since the 2003 invasion so, both young and foolish, I chose to offer my services to the army for the next two years. I figured it would give me time to think about my future while I played peacekeeper to the struggling Iraqi people.

The army welcomed me into its ranks and whipped my already lean and mean body into a fighting machine. I'd minored in football and lacrosse at Aurora, so I had a leg up on most of my fellow recruits. My drill instructor saw my potential and recommended me for the military's advanced studies program. In a little more than six months I could shoot the eye out of a weasel at a hundred yards, I could speak Arabic fluently, (I have a special gift I'll explain later) and I'd mastered more than twenty ways to kill an enemy combatant with my bare hands. I couldn't help thinking it was all a waste of time since I would be charged with keeping the peace in Iraq.

The transport plane carrying me, and my elite group of greenhorn soldiers landed in Baghdad on September 4, 2004, in the dead of night. I got my first inkling of what lay ahead when I spotted three separate explosive flashes in the city below. I could tell they weren't fireworks celebrations. Not for the last time I asked myself what the hell I'd gotten myself into.

The plane landed and taxied, and we filed out through the rear ramp, our gear weighing us down as we hiked to a nearby building. Our new commander eyed us critically as we entered. Once all of us were inside he yelled *Sit!* Widely spaced chairs faced the front where he stood, allowing us to set our gear down to the side before plopping our butts down on a chair.

I won't go over his entire welcoming speech, but one part of it still stands out in my mind. He said, "If you came here under the illusion that the fighting is all over and you're here to keep the peace, you've got your head up your ass! This is a fuckin' war zone and good men are dying every day. If you want to go home vertically instead of horizontally, you'd better be ready to kick ass and take names." I got a mind picture of a metal coffin draped with Old Glory, me in it. A hell of a welcome to old Baghdad.

The next day was designated as orientation. We learned how to get to the mess hall from our barracks. We also got a tour of the supply depot where we could replenish ammo and ordnance when needed. Last of all was a walkthrough of the transport depot where the trucks and Humvees were repaired and readied for the next foray. We missed a visit to sick bay and the hospital. No doubt they figured we'd find it if we needed it.

That afternoon found us back in the same building they'd used as a welcome center the night before. It was there that our assignments were doled out to us. I learned that I would be joining a search team. My first thought: if a soldier got lost, we'd go find him.

Not even close, it turned out.

With my gear bags hanging off me, I was driven by Jeep to another military facility on base. The gunny sergeant in charge eyed me critically as I climbed from the Jeep and strode towards him, my packs slapping time on my thighs. I managed to free my right hand and toss off a salute at him.

"Cut that shit out!" he hollered at me, his face going crimson. "You trying to get my ass killed?"

The puzzled expression on my face must've given me away. I hadn't a clue what he was screaming about.

"Look around, jarhead! You see all the Iraqis? One in five is an infiltrator. They see you saluting me, they know I'm a leader and they'll come gunning for me. Get it?"

"Got it, Sarge."

"And don't for Christ's sake call me sarge! My name is Mike! Mike-Mike-Mike."

"Okay, Mike."

I had the chance to size up Mike the Sarge as he ranted. I'm six-four so I looked down on him. He was maybe five-ten with a tight, wiry build. His craggy face showed signs of near misses, with the most prominent feature a ragged scar along the right side of his face that bisected his right ear, leaving a hole big enough to stick a finger through. I guessed that a bullet creased his cheek and punctured his ear as it blew by. Or maybe he got it in a whore house fight. He'd maybe tell me which it was in good time.

"Inside, kid!" he ordered, his hand pointing the way. I turned sideways to duck through the doorway, my packs making it a challenge to get inside. Once in the relative gloom of the billeting room I saw that all the bunks were occupied, save one. I counted five double decker beds. Mike pointed to the empty double decker single and said, "You're on top." I planted my packs on the floor at the head of the bed and rolled my shoulders to shake off the tightness, now relieved of their burden.

I turned to face Mike and said, "My name is—"

He cut me off by saying, "I can see the name tag on your shirt, Roberts. If you're still alive at the end of the week, I'll ask you for your first name. Saves me a lot of trouble, remembering, when it can be a waste of my time. What's your specialty?" he asked, his eyes assessing me.

"I'm a sniper, sir," I said.

"Cut that shit out! It's not sir, it's not sarge, it's Mike! Mike-Mike-Mike! Don't fuckin' forget it!"

"I got it, Mike," I said, chastened.

"I don't know what good your sniper skills will be when we're doing mostly close-up combat shit," said Mike.

"I can shoot accurately at 400 yards, or I can shoot straight at four yards. It's all the same to me," I said.

"You ever killed someone?" he challenged me. His thick eyebrows lifted with the question.

"Not that I know of," I said.

"What've you killed that you *do* know about?"

"Deer, moose, elk, coyotes."

"Animals. Want my advice? Until you get used to it, picture the enemy facing you as an animal. Once you've taken out a half dozen of them you can picture them as the ragheads they are."

"Thanks for the tip, Mike. Makes sense."

"That's if you make it to that point, Roberts."

"So, tell me, Mike. What do we do as a search team?" I clung to the image of going out to find lost GIs.

Mike stared at me a moment. "You don't have a fuckin' clue, do you? I can see it in your eyes. You don't have a fuckin' clue!

"Search, as in search and rescue?" I said, hoping I was getting warm.

"You got search right but forget the rescue part. We get tips, go out at night and raid houses looking for bad guys and arms caches," recited Mike.

"And then we get the daytime to do what we want?"

"Yeah. After you've washed up, changed clothes, and grabbed some sleep, the rest of the day's all yours. Then we're out the gate the next night and do it all over again," said Mike, a sarcastic smirk taking over his thin face.

I had a looksee around in the gloom of the billet area. Tight quarters. Eight soldiers stretched out and sleeping, undisturbed by our loud talking. I peered at my watch face. Four-twenty. Late afternoon. I guessed that the team, my team now, had had a rough night of it and were sleeping in.

"Are we going out tonight, Mike?" I asked, wondering what the schedule might be.

"We go out every night we get leads handed to us. Last time we had a night off was like six weeks ago," said Mike, a grim expression on his face. I thought maybe I was seeing the real Mike.

"When'll we be heading out?" I asked, speaking in a low voice so I wouldn't wake up the sleeping men.

"We hit the chow line at six and then come back here to gear up. We head out at dark-thirty, and this time of year that's around nine. We go on foot so's not to alert our targets with engine noise. If our point man spots a lookout, we take him out. We try to get a man to circle behind him and cut his throat, but if the raghead's keyed, wired, we settle for a suppressed round to the head. It makes a little more noise, what with the rifle action working, but sometimes we have no choice," said Mike, all matter of fact.

"What do you see me doing?" I asked, trying to get a picture of how I fit in with this murderous crew.

"When we head out tonight, you'll be our six, take up the rear. It'll give you a chance to see how things are done, and maybe come back to base without bullet holes or grenade frags in you. On the job training at its best," Mike added, his eyes watchful for a reaction from me.

"You don't expect me to do any shooting, right?" I asked.

"Someone comes at you in your rear position, you'd better fuckin' shoot or you're going back to base horizontal, not vertical. Just so you know, the team hates like hell to have to carry someone back," Mike added with a sweep of his arm at the sleeping men.

"I get it," I said, thinking how far off I was, picturing my new job as search and rescue.

"Right now, you've got time to get settled, square your gear. There's an empty footlocker at the end of your bunk. Consider it yours. The team will be waking up soon, and you'll have time for intros before we head to mess at six," said Mike.

"I'm on it," I told Mike. He made his way to the only empty lower bunk, his home away from home, while I headed for mine. My sky view box.

A green canvas rig with pockets in it, tucked under the mattress and hanging down a foot or so, is a place to stow frequently used gear like razors, toothbrushes, that sort of stuff. I busied myself by tucking my own gear in it. As I did so, I wondered how many different sets of toothbrushes had been there before mine. Mike made it sound like I'd be lucky to make it to the end of the week.

I finished getting all my gear in order when the first team member showed signs of life. He groaned, stretched his arms, and swung his legs over the side of his bunk, then rubbed his face. His eyes swept the room and locked on me. His bushy eyebrows lifted with the sight of me. "Sonofabitch, will you look at that? Pete's been gone a little over twenty-four hours and we already got his replacement," he said. His voice loud, meant to reach the others.

That caused several more sleeping team members to come around. Faces were turned my way. I felt a little like a puppy in a store window. I watched as faces were rubbed, beards scratched, and an increasing number of eyes passed over me, assessing me. Not knowing what I should say, I kept my mouth shut.

Mike came to my rescue, sort of. "This here is our new team member, last name Roberts. He tells me he can shoot so I guess we'll let him carry a gun."

A ripple of laughter rolled through the room as the rest of the team regained consciousness, sat up and turned to face me. "Like Mike said, my name's Roberts. He told me he'd ask me what my first name is if I'm still vertical at the end of the week," I said by way of testing the water.

Easy laughter rolled through the group. I figured it wasn't the first time Mike had made that announcement to new recruits. Then a surprising thing happened. The men stood as one, formed a line and shuffled over to me. One by one they shook my hand, gave me a hug, and told me their names. All eight of them. When the last man got done, the first man, Leo Martinez said, "Okay, Roberts. Do you remember any of our names?" A broad smile played across his swarthy face as he questioned me.

"You want them in the order you each spoke to me, or in alphabetical order?" I asked Leo. I could tell by expressions the men were having fun with me, waiting for me to stumble, stammer and fail.

"Hey, take us in order," said Leo, thinking he was making my work harder.

"Okay, here you go," I said. First to greet me was you, Leo Martinez. Second was Harry Hudson. Then came Bob Harrington, followed by Victor Bono, then Chip O'Neal. Next in line was Donnie Stankovic, followed by Vlad Mir, and at the end was Marty Passionata. Nice meeting you all," I said, finishing up.

Stunned silence filled the room for a good thirty seconds. Finally, Mike broke the silence. "How the fuck did you do that, Roberts?" I glanced around at the faces turned my way. Surprised expressions dominated.

"Simple. I concentrated," I said. Then I thought I'd better start off on the right foot, so I explained that I had one of those memories that allowed me to remember everything that ever happened to me. "They call it eidetic," I added.

"Everything?" asked Mike.

"Yeah, for better or for worse," I said.

"I can see how it could be sweet to remember every piece of ass you ever had, but the bad stuff, you remember it, too?" asked Mike.

"That's where the fun stops. I need to put walls up in my head to block out the bad stuff. And it doesn't always work. So, if you hear me groaning, yelling out in my sleep, you'll know the walls aren't working."

"Pretty fuckin' amazing," said Mike by way of defusing the tension. "What'd you say your name was again?"

Easy laughter rolled from the men.

At ten of six we headed out, looking like a ragtag group for all to see, but I already knew otherwise. It turned out to be a ten-minute stroll to mess hall, giving me the chance to exchange short greetings with most of my new team members. At that hour the mess hall line was short, and we were inside, getting our trays loaded by ten past six. Featured meal of the night was shit on a shingle, good old creamed chipped beef on toast. If you took enough, it filled you up and stuck with you. The army had it down pat. We added sides of vegetables, plus rolls to sop up what the toast couldn't handle, ending with a dish of some dessert concoction that defied identification but had a sweet taste. Most of us took coffee, plus water to drink.

More light conversation took place while we sat and ate our meals. The man next to me, Vlad Mir, looked me over and said, "You look like you got Oriental in you. How'd you end up so tall? I thought all Orientals were squirts," he said, smiling to defuse the sarcasm in his voice.

"You're right, Vlad. My mother is Japanese She was born in Hokkaido which is the northernmost island of Japan. There are a lot of tall Japanese there, and my mom has those genes. My dad's six-two and mom's five-ten.

I ended up at six-four. Mom tells me there are guys even taller than that back in Hokkaido. Must be something in the water," I said with a grin.

We finished our SOS, dropped our trays on the dishwashing chute and ambled back to our billet, enjoying the drop in temperature as the shadows lengthened. I knew we had a couple hours before sunset so there was no rush to get ready. Some of the guys wrote letters, but most sat sprawled on their bunks shooting the breeze. I got to speak to a couple more of my team members before Mike yelled, "Thirty minutes!", bringing us back to the here and now. I stripped out of my BDUs and put on my tactical clothes, which were much lighter and allowed free movement. Back on went my boots with their soft rubber soles. I wouldn't go clickety-click as I moved along the quiet streets of old Baghdad, giving us away. I checked over my plate carrier with its add-ons that held my tactical light, six 30-round mags for my M4 and my tac knife. All was in order. I shrugged into it and fastened the front straps. With my cleaned and oiled M4 lying across my bunk, I set my helmet with my night vision goggles next to it. My fingerless gloves sat inside the helmet. I was as ready as I'd ever be. I said a silent prayer that I'd come back under my own power, and then Mike was telling us to form up. For me that meant going to the end of the line.

Ten men, nine seasoned veterans and me, strolled out of our billet in a ragtag line. To the casual eye, we were off to see the town, or maybe see the Wizard if he was anywhere nearby. Once we cleared the base gate the team's movements became more purposeful and I began taking my position more seriously. My job was to watch our rear, our six if you think of a clock face, with the team moving towards twelve o'clock.

The streets we covered were well-lit at first. As we moved further into the old part of the city, the street lighting became increasingly dimmer. I watched night vision goggles being dropped into place, and I followed suit. My right eye saw everything as a pale green picture. The next time I looked back the way we'd come I spotted a man following along in our direction. He slipped along from cover to cover, clearly stalking us. When he got within fifty yards of me, my night vision goggles highlighted something shiny in his right hand. Knife. Any thoughts that he was out for an evening stroll went out the window. I added the fact that he was right-handed into my calculations.

I let him get within twenty-five yards of me before I pulled my tactical knife from its scabbard and held it close to my chest. Then it became a waiting game, with me taking quick glances at the advancing man, his intent crystal clear. I calculated his height at around five-nine and entered it into my calculations. When he was ten yards back, I heard his sneakers slapping the roadway as he charged at me. Now it was all about timing, positioning. He raced at me, and when I guessed he was a yard back, I pivoted away from the direction of his charge and held my tactical knife out where he'd be when he raced past. My calculations were dead-on, excuse the pun. He ran into my knife, or rather his neck did, and his impetus resulted in my sharp blade bisecting his trachea and his major arteries as he blew past. My dad and I had drilled on a scene like it over the years, though the sides of our hands had taken the place of a knife.

He kept running for three, four steps, amazing me with his stamina, but it was all show. My goggles showed a spray of blood from both sides of his throat, and he collapsed in ten seconds, his brain starved for the blood that no longer reached it. It occurred to me as the man collapsed on the roadway that I hadn't killed him. He'd committed suicide by running into my knife.

The team member ahead of me heard the commotion, saw what had happened through his night vision goggles, and used his comm to tell Mike. I was shaking badly when Mike reached me and surveyed the scene, adrenaline in control of my bloodstream.

"Well, lookee there, Roberts. You done good work. What'd you picture him like? A deer? An elk?"

"I took cleansing breaths, blowing off the adrenaline rush. "Guess I didn't have time to picture him anyway but as a man," I said, an adrenaline tremor in my voice.

"That's good. Your next kill will be a piece of cake."

"I didn't kill him. He committed suicide, running into my knife," I said.

Mike's laugh came out more like a bark. "I like it, Roberts. From now on I'll say the militants who fall when I shoot them are committing suicide, running into my bullets!"

Mike told a couple team members to drag the body between two houses and he picked up the man's knife. He held it out to me. "Souvenir?"

I glanced at it, shook my head, and said, "I got one that's way better than that."

Mike hurled it between the building where the body lay. It clattered against the stony ground, breaking the silence. We moved on.

The first house we breached turned out to be poor intel. We scared the hell out of a couple and their two kids, and our search came up dry. Mike gave them money for a new door and a little extra for their trouble, and we moved on.

House two started out like the first. I kept my eyes on two men sitting on a couch while my team members combed the place for contraband that included guns, ammo, and other armaments. I heard one whisper to another. "They'll never find it." Arabic. Guess they didn't think I'd understand. One of them glanced at the rug in front of the couch. Then I knew.

I yelled at them in Arabic to stand up and go over against the wall. The surprise on their faces said it all. They did as I asked. I told Victor, who'd been sharing the duty of guarding the two with me, to watch them closely as I strode towards the couch and pulled the rug aside. I spotted the trap door at once. Without the rug to cover it, it stood out like a wine stain on a bride's dress. I lifted it away and grabbed my tac light, shining it down the opening. It illuminated a basement with a dirt floor. A makeshift ladder led the way down.

"Don't fuckin' move!" I heard Victor yell at the two men as I started down the ladder, my tactical light shining the way. And what to my wondering eyes should appear, but one hell of a cache of arms and ammo. I calculated that there must've been close to fifty AK47s and more than thirty cases of ammo to feed them. Then I spotted a curious looking addition. It was a baby goat hide, the legs stitched off to make a crude bag, the neck flap folded over and closed by a skewer that may have been used to hold the goat meat to cook it, who knew? The hair was still on it. It was about the size of one of my mom's handbags that she loaded with all her stuff.

I picked it up, hefting it, and felt what seemed like pebbles shifting around inside. "My first souvenir," I thought as I crammed it behind my plate carrier. Then I called out to Vic to get guys down there. "We hit the jackpot," I shouted up at him.

The rest of that night was spent hauling all the guns and ammo from that spider hole. Mike called for an armored personnel carrier to come to the scene, cram the stuff inside and haul it all back to base. The two handcuffed men who'd made the mistake of talking too loudly in Arabic were included. They were facing some serious questioning by the intel guys on base.

It was past three in the morning when Mike announced that we'd done enough for one night and suggested that we head back to base. I heard no arguments. As we retraced our steps, Mike came up alongside of me, slapped a hand on my shoulder and said, "I'm ready for your name, Roberts."

"I thought you were going to wait till Friday, if I made it through till then," I said, looking askance at him.

"Rules are made to be broken. C'mon, Roberts. What's your first name?"

"It's Tojo. Joe for short."

"Tojo Roberts? No shit?" said Mike.

"Yeah. My mom and dad had fun naming me. Since I'm half Japanese Mom held out for a Japanese first name. Dad made sure it got shortened to Joe," I said as we worked our way back to base.

"Now that I know, I could kind of see it in your eyes. There's a hint of slanty eyes there," said Mike, smiling to defuse his bluntness. I'd heard it a thousand times before. I brushed it off.

"Welcome to the team, Joe. Looks like you'll fit in just fine," said Mike.

"Yeah, if I make it to Friday," I tossed back at him.

You guessed it. I did.

Two

L IFE WITH THE team was always a roller coaster ride. Some nights turned up nothing while other nights turned up a whole row of lucky sevens on the one arm bandit. Jackpot. We lived for the jackpot nights but loved the nothing nights more when we returned to base unscathed.

I came upon my second baby goat pouch around six months into my tour. I'd tossed the first one into my footlocker and forgot about it. Seemed like there were other things occupying my time. When I found the second one under a pile of AK47s I thought back on the first one. The second one felt the same: a goat skin full of pebbles. Nobody saw me stuff it behind my plate carrier. I wondered what kind of souvenir I'd collected.

Back at our billet I tucked it in the bottom of my footlocker next to the first one. Resting there together they looked eerily similar. Maybe they were made by the same baby goat skinner. Who knew? I shut the locker top, stripped, climbed into my bunk, and promptly forgot about them as blessed sleep carried me off.

I was within days of the end of my one-year tour of duty when I got called into the commander's office and was told I was being transferred to the Second Battalion, 325th Infantry Regiment. They were recruiting snipers for an operation in northwest Iraq, and a review of my dossier showed that I had the right stuff for the job. You don't argue with commanding officers, so I packed my gear, including my Barrett 50 caliber rifle and scope, was introduced to Patrick O'Neal my assigned spotter, and joined the mechanized column headed northeast for a city called Tal Afar. On the way I learned that Patrick was available because the sniper he worked with took a round. I hoped bad luck didn't run with Patrick.

We were told that Tal Afar had been overrun by Al Qaeda in Iraq and we were going to kick them the hell out. It all sounded like a walk in the park. Reality turned out to be different.

The fighting in Tal Afar started on September first, 2005, and ended on September 18th, with Al Qaeda forces dead or on the run. My spotter Patrick and I set up shop in building windows or rooftops all over the city in the next two weeks and I managed to punch unrepairable holes in scores of Al Qaeda bad guys. My spotter and I both lived to fight another day. Oh, and I came across another one of those baby goat skin pouches, only this one was heavier than the others. I estimated that it weighed close to twenty-five pounds as I tucked it behind my plate carrier and went about the business at hand. I now had three custom made goat skin bags, contents unknown. How cool is that? Tojo the goat bag man.

The 325th thanked me for joining the fight at Tal Afar and released me back to my search team. I said farewell to my new buddy Patrick and wished him well. Back at my billet, Mike met me at the door with a letter in his hand. "Sounds like you done good, Tojo. Nice note from 325th saying you did your part in, ah, 'Operation restoring rights against Al Qaeda in Iraq.' No mention of any medals, though," he said with a shake of the letter in his hand.

"Medals? Who needs medals? Another way to remind me of the shit I dished out. I'll struggle to forget about it for a long time, maybe for the rest of my life. If you write them back, tell them thanks for not giving me a medal, you hear?" I realized I'd raised my voice.

"Got it, Joe. I see your point," said Mike, chastened.

I hurried to lighten the atmosphere between us. "It was a major change of pace, going up there and kicking Al Qaeda's ass, but it's good to be back here with the team," I said.

"Glad you're back in one piece, Joe. I know the team missed you."

I figured that was as close as I'd come to a compliment from Mike.

My tour was officially up, having served a year in a war zone, but when I thought about going stateside, I realized I still hadn't made any decisions about my future. I'd joined up thinking that the time in the army would give me the chance to figure out what I wanted to do with the rest of my life, but I wasn't any closer to a decision than I was two years ago. In a way that made it easier to stay on. I'd grown close to the team members and going out every night had become part of me. It was like pulling the handle on that old slot machine. You never knew what was going to show up. Kept us on our toes.

The night of November thirteenth changed all that. It wasn't Friday the thirteenth, but it might as well have been. We blew open the door to a house and rushed into a shitstorm. Half a dozen armed Iraqi militants waited until we'd all cleared the entrance before laying down murderous fire that cut through us. I hit the deck as soon as I saw what was happening, but not before a round struck me in my left upper arm. I could still shoot, and shoot I did, emptying two mags at the militants.

The militants must've thought that they'd hit us so fast that we wouldn't be able to shoot back. They stood there firing their AK47s into us, giving me and at least one other team member easy targets to shoot at. When the last militant fell, silence returned. My ears were ringing, and my lungs were full of the stink of cordite and the copper stink of blood. Anyone says blood doesn't stink never went through something like that.

I slowly climbed to my feet and glanced around the big room at the chaos. My first thought was to make sure all the militants were dead, not faking it until they had a chance to shoot some more. With a fresh mag in my M4 I inched my way forward, my eyes searching for movement amongst the downed militants. I erred on the side of caution, putting a bullet into every one of them that didn't display a gaping head wound. One of them twitched and went still after my shot.

Satisfied that the threat was over, I turned back to assess my team members. The horror before me will haunt me for the rest of my life. Six of my team members had taken rounds to their heads. There was no saving them. Mike was gone, his blank eyes staring up at me. Harry took one through his left eye. Victor had a round enter his mouth and sever his spine. Chip was missing the top of his head, his helmet gone. Donnie took one through his neck. There was blood everywhere. Martin had a small hole in his forehead and the back of his head was missing.

Lee was bleeding from his right arm and right leg. His plate carrier saved his chest and abdomen. Bob sat with blood running down his right hand. Vlad must have been the other one of us returning fire because he took fire to his left leg but was otherwise intact. And talking. A good sign.

I used my radio to call back to base for medics and transport, and then moved among my shot-up team to confirm the deaths and tend to the wounded as best I could. My own left arm hung useless by my side, making my efforts difficult. Vlad, seeing me, dragged himself over to help. Between us we were able to stop the blood flowing from Lee and Bob. I worked on Vlad's left leg wound and he did the same on my left arm.

We'd finished when I heard two Humvees and an APC pull up outside. The cavalry had arrived. Two armed soldiers rushed through the door and quickly assessed the situation, and then medics followed behind. They moved from downed man to downed man, assessing, then focused on the four survivors.

The two lead soldiers went forward to check out the militants and found them to be beyond repair. Six of them dead. Six of my team dead. An eye for an eye.

Our dead team members were loaded into the APC and our four wounded, which included me, were helped into the Humvees. They delivered all of us to the base hospital, six to the morgue and four to the ER. Hell of a night.

Three days later, after a surgeon had put my left arm back together, I had visitors. The base commander and two escorts appeared at my bed, and he told me he was there to award me the bronze star for valor and a purple heart for the damage to my arm. I told him he could stick the medals where the sun doesn't shine. He tossed me a crisp salute, did an about face and left without another word. I didn't need medals to remind me of that nightmarish night every time I looked at them. I was sick and tired of death and dismemberment, and I was ready to put it all behind me.

Bob, Lee, Vlad, and I were sent stateside when our wounds had healed enough to tolerate the travel. They told us they were putting together a new search team and they offered me the lead position. I told them to go fuck themselves in so many words, that I had served my two years and I was applying for an honorable discharge. They reviewed my record and put up no argument. They may have figured I suffered from PTSD, considering what I went through. Maybe I did.

Three

M Y PARENTS WELCOMED me back into their home in Surprise, a short drive from Phoenix. My arm was nearly healed. My head was a different story. I've had nightmares. Hell, who hasn't? You wake up with images fading fast, you shake your head, and you go back to sleep. This new round was different. A bunch of images from Iraq started things off, and the last one was a playback of the night when six of my team were cut down. The sound of the gunfire in my dream would bring me back to Surprise, but not before I was soaked in sweat and shaking like a baby. I guess I called out in my sleep more than once. On one occasion I came out of it to find both Mom and Dad at my bedside. They stared down at me, their faces contorted with a combination of anxiety and concern. Mom sat on the side of the bed and cradled me in her arms as she rocked back and forth, her tears rolling down her plump cheeks and landing on my sweat-soaked chest. Dad looked on, his hand resting gently on Mom's shoulder, completing the connection.

"What is it, my dear sweet boy?" Mom whispered in my ear as she continued to rock me in her arms. With my eyes closed tightly, it took me back to my childhood and the times when I needed comforting for what were now insignificant problems.

I struggled to find my voice. "A bad dream," I managed to say.

"Can you tell us about it?" she whispered, including Dad with her question.

"It's like a loop tape playing over and over, every time I go to sleep. It's all about the night my team got shot up," I managed to say. "It's getting so I'm afraid to close my eyes, knowing what's waiting for me," I added.

"You need help, Son." Dad, getting right to the point.

"Yes, sweet Tojo. Your dad is right," Mom murmured in my ear.

I sat up. "Who can help me?" I asked them, thinking I already knew.

The V.A. Hospital, Son. Surely they know how to deal with the pain you are going through." Dad again.

Mom got to her feet. "I'll go and call them for you, Tojo." She enjoyed using my full first name.

My appointment at the Phoenix V.A. Hospital was a week away. A week of night sweats, loop tape replays of that awful night so far away in Iraq, nights when I feared falling asleep, knowing what was inevitable.

I had a look in the mirror before Dad drove me to the V.A. My eyes looked like I'd stolen them from a raccoon. *The Lone Ranger rides again.* Not funny.

Dad walked with me to the reception desk and told me he'd wait for me in the coffee shop. Since it was my first visit to the V.A. hospital, I had paperwork to fill out. I found the kicker at the end of the third page: *What is the reason for your visit today?* I thought a moment, then wrote, "Insomnia."

The reception guy whose name tag said he was Walter Ocanoa scanned the three pages, and when he read the last page he looked searchingly at me, taking in the haggard expression on my face. "Are you having bad dreams?" he asked, his eyes on mine.

"No. Not bad dreams. One bad dream," I mumbled.

"Do you think it's service-connected? he asked.

There it was. The big question. If it isn't service connected, go someplace else.

I glared at him and said, "It's a replay of the night when sixty percent of my team got killed," I said.

"I'm sorry. I had to ask. It's one of those government-issue standard questions," he said, his voice apologetic.

"I get it," I replied, working to get the anger out of my voice.

"Hold on while I make a couple phone calls, okay?" he said.

"I'm not going anywhere," I said.

Walter picked up his phone and made a call. When it was answered, he turned away from me and cupped his hand over the mouthpiece, shielding me from what he said. He spoke for a minute and hung up. When he turned back to face me his face wore a bright expression. "A counselor is on his way down to meet with you," he said.

"That was fast," I said.

"He was in between patients," said Walter. He busied himself with running my papers through the copy machine to the right of his desk.

The elevator door opened soon after and a tall, lean man strode towards the reception desk, a smile leading the way. I guessed him in his early forties. He wore glasses and his brown hair was close-cropped. He radiated ex-military. As he approached, he stuck out his right hand. His fourth and fifth fingers were missing.

"You must be Joe Roberts," he said, taking what was left of his hand in mine. The grip was still there.

"Guilty," I said.

"I'm Larry Jenkins. I'm a counselor here. Let's go to my office," he said as Walter handed him copies of my papers. I followed him back to the elevator bank and up to his office. He made small talk along the way, questions about my service, blah de blah blah. I answered blah de blah blah.

When he closed his office door behind us, he said, "You look like shit, Joe. What's going on?

I told him. About Iraq. About the ambush. About the nightmare that wouldn't go away.

He nodded his head at me and asked, "You heard of PTSD, Joe?"

"Sure. Post-Traumatic Stress Disorder. Who hasn't?"

"Do you think you could have it?"

"Yeah. It's a possibility," I admitted.

"No, Joe. It isn't a possibility. It's fuckin' real, and you got it," said Larry, his eyes locked on mine.

I didn't know what to say so I kept my mouth shut.

"You want to know how I know?" he asked.

"How?"

"Because I have it, too." Larry paused, letting that sink in.

"Oh," I managed to say.

"Yeah, oh. I know you saw I'm missing fingers on my right hand. There's more you can't see. PTSD is two-faced. The side you can see and the side that's there, but you can't see. Got it?" he asked.

"Got it," I said.

"Let's talk about the nightmares you've been having."

"Nightmare," I said.

"So, it's one nightmare that keeps coming back, is that right?"

"Right. Like a loop tape playing in my head when I sleep, a replay of the night my team got shot to hell," I said.

"And when you sleep you relive that night."

"Yeah. Sometimes it comes on right away, sometimes I sleep some before it starts, but it always wakes me up and I'm soaked in sweat. No matter how many times I relive it, it seems as real as if it's happening for the first time," I told Larry.

"Yeah. PTSD is a bitch. But you know what?"

"What?"

"You can make the bad dream a bad dream. You can shove it into a container in your head and slam the door on it."

"I've done that," I said, thinking back on the times I built walls in my mind to shield me from bad memories.

"Tell me about it," Larry urged.

I told him about my eidetic memory and how I dealt with bad situations in the past by mentally creating a wall around them.

"Shit, Joe. You're halfway there already. The big difference is this situation you went through in Iraq is much bigger, nastier, harder to control than the ones you dealt with before. It's causing you constant nightmares, some people call them flashbacks, and so far, you haven't been able to get control of the situation. But I'm here to tell you, you can," said Larry, his voice going gentle at the end.

"I guess you're going to wave your magic wand over my head and make all the bad memories vanish into the ether," I said while I pulled myself upright in the armchair that I'd dropped in.

"No. There's no magic here. There's plenty of hard work for you to do but consider me along for the ride. I'll guide you, keep you on the straight and narrow as you move forward, but if you don't have the strength and the willpower there's nothing much I can do."

"Here's the deal. Guys with PTSD can go two ways. With strength and willpower, they can work their way past the flashbacks, the anxiety, the paranoia and come out the other side functioning human beings with meaningful lives. The ones who can't do that end up on drugs for the rest of their lives, or until they can get a handle on their problem. Which guy do you want to be?" he asked, his eyes boring into mine.

"When do we start?" I asked him, holding the eye contact.

"We just did."

He let that soak in a minute before he began outlining the plan that he created for me. I listened intently, not wanting to miss a single word. When he finished, he said, "Let me print off a copy of that."

"There's no need," I said.

"You think you can remember all that? Oh, yeah. That amazing memory of yours. To reassure me, tell me what Step Two is."

I recited it back to him.

"Okay. You've convinced me. Work on those things and come back to see me in a week." He took a card out of his desk and started to write on it.

"What time?" I asked him.

He raised his eyes to me, smiled and said "Ten."

"See you then," I said, returning his smile.

He dropped the card back in his desk drawer and stood, extending his three-fingered hand to me. "See you then, Joe."

I gave it a good shake, thanked him for his time, and turned to go.

"This isn't going to be easy, you know, even for you, Joe."

I turned back to Larry. "Nothing worthwhile ever is, right?"

"Good. We're on the same page. See you in a week," he said

"See you in a week."

That night I lay on my bed in the silence surrounding me and mentally constructed an elaborate concrete block enclosure, finishing with a solid concrete slab for the top. When I was satisfied, I conjured up the scenario of that terrible night in Iraq when my team got ambushed, and I forced it all inside my concrete enclosure and sealed all access to it. Satisfied with my work, I turned over and went to sleep.

I woke up three hours later, drenched in sweat, my nightmare slowly dissipating in the light of my bedside lamp. With my body shaking, I turned inward to examine my concrete enclosure and found it blasted into thousands of pieces. It reminded me of the rubble of buildings in Iraq after a missile struck them. Clearly my nightmare had won round one.

After thinking about it most of the next day, I set to work building a thick steel enclosure in my mind. The steel plates were slabs, each a full four inches thick. The top was another four-inch slab, and I mentally welded every seam on both sides. The plates on a battleship couldn't match my workmanship when I was done.

Satisfied with my construction, I once again pictured that nightmare in Iraq when six of my team were massacred and forced it all inside my steel enclosure. When I finished welding the entrance so an observer couldn't discern any access to it, I rolled onto my side and let sleep overtake me.

My nightmare, or flashback, or whatever it was made its appearance like clockwork. I woke from it as always, my T-shirt drenched with sweat, and switched on my bedside light to chase the last vestiges from the room and from my mind. Once in control again, I searched my mind for the steel container I'd so carefully and meticulously built. What I found shocked me to my roots. Not a single steel plate remained welded to its neighbor. Plates were scattered about like sheets of paper in the wind, each one displaying a bulge in its center as if an immense explosion blasted them apart. My first thought was, I'll never be able to rid myself of this nightmare, this flashback. The thought of suicide reared its ugly head.

I tossed and turned through the remainder of the night, searching my mind for a solution. As dawn was breaking, a thought came to me.

I spent the rest of that new day examining it from every angle in my mind, and ultimately decided that it was worth a try.

All my previous efforts at 'forgetting' the bad events encountered during my life involved building walls to shield them from my conscious thoughts. My active mind stood on one side and the bad memories huddled on the other side, where they made no effort to climb the wall and confront me. Until now. My Iraqi flashback had a mind of its own and no wall or enclosure I built had any effect on it. It came at me every night when I was vulnerable in sleep.

When I crawled into bed that night, I closed my eyes and began a new construction. Rather than trying to build a wall or enclosure to surround and contain my nightmare, I chose to build defenses around me, and leave the nightmare in the open area in my mind. With European castles as a reference, I built a high wall with parapets from which boiling oil could be poured down on attackers and surrounded the whole thing with a moat filled with caustic nightmare-dissolving acid. I manned it with loyal subjects who would remain watchful while I slept, ready to act against any invading nightmare. Once satisfied that I had everything in place, I pulled the covers over my shoulders and let sleep claim me.

The light of dawn was filtering through my window when my nightmare awoke me. The usual sheen of sweat enveloped me, but I had achieved a small victory. I had slept undisturbed for nearly eight hours. It was a huge achievement. I felt refreshed, renewed, full of the energy I had been missing for a long time.

I closed my eyes and searched out the defenses I'd built the night before. There was damage to see, but it was scattered, helter-skelter, not focused in one area. Three of my loyal subjects were dead, caught in the act of pouring boiling oil onto my nightmare. A bloody trail led from the moat to the castle wall, evidence of the effect the nightmare-dissolving acid had wreaked. Would the damage to my nightmare carry over, or would it be shaken off, the nightmare restored to its full strength? Time alone would tell.

No question about it. I was onto something. I used every bit of my free time during the day thinking of ways to improve my defenses. By bedtime I added to my already-established bulwark and drifted off to sleep.

The nightmare yanked me sodden and shaken back to reality. It was a little after one in the morning. Three hours of sleep. Something had gone wrong with my defenses. I put on a dry T-shirt and lay back down, my thoughts probing for weaknesses in my defense. I closed my eyes and concentrated on the moat and the parapets that had worked so well the night before. The destruction I saw shocked me.

For starters, the moat had been drained dry, rendering it useless. The tops of all the parapets were gone, the jagged remains a testament to the forces that had struck them. All my loyal subjects lay dead, their bodies scattered about like chaff in the wind. My fortress that had seemed so indestructible the previous night lay in tatters, destroyed.

What was different? I lay there thinking, and then it struck me. My nightmare, my flashback, was a living, learning force. It had learned from the first night and it didn't make the same mistakes twice. Its mission, to disrupt my life, was not to be stopped.

Unable to accept a life of recurring nightmares built on one horrific life experience, I considered my options. The thought of succumbing to them and taking mind-numbing drugs for the rest of my days offered no appeal. Although suicide offered a permanent solution, I wasn't to the point of embracing it. Not yet. There had to be a way to gain control and lead a normal life, whatever that might be. I bolted upright, swung my legs over the side of the bed and rose to my feet, determined to find relief from my nightmares that didn't include suicide, inviting as it seemed.

As I dressed and prepared to join Mom and Dad for breakfast, I considered the cleverness, the flexibility of my nightmare. If it could learn to avoid my defenses, what could I do to keep it at bay? An idea struck me as Mom saw me coming down the stairs. "Good morning, Tojo. How was your sleep?" I'd told her of the improvement two nights before, and she was hoping for another good report, though the haggard expression I bore must have told her otherwise. I tried to put on a brave face.

"It wasn't as good as two nights ago, but I may have come up with a way to make things better," I said, putting a touch of cheer in my voice.

Dad heard my comment. "We raised you tough, Joe. You can get through this," he said while squeezing my shoulder. I wished I shared his confidence.

My plan seemed simple, in a complex way. It had its roots in what I'd been involved with for the past two years. Military science. In the early days of warfare, when one army was entrenched and the other army was on the offense, the smart defenders moved their men and fortifications around daily. The army on the offense made probing attacks on the enemy defenses, and if they found a weakness, they focused their attack there. If the defenders moved forces and fortifications before the attack, they could defend their position successfully.

I needed to think like that. I was the defender, and my nightmare was the attacking army. If it found a weakness, my defenses would be overrun. If on the other hand I could make changes in my defenses that confused and slowed, maybe even stopped the invading nightmare, then I could get through the night unscathed. Uninterrupted sleep would be my reward.

I faced an unrelenting battle; one I would need to work hard to win. A single miscalculation could bring the full force and fury of the nightmare upon me. I needed to use every defense ever employed by the military to achieve a complete victory. The prospect of nights free of flashbacks urged me on.

As night took control of the day, I began my preparations. At this point I had one line of defense and my nightmare had found a way through it. A single castle wall and a toxic moat had worked well once, but it wasn't enough to stop the clever nightmare. My fortifications needed to be much more complex. If I could design a defense line that defeated my nightmare's efforts to break through to me, I could dismiss the lure of suicide as a solution.

Enter my incredible memory. The military science courses I took in college gave me an insight into battles from the Revolutionary War to Teddy Roosevelt's charge up San Juan Hill, from the French and Indian Wars to the bloody Civil War, from World War One to World War Two, from Korea to Viet Nam, and all the minor skirmishes that never made the distinction of being called a war. I crossed my fingers and hoped my flashback memory hadn't taken a military science course. If it had, I might as well write my obituary and plan my suicide.

My first efforts, using a castle and toxic moat, had started out well, so I returned to it, only this time I added many more defenses.

The defenses employed by both sides in Viet Nam came to mind, so I started there. I dug pits all around the castle and put punji sticks at the bottom, a la Viet Cong, then covered the openings with good camo netting. If my nightmare ventured that way it might fall into the pits and land on the punji sticks below, causing serious harm to it. Then I used American-made Claymore mines around the perimeter of my castle, with tripwires concealed in front of them. When my nightmare tripped the wire, the Claymore would fire hundreds of steel balls at it, hopefully disabling it or ending its existence. What a sweet thought that was. I went to bed and closed my eyes, feeling hopeful.

An ear-piercing shriek woke me with a start. I felt my T-shirt. It was dry. I closed my eyes and pictured the defenses I had constructed and saw at once that the camouflage cover that I'd used over one of my punji stick pits was missing. I went to the edge of the pit and peered down. The stakes were in disarray, and they were wet with something that had landed on them. My nightmare had been wounded. Its shriek had wakened me. Round one to the good guy. I closed my eyes and slept like a baby until morning.

The next night a loud explosion woke me. Once again, my T-shirt was free of sweat. I closed my eyes and saw at once that a Claymore had been tripped and shards of my nightmare were scattered on the ground in front of it. I could tell it wasn't the entire nightmare, but clearly the Claymore had done serious damage to it.

I went to bed the next night without making any changes to my defenses, curious about what might happen. My nightmare came to visit me, but its force and effect were greatly diminished. It was frightening, but it didn't have the mind-numbing effect on me that it had before I built up my defenses. My shirt was damp, not soaked. I knew I was on the right track.

At my next meeting with Larry, my VA counselor, he was surprised and delighted with my progress. "I'll share this with my other patients. Maybe they can use their minds to construct defenses like the ones you've built and get the upper hand on their flashbacks." I went home with a bounce in my step I hadn't felt in ages. I hid my thoughts of suicide in the back of my mind. I could see a faint light at the end of the tunnel.

From that day forward I continued to gain control of my flashbacks, my demons. They would visit me in my dreams, but most nights they didn't have the same raw power over me that they'd had before I built my defenses. I felt confident that the techniques I'd learned would serve me well in the future, providing that I took the time to make subtle changes in my defenses every night.

During my struggles to gain control, Dad offered me a huge distraction by sparring with me. It took me back. For me it was a taste of the old days when he taught me all he knew of self-defense, some taught to him in the military, much more picked up while he was serving in Japan. I remember him calling me his little Samurai as I was growing up. The meaning of the term became clear to me when I did my stint in the army.

Four

Y FOOTLOCKER SHOWED up two weeks after I got home. I ignored it. Looking at it brought back bad memories. Dad, curious as ever, goaded me into opening it. "Come on, Son. I want to see what you thought was important enough to keep."

Dad won out.

I took off the padlock and lifted the cover. The smell of pent-up goats poleaxed my senses.

When the stink hit Dad he reeled back, his head shaking. "What's dead in there, Joe?" he asked, his hand cupped over his nose.

I realized what it was. I reached in and lifted out one of the baby goat skin pouches, the pebbles inside clittering against each other as I did so. Dad stared at it, his curiosity reaching a crescendo. I explained how I'd found it draped over a stockpile of arms in a hidey hole, and on two other raids had found two others like this one, gesturing at the inside of my footlocker as I said that. It surprised me that the MPs, military police, hadn't confiscated them. They removed my rifles and handgun. I guessed they thought smelly goat pouches posed no threat.

"What's inside it? Have you checked it out?"

"Nope. I tossed them into my locker and forgot about them. Two of them feel like they're full of pebbles and the third one is much heavier."

"Open it, Son. The suspense is killing me," urged Dad.

I turned it in my hands until the neck flap was uppermost, and slowly pulled out the skewer that held it closed. Opened, I cupped my hand under the opening and poured out a handful of pebbles.

Dad found his voice before I did. "Those look like diamonds, Son,"

"You're right, Dad. They do. But what would they be doing on a heap of small arms?"

Dad came up with an explanation. "They were to pay people off in the chain of arms transfers. If those are real diamonds, there's some mighty pissed-off militants out there."

"How can we test them to see if they're diamonds and not glass?" I asked as I rolled the handful back and forth, the light making them sparkle and shimmer.

"Let's take them out to the garage. I've got a vise. If we put one in it and crank it tight, glass will crumble under the pressure. We can also see if they can scratch a spare pane of glass I have out there."

We found out two things. The vise didn't shatter it and it etched a visible trail in Dad's window glass.

"I'm pretty damned sure you got yourself a goat full of diamonds, Joe," said Dad, a wolfish grin crossing his face.

If he was right, I was holding a treasure trove of unexpected wealth.

I fished out the other two goat pouches. The pebbly one yielded more stones that looked like diamonds. I tilted the neck opening of the heavy one over my hand and coins spilled out. Heavy yellow ones. Gold, if I had to guess. Dad plucked one of the coins from my hand and eyed it closely, then turned to me, his grin huge. "It's a Krugerrand, Joe. One ounce of pure gold. Let's weigh the bag on the scales in the bathroom."

I followed Dad into the bathroom, the goat pouch held against my chest. Dad set the scale down and I stepped onto it, holding the bag close to me. "Two seventy-two," said Dad, reading the dial.

I set down the bag and stepped on again. "Two forty-three," said Dad.

I did the math as I stepped off the scale. Twenty-nine pounds of Krugerrands. At an ounce apiece, that added up to four hundred and sixty-four coins. "Any idea what a Krugerrand's worth, Dad?"

"Nope, but my computer does," he replied as he led the way to the den.

He found the price with a couple clicks of his keyboard. "It's right around $575 an ounce," he said with a smile directed my way.

"Okay. What's 464 times $575? I asked him while I ran the numbers in my head.

Dad picked up pen and paper and began scribbling. "I come up with $266,800," I told him, and then the enormity of the number struck me speechless. The Krugerrands alone were worth over a quarter of a million dollars, and we had no idea what all the diamonds were worth. That is, if they were really diamonds.

"Do you know any jewelers we can take the diamonds to? They may have more sophisticated ways of checking them out. I'd be surprised if they use a vise and a pane of glass," I said, tempering my comment with a broad smile.

"Yeah, good idea. Dump some out and pick out a representative sample of them while I check the Yellow Pages," said Dad. He left me to pick out samples while he looked up jewelers who did appraisals in the Phoenix area. I chose a half dozen stones of different sizes and found an envelope to put them in. After Dad located a string of jewelers who advertised appraisals, he picked the one closest to us. As we headed for Dad's car, Mom came out of the kitchen and asked us what was going on.

"Joe brought back some stones he wants a jeweler to have a peek at," said Dad, his voice calm, matter of fact.

All right, you two. Drive safely. See you when you get back." She strolled back to the kitchen and her dinner preparations, leaving a trail of fantastic aromas behind in her wake.

The jewelry store had one other customer when we stepped inside. A young woman shuffled along the display cases, her right hand tapping out a rhythm on the glass to a song playing in her head, or so it seemed. She'd pause, stare at a piece of jewelry and then resume her tapping shuffle. When she reached the end of the last case, she bobbed her head from side to side and said, "Thank you. I'll be back," to the lone man behind the counter. He smiled and said, "Hurry back, Esther," as she made it out the door. He turned his attention to us.

"May I help you, gentlemen?" I sensed a defensive reaction on his part when he looked at me.

I stepped up to the counter and improvised by saying, "I won some stones in a poker game. The man who offered them as an ante said they were genuine diamonds. I came to see what you think of them." I pulled the envelope from my pocket.

"Very good, sir. I'll be happy to have a look," he said. He picked up a red velvet pad and placed it on the glass counter in front of me.

I opened the envelope and poured the stones onto the pad. Dad stood at my side as we watched the jeweler. He took out a pair of fine pliers and a little magnifying gizmo, picked up one of the stones with his tweezers and held it in front of his magnifier, turning it about as he stared at it. He slowly shook his head. "Not a diamond," he said as he dropped it on the pad and took up another one. He came to the same conclusion with each of the six stones.

"I'm sorry to disappoint you, but none of them are diamonds. Someone did a nice job cutting the glass to look like diamonds, but they're worthless, sad to say. You got fooled by a clever card shark. If you want, I'll dispose of them for you," he said.

"Thanks, but I think I'll keep them to remind me of what a fool I was in that card game," I said while I scooped them back in the envelope.

"Are you sure, sir? It's no trouble on my part," said the jeweler.

"Yes, I'm sure. Thanks for your time." With Dad at my side, we turned and left the shop.

Once outside, I turned to Dad. "Something didn't feel right about that guy. Let's go to another jeweler for a second opinion, okay?"

"I got the same vibes. There's another store not far from here."

We drove to the second jewelry store, and I used the same story. Out came the red velvet pad and the tools of his trade. We watched the jeweler's eyebrows dance with each stone he examined. Finished, he looked up at me, assessing me. I could see the wheels turning. He was looking at a con artist, or worse. "Where did you say you got these stones?" he asked, his eyes hard on mine.

I stuck to my story. "I won them in a poker game."

He stared hard at my face, waiting for me to break. I held on.

"All right, young man. Turns out you're one lucky poker player. These diamonds on the wholesale market, what I would expect to pay for them as a jeweler, are worth between forty and fifty thousand dollars. Does that surprise you?"

I wanted to say yeah, especially since another jeweler just finished telling me they were worthless glass forgeries. Instead, I said, "Yeah. The bet was for ten thousand. Looks like the guy didn't know what he had."

"Or maybe he stole them?" suggested the jeweler.

"He didn't act like a crook," I said with a shake of my head.

"What's a crook act like?" countered the jeweler.

"I don't know. He seemed at ease, and he took them out of his pocket to continue betting. He must have thought he had a winning hand," I said, improvising like crazy.

"But he didn't. You did. Do you want me to buy them from you?" asked the jeweler, his eyes on mine.

"Not right now, but it's good to know that they're valuable. Is there anywhere else I could sell them for more than what you said they're worth?"

"The only other way is to run an ad in a local paper, but you should know what each stone is worth and have a letter of appraisal for each one," said the Jeweler.

"Sounds like that's where you come in. What do you charge for a written appraisal?" I asked.

"If you want an appraisal for insurance purposes, I can do that. However, if you want an accurate assessment of a diamond's value, you should get a certificate. It's much more detailed and accurate, and an examiner will charge around fifty dollars an hour to do it. A certificate of value will go a lot farther in selling loose diamonds for their fair value," he said.

"Thank you for your time and expertise. You've given me an education in diamonds and their worth. If I decide to sell, I'll come back to see you, for sure."

"That's very kind of you. I'm glad to be of assistance. You have six impressive diamonds there," he said with a wave of his hand at my shirt pocket.

Dad and I left the store, the shock of what we learned making me weak in the knees. Once back in the car I thought about the first jeweler who said my stones were glass. Unless he was an idiot, and he didn't act like one, he knew my diamonds were real and he thought he'd take possession of them by offering to throw them in the trash for me. I considered what I could do to repay the favor, something that wouldn't get me in trouble with the law. I knew it would be his word against mine if it went to court.

"Dad, I want to go back to that first jewelry store, confront the guy," I said, decision made.

"Only if you promise not to kick his ass, Son."

"It's a temptation, but okay. I want to hear what he says when I tell him another jeweler said they were real diamonds," I said.

"All right, Son. I want to hear his side, too."

When we walked into the store the jeweler looked up at us, a surprised expression on his pudgy round face. "Gentlemen. You've come back," he said. His expression said his statement sounded lame, even to him.

"I've come back because we had another jeweler examine my stones. He said they were real. You told me they were worthless and offered to dispose of them for me. That sounds like grand larceny to me. You get my diamonds and I get the shaft." I stared at him, waiting.

"It's complicated," he said, his words coming out soft, barely understandable.

"Nothing's complicated about thievery," I countered.

"I need to tell you a story. When I was eight years old, living in San Francisco with my parents and younger brother, a Chinese gang member snatched my mother's purse. When she put up a fight, he shot her. Killed her for her purse. When I saw you were Asian, it shows in your eyes, I flipped out, remembering what happened to my mom. I guessed that you were a thief and wanted to peddle your stolen diamonds, so I made up the story that they were worthless. Offering to dispose of them for you was stupid, I shouldn't have said that. There's no way I wanted to have anything to do with stolen diamonds being fenced by a Chinese man," he said, lifting his eyes to look at me as he finished.

"I'm not Chinese. My mother's Japanese and this is my father," I said with a gesture towards Dad.

The jeweler glanced at Dad and back to me. "I'm so sorry. I should never have let my emotions get the better of me. When I saw your eyes, your oriental features, I was taken back to that horrible day in my childhood. I've made a terrible error in judgment, and I offer you my sincerest apology, though I won't blame you if you don't accept it. If I were in your place, I doubt that I would."

I considered the jeweler's words. It wasn't the first time I was picked on because of my oriental eyes, and I doubted if it would be the last. Kids in school made fun of me, but my size kept things from getting out of control. I was already six feet tall and weighed 150 pounds as a high school freshman, and Dad had already taught me a lot about self-defense. The one kid who pressed his luck went home with a broken nose.

"I understand where you're coming from. I accept your apology," I said, holding his eyes with mine.

"Thank you! I can't begin to tell you what this means to me. It will help me sleep tonight. If you still have the diamonds, I'd be more than happy to take another look at them," he said in a rush of words.

I pulled the envelope from my pocket while he retrieved his instruments. Dad and I watched him carefully as he went through the same routine, examining each diamond. Done, he raised his eyes to mine. "I have to tell you, sir. These are not good diamonds." He paused a moment, then added, "These are beautiful, flawless diamonds, I'm happy to tell you."

I struggled to get my lower jaw back in place after his statement. He smiled at my expression, happy with the effect he'd had on me. When I got my speech back, I asked him what he thought they were worth, keeping in mind what the second jeweler had told us.

"The smallest diamond is a caret and a half, and the largest is close to six carets. The six-caret stone by itself is easily worth sixty thousand dollars, It's exquisite. Flawless. Perfectly clear. I would be happy to purchase it from you," he added.

After I managed to close my mouth again, I thanked him for his appraisal.

"Is it true that you won the diamonds in a poker game as you said before?" he asked.

I've always preferred telling the truth, something Mom drilled into me, beginning ten minutes after I was born, with reminders whenever she thought they were needed.

"I'm a lousy poker player. No, I picked them up while serving a tour in Iraq," I said.

"Iraq? Interesting. I'd never have guessed that they came from Iraq," he said with a slight shake of his head.

Since I had no reply, I kept silent. I knew most diamonds came from South Africa, but Iraq? Maybe Dad could check it out on his computer.

The jeweler stood my silence for a moment, and then he got a quizzical look on his round face and said, "You've got more than these six stones, don't you?"

"A couple more," I said, maintaining my commitment about honesty with Mom.

"Well, perhaps you'd like me to make a ring, or maybe a pendant for a wife, a mother, a sister?" he said.

"There's no wife, but I'll check with my mother and sister, see what they think," I said, thinking that it was a great suggestion. I was starting to like this guy, despite the lousy first impression he'd made.

"Very well, then. I'll put your diamonds in a proper container and I'll await your decision," he said.

While he busied himself with wrapping my diamonds I said, "I didn't get your name through all of this."

"Oh, so sorry. My name is Maximilian Smith," he said while gesturing at the sign on the wall that announced, 'Smith's Jewelry Emporium.' "Please. Call me Max. It's so much easier."

"Nice to meet you, Max. I'm Tojo Roberts, but everyone calls me Joe," I said, extending my hand.

Max took it and gave it a firm shake, which surprised me. I was expecting a dead fish. Must have been due to the work he does, hammering out rings and stuff. I didn't think it was from pushups.

"Let me know if there is anything I can do to set your lovely stones into a ring, a necklace, perhaps earrings," he said, smiling.

I'll find out if my mom or my sister have a hankering for some jewelry. I'd like to surprise them, so I'll have to be sneaky, finding out," I said with a smile back at him.

Max handed me my neatly wrapped diamonds and Dad and I headed home. On the way I asked him if he knew what Mom or Kimiko might want as a little bauble from me.

"Your mother never took much interest in jewelry, and Kimmie is a lot like her. Good luck getting them to tell you what they'd like. Might be better to surprise them with something you think they'd like, Son."

That hit me as great advice. I salted it away in my memory banks.

Five

LARRY SURPRISED ME at the next PTSD session by offering me a job. "I think you could be a huge help to the other patients. If you can explain to them how you built your defenses against your flashbacks, your nightmares, show them how they can do it against theirs, there's no telling what kind of success you'll have, and they'll have. It could be a monster breakthrough, no pun intended," he said.

"You serious?" I asked, surprised.

"Fucking A I'm serious. You willing to give it a shot?"

Okay, sure. Wait. What does it pay?" I asked, topping off the question with my Cheshire cat smile I got from Mom.

"The pay is for shit, but if you end up helping even one vet, the reward will more than compensate you."

I got what he meant.

"When do I start?"

"I'll set it up for next week. Spend the time until then thinking about what you'll say, how you'll say it. I know you'll do fine," said Larry with a wave of his three-finger hand.

"How much talking time do I have?"

"An hour. But if you don't get through it all in an hour we'll take up where you leave off the week after, okay?"

"More than generous. See you in a week."

I arrived at Larry's office five minutes before our appointed time. We exchanged pleasantries and he told me to follow him. He took me to a large room crowded with vets of every sex and age. Some of the men were clean-shaven while others looked like they'd been born with beards. The six women were divided equally between close-cropped and long tresses. All eyes turned to examine me when Larry and I walked in.

Larry raised his three-finger hand for silence and gave them a brief intro while my stomach turned over, wondering what I'd gotten myself into. "And with that I'll turn the discussion over to Joe Roberts."

My cue. I drew in a long breath and silently exhaled, then jumped in with both feet. I spoke briefly of the ambush and deaths of my comrades, and then about the recurring nightmare that visited me every night after that, waking me, soaking me to the skin with sweat. Many heads nodded, understanding. I had nearly everyone's full attention.

I spoke of my earlier experiences of bad memories and how I had closed my eyes and mentally built a wall around the memory. It had worked. The bad memories stayed on the other side of my wall, and I was able to go on with my life.

I went on to say that my attempts at controlling the Iraqi flashbacks were met with failure. "Building walls around them did nothing to stop them. Both concrete and steel enclosures were blown apart by them as if they were nothing. I was near despair, with thoughts of suicide taking over my thoughts."

Many heads nodded, understanding.

"After thinking some more about it, I thought maybe I could build defenses in my mind, defenses that would hold off the flashbacks. I built a castle wall, circled it with a moat full of toxic acid, and set loyal subjects on the parapets to pour boiling oil down on the attacking nightmare. I went to bed, hopeful that my defenses would work."

"The light of dawn was filtering through the window when I woke up. I closed my eyes to check my defenses and saw that the toxic moat and boiling oil had been effective. The uninterrupted eight hours of sleep I'd had buoyed me up, gave me a surge of energy that I hadn't felt in weeks. Correction: make that in months."

"I went to bed the next night without making any changes to my defenses. Big mistake. The flashback jarred me awake after three hours, my T- shirt soaked through. When I recovered, I closed my eyes and examined my defenses, and what I found shocked me to the core. My moat had been drained dry and all my loyal subjects lay dead. Reality struck me. The nightmare was a living, thinking thing with the intelligence to avoid my defenses once it learned what they could do to it."

"Enter Plan B," I told the assembled vets. "With my knowledge of all the battles and sieges the U.S. had been involved in, I set out to build defenses that couldn't be breached. Keeping my castle, I set out Viet Cong punji stick pits covered with camo and deployed Claymore mines with tripwires set ahead of them. That night a piercing scream jarred me awake. My shirt was damp but far from soaked. When I examined my defenses, I saw a pit cover gone, and looking into it I saw wetness on the punji sticks. My nightmare had been wounded. I slept peacefully the rest of the night."

"The next night a loud explosion jarred me awake. My shirt dry, I closed my eyes and saw that a Claymore had been tripped, and shredded parts of my nightmare were scattered about. The main body of the nightmare survived, but the injury to it was impressive."

"From that night on I've been able to sleep. I continue to add defenses and modify my plan, and occasionally the nightmare breaks through, but with far less power and effectiveness than before. I urge all of you to experiment with your own strong defenses. If you are successful, and there's no reason why you can't be, you can get your life back."

When I finished, a long silence hung in the air. At length one of the men in the back row stood up and began to clap, and it triggered everyone to join in, filling the room with a thunderous applause. It brought everybody to their feet. I stood before them in awe of their response. I had never experienced anything even close to that emotion. I felt hot tears of joy run down my cheeks.

Larry came to my side and draped his three-fingered arm over my shoulder. I say draped, but the truth is, it was a reach for him to place his hand on my high shoulder. His simple touch felt comforting, reassuring. His words broke the spell. "Ladies and gentlemen, you have just heard one of the finest explanations of the horrors of flashbacks and one man's solution to the problem. I think there's questions out there, so raise your hands and fire away," he said with a wave of his famous service-connected hand.

The questions came, and I did my best to respond as positively as I could. Eventually they dwindled down to a scattered few and Larry stepped in again. "We're way over the time I scheduled for Joe's presentation, and I think we should cut him some slack and let him go, but on one condition. That he agrees to come back for another session, to answer all the questions that are there at the tips of your tongues and the ones that are hanging there, ready to pop out as soon as he leaves. You okay with that, Joe?"

"Hell, yeah. I want to see all of you kick your nightmares out the door for good," I said while my eyes swept the audience. I saw faces upturned to me, bearing one common expression: hope. Those faces buoyed me up, filled me with energy, gave me hope that I might be able to ease their pain.

As the room began to clear Larry turned back to me, a warm smile lighting up his rugged face. "God speaks in mysterious ways, Joe, and He brought you to me and to my group. I don't know how else to say it. Your words affected everyone. I could see it in their eyes, in the way they hung on every word. You have a gift," he said as he gripped my arm with his strong right hand.

"Now don't go getting carried away, Larry. All I did was explain to them what I found out about my own nightmares and how I went about fending them off, maybe weaken them with my efforts," I said, struggling to deflect his praise.

"You don't get it, Joe. You spoke to a roomful of vets who suffer from PTSD, from flashbacks, from nightmares as bad as, maybe worse than yours. Some of them have carried the curse since Viet Nam, one of them since Korea. They've tried everything we can offer them, hoping to recover their energy, their sanity even, and sadly many of them have fallen into a reliance on drugs to get them through the day, as well as through the night. You just finished offering every one of them a miracle. It's called hope," said Larry.

"It's true," came a woman's voice behind me. I had been so caught up in my conversation with Larry that I was unaware that one of the attendees had remained behind. I turned towards the voice to see a tall, willowy young woman regarding me. Her eyes caught my attention. They were almond-shaped, like mine. She had silky black hair tied in a bun that framed her round face, and her aquiline nose, prominently Caucasian, drew my gaze down to her slightly rounded lips.

Nice package.

"Lisa, meet Joe. Joe, this is Lisa," said Larry, breaking the spell. I reached out to shake her hand. Her returning grip was both warm and firm.

"I stayed behind because I wanted to thank you personally for your encouraging presentation," she said, her smile lighting up her face.

A glance at her left hand showed no wedding band, but I knew that meant nothing. "You're sweet to take the time to thank me. I appreciate it. This is my first attempt at talking about my trials of fighting flashbacks," I said, feeling like the world's biggest bonehead as I struggled to say what I meant.

"I never would have known it. I thought you were a professional speaker going from one VA hospital to the next," said lovely Lisa, an impish smile overspreading her face.

"Truth of the matter, I live in Surprise and this VA is the closest for me," I said, holding her eyes with mine.

"I couldn't help noticing, you have Asian eyes. What nationality is your mother?" she asked.

"How'd you know it's my mother who's Asian?" I asked.

"Well, Larry introduced you as Joe Roberts, and Roberts isn't very Oriental," she said, her smile broadening.

"I did not see that coming. You're right. My mother is Japanese," I said, my assessment of her going up a couple notches.

Larry jumped in. "Joe, I'll give you a call to discuss continuing this discussion. You two can talk for as long as you want. The room's vacant for the next hour. Take care, you two." He reached out to give me his famous three-finger handshake and was gone.

Lisa broke the brief silence. "I got my almond eyes from my mom, too. She's also Japanese," she said.

"That's nothing short of amazing. The only Japanese-American girl I know is my sister, Kim, short for Kimiko," I said, feeling dumber by the minute in front of this charming young lady.

Lisa rescued me by saying, "And you're the first Japanese-American boy I've met other than my brother, Hito. Hey, do you want to sit down? You've been on your feet a long time."

"Invitation accepted," I said. I picked up one of the folding chairs so I could face her. Once she was seated, I positioned my chair at a non-invasive distance.

"How long have you been fighting your nightmares?" she asked while she swept an errant strand of black hair behind her right ear.

"It's been close to three months now. I went through a bad time in Iraq," I said.

"I got my nightmares in Iraq, too, but I'm sure the source of mine is different than yours," she said, a wistful expression on her attractive face. "You tell me your story and I'll tell you mine," she offered, her warm smile encouraging me to respond.

"Okay. My ten-man team walked into an ambush. Four of us survived. I was one of the lucky ones," I said, my head lowered, remembering.

"That gives you survival guilt on top of the trauma you went through." It was a statement, not a question.

"You got it. What did I do that allowed me to live while six pf my teammates died?"

"From all I've heard, it's likely that you'll never get a satisfactory answer. It's probably better to think that God, or whatever you believe in, spared you for a reason, that He has plans for you that will take time for you to understand."

"I like that. What, are you on Larry's payroll too?" I asked Lisa, fixing her eyes with mine.

Lisa laughed, a high throaty sound. It was open and alive, drawing me in, including me in a way that startled me. Her smile completed the package. "No. He can't afford me," she said, a warm smile punctuating her laugh.

"You're a counselor with your own practice?" I asked.

"No. I'm an upholsterer. I restore people's old sofas and chairs. I found out all that stuff about survival guilt when I read up on it at the library," she said brightly.

"That means you know how to swing a hammer," I said, nodding at her.

"That and other things, yes."

"Okay. Your turn. What caused your nightmares, your flashbacks?" As I said that, I watched all the joyful expression drain from Lisa's face. My words had burst her bubble. I opened my mouth to tell her never mind, we can talk about it later when she responded.

"I was raped by my supervisor in Iraq." The words came out in a monotone spoken by a stranger. The Lisa I'd seen before had withdrawn to another place, another time.

"Shit! I didn't see that coming," I said with force.

"Neither did I. I was working alone one evening. He came up behind me while I sat, doing my paperwork, and circled my neck with his forearm, squeezing so hard that he stopped the blood flow to my brain. He surprised me so completely that I barely had time to put up a fight before I passed out. When I regained consciousness, he had me on the floor, my pants were gone, and he was hammering inside me. He came with a jerking spasm, pushed away from me, and told me to keep it to myself or he'd see me dead. I knew he meant it."

"After thinking about it for a week I decided to take it to his superior. I explained what had happened and he looked me in the eye and asked what proof I had. I told him there was nothing and there were no witnesses. His superior shook his head and told me I didn't have a case. It would be my word against his and a judge would throw it out for lack of evidence. Then the nightmares started," she said in a scary, matter of fact tone.

I reached out and put my hand on her arm in a protective gesture. A jolt of static electricity jumped from her to me. "Let's get out of here. There's a coffee shop around the corner where we can be more comfortable."

She stood without a word and followed me out.

The coffee shop was relatively quiet, lunch hour already in the rearview mirror, and we took a table against the wall and away from other patrons. We both ordered sandwiches and black coffee. While waiting I asked her what she knew of her attacker.

"I know plenty. I got my hands on his records, which turned out to be easy since I worked in communications. He's single, lives with his mom and dad when he's home in Schenectady, New York. Oh, and his next leave is coming up in a month," she told me.

"If you had the chance to even the score with him, what would you like to do?" I asked as the waitress showed up with our lunch.

"You don't want to hear that," she said with a subtle shake of her head.

"I wouldn't have asked if I didn't want to hear," I shot back.

Lisa took a long drink from her water glass and set it down. "I have this fantasy where he's unconscious, like I was, and I take my upholsterers' hammer and drive one of those broad-headed brass tacks through his offending member," she said, her head lowered, her voice a mere whisper.

"That sounds like perfect poetic justice to me," I said.

"Yeah, a perfect pipe dream anyway."

"Let's talk about ways to make your fantasy come true," I said.

"You're kidding, right?" Lisa challenged, her head aslant.

"No. I'm dead serious. I'd enjoy helping you to even the score with that bastard." The loudness of my voice surprised me. I glanced around the room to see if I'd caught the attention of other customers. Nobody looked in our direction, I was relieved to see.

I'd made a statement that I wasn't sure I could keep so I made a fuss over polishing off my sandwich while I thought about it. Lisa copied my example and silence stole the show. I considered all my options. I knew money wasn't an issue, what with my stash of diamonds and gold. What concerned me was the possibility of jail time in Schenectady, New York, or anywhere else, for that matter. The immediate question became, how much do I tell this charming young lady who I've barely met? Is she trustworthy, loyal, helpful, et cetera? Maybe she isn't who she says she is. I decided to back away for the time being.

My lunch disposed of, I daubed the corners of my mouth with my napkin and turned back to Lisa. Seeing me seeing her, she offered me a broad smile and an expectant expression that evaporated my resolve. I leaped into the void. "If you're going to be successful in tacking this guy we need to plan carefully. I'm sure you wouldn't want to share a jail cell in Schenectady with me, so our plan needs to go off without a hitch. Could you take off, say, a week or ten days from your business to travel to New York?" I asked as I lost myself in her lovely coal-black eyes.

"I'd arrange things so I could," was her instant answer.

"Then let's make some plans," I said.

"I've done some planning already. I Googled his parents' address and did a Google Earth search of their home. I've also scanned the neighboring area and made notes of the businesses and landmarks," said Lisa, a coy smile flittering about her mouth as she spoke.

"Google Earth? What's that?"

It's a new app from Google. They use satellite images taken of the earth. They show the telescopic images of every place on earth. You can look down on an address from, like, thirty feet above, and see all the details."

"That's impressive. So, you were going to do something all by yourself, weren't you?"

"It was all a pipe dream, as I said. There's no way I can carry out anything by my lonesome."

"And now you have a co-conspirator," I said as I observed her face. The smile that lit it up seemed genuine. But then again, who knew? I'd met this charmer less than two hours ago.

"I don't know why you'd be willing to help me. We've barely met, and you don't know anything about me," she said. I wondered idly if she could read minds. Scary thought.

"You're right. Let's get better acquainted so both of us can feel comfortable and confident with each other," I said.

"I'd like that," she said, the coy smile back.

"What time should I pick you up for dinner?"

"Do you like Miso?" she asked, head tilted.

"I was raised on miso. I love it. Why?"

"Come to my apartment at seven and I'll make miso nikomi udon for dinner," she said, her happy smile holding down the fort.

"One of my favorites! What should I bring?"

"Beside yourself, a bottle of cheap white wine, if you like."

"What about a dessert?"

"I'll pass. Bring something for yourself if you want," she said.

"Nah. A dessert would be an insult to good miso."

Lisa gave me her address, I paid for lunch, and I walked her to her parked car. Dad's loaner was close by. After saying our goodbyes, we headed out in opposite directions.

When I pulled into the driveway Dad was standing outside, maybe waiting for me. I got out and tossed him the keys which he deftly caught and pocketed. "Did everything go okay, Son?"

He knew I was scheduled to talk to the PTSD group at the VA. He also knew that it was supposed to take an hour, and I'd added two additional hours to my outing.

"Everything's great, Dad. I met a young lady, is all."

"Uh oh. We'd better go inside and share that with your mom. She'll want all the details," he said, his sly smile leading the way.

When I told Mom that Lisa was half Japanese an expression came over her face that I'd never seen before. Happiness? Pride? Joy? Maybe a little of all three. "Why is she in the PTSD group, Tojo?"

Oh boy.

I paused a moment. She raised me to be honest in everything I did or said so there was no dodging the question. I told her what had happened to Lisa and how her nightmares had grown out of it.

Mercy me! The poor girl. You tread lightly with her, you hear me, Tojo?"

I knew what she meant. "Don't worry, Mom. I will."

"That's my boy. Now tell me about the rest of your day," she said.

I started from the beginning, told Mom and Dad about speaking to the group, said that my little talk was received with a lot of enthusiasm and Lisa had come up to me afterwards to thank me for my encouraging words. "After we'd told each other what caused our PTSD, I took her to a coffee shop for lunch and we talked some more. I asked her out to dinner, and she did one better. She invited me to share a miso meal with her at her apartment," I said, watching Mom for a reaction. I got it, in spades.

"Miso? That's wonderful, Tojo! It sounds like she knows how to cook." I heard a lot more in her voice than her words alone. My mom, the matchmaker. She went to the refrigerator and came back with a bottle of white wine. Handing it to me, she said, "This will go perfectly with Lisa's miso, Tojo. Don't tell her it came from me, though."

"You want me to lie, Mom?" I sensed an opening I'd never seen before.

"Of course not! You just tell her you picked it up on your way over to her apartment. That isn't a lie, now, is it?"

Not for the first time I realized what a smart mom I had.

Six

I HIT THE buzzer for L. Goodweather outside her apartment building door and in seconds I heard the door lock open. Lisa's apartment was on the third floor, so I ignored the elevator and took the stairs to burn off my nervousness. When I emerged from the stairwell she stood in her open doorway, a warm smile beckoning to me. I closed the gap in easy strides and held the bottle of wine out for her. "This comes highly recommended to share with miso," I said brightly. I omitted saying that the person recommending it was my mom.

Lisa took the bottle from me and led the way inside, closing the door behind us. Her apartment, though small, was neat and tidy. The foyer led to a living area with a two-place sofa and two upholstered chairs surrounding a coffee table of light wood. The kitchen was adjacent to it, with a small dining table and four padded chairs set around it. A swirl of enticing aromas reached out to me. A closed door behind the living area, I guessed, led to her bedroom.

As I completed my brief inspection, Lisa handed the still-cool wine bottle back to me and gestured at an opener on the counter. Next to it sat two glasses. I smiled at her and set to work, cutting the foil and extracting the cork. I poured wine in both glasses. I handed one to Lisa and claimed the other one. She smiled at my handiwork and reached forward to touch glasses, then took an exploratory sip. "Mm, that's really good, Joe," she murmured. She leaned in to examine the label and lightly contacted my left arm with her side. I felt an electric jolt pass through me. Static electricity. We'd been going through a dry spell and static electricity was rampant. At home, when I stood up from the upholstered couch and touched the lamp, *blammo!* I got a shock.

"I'll have to remember that label," said Lisa, ignoring the static electricity. She turned to the stove to check on our meal and I walked into the living area. A framed photograph on the wall drew me to it. I saw at once it was a family photo. Lisa stood next to a man I guessed was her dad, a tall, solidly built guy with dark close-cropped hair and glasses. A tall, thin Japanese woman with a broad smile stood next to him. Lisa's mom. She was dwarfed by the young man to her right. Tito, her brother. Tall and broad-shouldered, he looked like he and I could have played on the same lacrosse team. A worthy competitor.

"Ah. You spotted the family photograph," said Lisa, coming up to my right side that still tingled from the earlier contact.

"Your mother's tall, like mine. Is she from Hokkaido?" I asked.

"You know about the tall Japanese from Hokkaido? Yes, my mother was born and raised there, but she was living in Tokyo when she met my dad," said Lisa.

"And both you and your brother inherited her height and good looks," I said, moving my eyes back to her.

"Flattery will get you---" she paused briefly, then said "a nice miso supper. And it's ready." She led the way to the kitchen where ceramic Japanese bowls and spoons waited on the counter. She removed the lid from the pot on the stove and the inviting aroma of miso enveloped me.

"You go first, Joe," she said while sweeping a hand at the steaming pot.

"You won't have to ask me twice," I said. I picked up a bowl and the ladle and scooped up chicken, egg, udon noodles, mushrooms, shallots, and pieces of fried tofu from the pot, being sure to add the right amount of the aromatic miso broth. When my bowl was as full as I dared to make it, I carried it to the table and set it on the colorful straw place mat. Lisa had set the wine bottle in a round aluminum dish that bore the message, *Wine makes the world go round.*

I watched her fill her bowl and carry it to the table. I moved over and pulled her chair out for her. As she bent to sit, she rested her hand gently on my forearm for a brief second. I felt the static electricity run up my arm as she said, "It's nice to see you're a gentleman. Your parents taught you well."

"My father and I took turns seating Mom and Kim at each meal," I said as I helped push her chair in.

"It's a nice gesture. So many men these days don't lift a finger for a woman. In some ways, I think women's liberation is responsible," she said.

As I took my seat, Lisa pyramided her hands in front of her. I knew what it meant. I did the same and together we said, "Itadakimasu." Japanese grace.

After, she looked at me with what could only be interpreted as an apologetic expression and said, "I hope this isn't too terrible. I know I'm competing with your mother and her Japanese cooking skills."

I picked up my ceramic spoon, scooped up a healthy amount of Lisa's miso soup and touched it tentatively to my lips to test the temperature. The temperature was perfect. I put it in my mouth. The fine flavors rolled across my taste buds and the textures of the different ingredients were fantastic. I chewed and swallowed and noted that I had Lisa's undivided attention. I set my spoon down and looked at her. "I'm sorry, Lisa. This isn't good miso."

Hearing my words, her face dropped, and all animation left it.

I felt terrible for the effect my words had on her and hurried on. "No, Lisa. This is not good miso. It's *incredible* miso. My mother would be proud to enjoy a meal of this at your table."

Hearing this, the light came back to her face. She pushed back her chair and came around to me. She surprised me by whacking my upper arm with her fist. She surprised me further by leaning over and gently brushing her lips against mine, sending another jolt of electricity through me. Before I could respond she had returned to her chair and picked up her spoon. My turn to sit, stunned. Two messages delivered. One, don't screw with my head. And two, I forgive you this time. Lesson learned. I scooped another delightful spoonful of miso into my mouth and chewed slowly, enjoying the intricate flavors and textures.

My silence prompted Lisa to speak. "Are you okay, Joe?" she asked, concern showing in her voice.

"I couldn't be better, Lisa. I'm enjoying a delicious dinner and I'm thoroughly enjoying your company. What more could I ask for?" I said as I lost myself in her searching eyes.

"Seconds?" she asked, her cute round face tilted to the side.

Now what could she mean? More of the miso soup? Or more of something else? Remembering my mother's admonishment to tread lightly with her, I chose the soup. "Thanks. As soon as I finish this I'll go for a refill. This is really good, Lisa," I added, frosting the cake I'd come close to destroying.

I had seconds, enjoying it as much as the first round, and we finished off the wine. By then it was past nine and time to bow out. There was an awkward moment at her door when we stood, facing each other, and the electricity in the air threatened to draw us together. I broke the spell by placing my forefinger gently on her lips and saying, "It's been a wonderful evening for me, Lisa, and I hope we can see each other again soon."

"The feeling's mutual, Joe. Maybe next time we can talk about settling the score with the creep who raped me."

She hadn't forgotten.

"Yes. I'll do some serious thinking. Let's see what we can come up with that will give him what he deserves," I said.

When she closed the door, I had the weird feeling that I'd left something behind. I reached out to knock, get back whatever I was missing, and the absurdity hit me. What could she possibly have taken from me? I patted my pockets. Nothing missing. I turned and walked for the stairway.

When I opened the front door of my parents' home my mother stood there, an inquisitive smile on her face. "I waited up to hear, Tojo. How did your evening with Lisa go?" Nothing shy about my mom. She got right to the heart of the matter.

"It was nice, Mom. She cooks a mean miso soup. I kidded her about it," I said, smiling at the memory Dory.

"What do you mean, you kidded her?" Mom pursued.

"She asked me how I liked it and I told her that it wasn't good. When the color drained from her face, I said it wasn't good, it was incredible, and that you would enjoy it as much as I was. Then she hit me," I said.

"She hit you?"

"After I said that, she came around and whacked me on the shoulder with her fist. It caught me by surprise. Then she leaned over and brushed her lips on mine. That surprised me even more," I said, remembering the shock it sent through me.

"My estimation of this young lady just went up a notch. She made her point by thumping you, and then she tempered it by giving you a light kiss," said Mom.

"One thing puzzles me, Mom. Her apartment was full of static electricity. Every time I touched her, I got a shock," I told her.

In response, Mom's eyebrows went up and a pleased smile spread across her face. "I'm glad you had a good time, Tojo. You deserve it, considering all you've gone through. Now I'm off to bed." She gave me a hug and pecked my cheek before heading up the stairs.

The next morning at breakfast Dad asked me what I planned to do with my goat skins full of treasure. "I worry about all that stuff lying around in the house, Son. I mean, somebody could break in the house and walk off with all of it."

The tatters of last night's small nightmare were still occupying my thoughts and his question caught me by surprise. I hadn't thought much about the diamonds and gold, and clearly Dad had a point. "What do you suggest, Dad?" I asked, thinking maybe he had a solution.

"I think it'd all fit into a safety deposit box if you lose the goat skin pouches and transfer the diamonds and gold into bags," he said. He took a sip of his coffee.

"What's a safety deposit box?" I asked, not having a clue.

It's a box in the bank's vault. You pay an annual fee to use it, and you get a key to access it when you want to. It's about the safest way to protect something of value that I could find," he said. Clearly, Dad had done his research.

"That sounds like a good idea, Dad. Does your bank have those boxes?"

"I checked and they do. You should get a checking account at the same time," he suggested.

I hadn't thought about doing that. I still had my army discharge check sitting in my room. "Makes sense, Dad. I'll repack all the loot after breakfast, and we can head for the bank afterwards."

"Why don't you take the time to sort the diamonds into, say, three different sizes. That way you don't have to mess with doing it later. I've got some cloth zipper bags you can use," he said.

"If you don't mind helping, we could get it done a lot faster," I said.

"Be glad to. The thought of handling all those diamonds puts a smile on my face," he said, the smile already there.

It took us close to two hours to sort through and package the diamonds by their approximate size, and we also divvied up the Krugerrands into bags so the weight of each was manageable. When we were done, we had twelve cloth bags full of diamonds and gold, and three goat skin pouches that had a date with the trash man. Dad said he wouldn't miss their lingering goat stink. I agreed with him.

It took longer to open a checking account than it did to get a safety deposit box. I left with a ten-pack of temporary checks and a small, flat key. The vault manager explained that if I wanted to access my box, I'd need to bring my key and my ID. There are two key slots, one for my key and one for the bank's key. Both are needed to unlock the box. All very secure. I felt a weight lift off me when Dad and I left all that loot behind.

On the way home he asked me what I planned to do with all my valuable assets. What with my nightmarish flashbacks I hadn't thought much about it. I was glad Dad brought it up. Other than telling Lisa that I could help her confront the creep who raped her I hadn't considered what else I could do with my stash. I took a chance and told Dad about Lisa knowing where her attacker lived and her wish to bring him pain, and that I'd volunteered to help her.

"What does she want to do? I hope murder isn't one of the possibilities," said Dad as he put the turn signal on and headed for home.

"No. I wouldn't agree to be part of that. She wants to hurt him where he hurt her."

"You mind elaborating?"

How do you tell your dad that she wanted to tack his pecker to a picket fence? While I considered how to explain her wishes, my silence must have been suspenseful to him. He asked me again to elaborate. Truth is always the best policy, ingrained into me by my mom.

"You know she has an upholstering business, right? She puts new faces on old chairs and sofas and stuff, and she's good at putting those little brass-headed tacks in a line." I paused, considering how to say the next bit. Dad beat me to it.

"She wants to hit the nail on the head. On his second head, the one with no brains," he added.

I couldn't have said it any better. "You got it, Dad."

"What's your role going to be in this vigilante action?"

"Lisa told me the creep crept up behind her, wrapped his arm around her neck and squeezed, shutting off the blood supply to her brain. When she regained consciousness, he was raping her. She'd like to replay the scene, this time with me putting him in a sleeper hold and her driving an upholstery tack through his offending member," I said.

"Poetic justice, sounds like," said Dad.

"So, you approve the plan?"

"As you know, I don't condone violence of any kind. But I have to say, if going through with that helps Lisa recover even slightly from the PTSD that she's suffering from because of being assaulted and raped, then I say, go for it." Dad glanced over at me when he finished. His way of putting an explanation point on his words.

"Thanks, Dad. It's nice to know that you'll put up my bail money if things go south," I said, grinning broadly.

"I expect that you and Lisa will plan this whole thing down to the smallest detail, so I won't have to worry about getting up bail money. With all that the army taught you, and all that I've taught you, I think you two will be fine. One more thing. Don't share any of this with your mother. She would worry herself sick if she knew what you two were up to," he said as he pulled into the driveway and brought the car to a stop.

"It'll be our little secret. I hope you don't talk in your sleep," I said.

"If I do, your mother never said so."

"Maybe she's saving it up, like money in the bank, letting it gather interest as time goes by."

Dad's reply was a sly grin which left me puzzled.

"I've been thinking about getting an apartment somewhere, try living on my own, Dad."

"You know you're always welcome here, Son."

"I do, Dad, but I'm a big boy now, and I think it's time that I found a place of my own," I said as I watched him for a reaction.

"It'd give you more privacy, if that's what you want."

"I want privacy, sure, but I also want the independence to go and come when I please, and maybe learn how to cook," I added.

Dad chuckled. "It'll be hard to come up with meals to equal your mom's, but it's worth a try. If you do move out, you can always come by for Sunday dinner, keep you from starving to death."

"I appreciate the invitation. By the way, is this car paid off?"

"That's kind of a personal question, but yeah, it's five years old and fully paid for. Why?"

"I need a car of my own so maybe we can do a deal. I'll look up the value and offer you more. You want paid in diamonds or gold?" I asked.

"Cold hard cash works for me," said Dad.

Seven

I N THE NEXT four days I did three things. I found a diamond merchant who could certify my diamonds. His name was Harold Whiteman, and his store was Whiteman's Fine Diamonds and Jewelry. He said he charged fifty dollars an hour to certify diamonds. He also agreed to purchase any I wished to sell, and at the certified price. He showed me his credentials. He was who he said he was. He went on to say that if he certified the diamonds inaccurately, in other words he undervalued them, he could not only ruin his reputation but end up in prison for fraud and grand larceny. I believed him.

Next on my list was a search for an apartment, I started with the newspaper classified section over a cup of coffee and circled the ones in nice quiet neighborhoods that looked promising. Then I made calls and set out to check them out. I quickly learned that the ones that seemed too good to be true, were. One was on the top floor, the sixth floor, and the only access was a stairway. I could do it, but Mom and Dad? I crossed it off my list and increased my budget by a hundred a month.

The one I settled on was relatively new, was on the fourth floor with views of open farmland and a playground, and a smooth elevator took me up and down. A stairway was there for safety reasons, and I could opt for it when I wanted to stretch my legs. The drawback? It was unfurnished. I needed furniture for the living area and bedroom, and the kitchen was bare of everything. I started a list.

Last on my list was a visit to the neighborhood Ford dealer. My plan was to get a new Ford Escape for Mom and Dad. Their 2002 Escape would be my set of wheels. Nice. All broken in. I opted for the limited edition for them. Leather, and lots of bells and whistles. They deserved it. I stuck with silver metallic clearcoat paint. It had been their color choice for as long as I remembered.

With totals for my apartment and new furnishings, plus the new Escape for Mom and Dad, I returned to the diamond certifier's store with a pouch of the smaller diamonds. As he poured them out on a large velvet pad, I watched his eyebrows arch. He turned to me, a wide smile on his narrow face. "You were serious when you said you had a few diamonds," he said.

"Honesty is the best policy," I replied, returning his smile.

"This will take some time to grade and value all these. I'm guessing that I'm looking at well over a hundred stones. If I do twenty an hour, that'll be five hours, maybe more. If you come back tomorrow, around noon, I think I'll be done."

"That works for me. See you then, Mister Whiteman." I nodded in agreement as he carefully returned my diamonds to the pouch. The little bell over his door dinged as I left him alone with his labors.

The next day the bell dinged as I pushed through into his store. A glance at my watch showed me I was twenty-seven seconds early. I've always prided myself on being on time. *Timeliness is next to godliness, or something like that.* Mister Whiteman greeted me with a warm welcoming smile. "Ah, Mister Roberts! You are as timely as I thought you'd be. Welcome back to my humble emporium," he said as he spread his hands to indicate his surroundings.

"It's nice to be back, Mister Whiteman," I said while noting one other customer in the store. A stout middle-aged woman was peering through the glass countertops at an array of bracelets. Mister Whiteman turned from me to ask her if she wanted to look at any specific items. I watched her point to an expensive looking diamond and emerald bracelet which Mister Whiteman retrieved and placed around her wrist. I watched a smile build on her round face as she rotated her wrist, examining the bracelet from different angles.

She lifted her eyes from the bracelet to Mister Whiteman. "It's perfect, Mister Whiteman. I will be the envy of every woman at tonight's charity ball," she announced.

"It is perfect on you, Misses Orbach. Shall I wrap it, or will you wear it?" he asked, his warm smile in place.

"Oh, wrap it, please. It will be that much more impressive to me when I put it on tonight."

While Mister Whiteman removed the bracelet from her wrist and placed it into a long hard-sided box I was reminded of my wish to give some of my diamonds in settings for my mother and sister. Neither of them wore rings or bracelets so I was at a loss for ideas. When Misses Orbach left with her bracelet and a sixteen-thousand-dollar charge on her credit card I asked Harold for suggestions.

"Why not make them pendants? They can wear them around their necks and be reminded of your generous gift every time they touch them. In that way they can wear them hidden or exposed, depending on their whims," he said.

"That's an excellent idea, Mister Whiteman. They're both avid Christians. Perhaps a cross would work well," I offered.

"Let me draw up some possibilities for you. If you like any of them, I can create them for you, using some of your diamonds, of course. Speaking of your diamonds, you have quite a collection there."

"Were you able to complete your appraisal, or what you call your certification?"

"Yes, indeed. You may be surprised to learn that my valuation of them was, let me see, two hundred twenty-three thousand, five hundred dollars," he recited from a paper he picked up from his desk.

Shocked, I grabbed the counter for support. "Really?" I managed to say, my question coming out in a hoarse whisper.

"Really, Mister Roberts. Most of your diamonds are what we call in the business, flawless," he explained as he brought his hands together in front of him.

"That's incredible," I mumbled while wondering how some low-life Iraqi arms dealer got his hands on stones like those. It became obvious to me that arms dealers were wheeling and dealing in the millions of dollars.

"Yes, and, true to my word, I will be more than happy to buy any and all of them from you," he said, his warm smile added for emphasis.

I took the paper with my current expenses from my pocket and smoothed it on the counter. "This is what I need now," I said, holding it out to him.

Mister Whiteman examined it briefly, noting the total, and turned back to me. "Here's what I suggest. I'll keep your diamonds in my vault and keep a record of payments made to you by me, with your signature of acceptance for each payment given to you. As I pay you, it will release diamonds to me valued for the amount paid you. Does that sound fair?" said Mister Whiteman.

"That works for me," I said, still feeling overwhelmed by the value of the diamonds.

"Excellent! I'll get you to sign a form I've prepared. It shows the amount I'm paying you against the total valuation, and it provides you with a check for the items on your list." He turned to his desk, opened a drawer, and took out a printed form with a fancy letterhead. It took him less than five minutes to fill in the blanks, time I used to regain my composure. Two hundred and twenty-three thousand, five hundred dollars!

He came back to the counter with a check and the printed form, setting them on the glass surface in front of me. The form stated that he was holding my diamonds, valued at two hundred twenty-three thousand, five hundred dollars, and was advancing me the sum of forty-five thousand dollars. There was a place for me to sign, acknowledging everything.

I signed, and Mister Whiteman passed me the check.

"Thank you, Mister Roberts. If you come back tomorrow at about the same time I'll have some sketches of possible pendants for you, most of them in the shape of a cross. If you like any of them, I will create them using a few of the diamonds you have brought me. How does that sound?"

"It sounds great, Mister Whiteman. Thank you for this," I said, waving the check he gave me in the air."

"You are most welcome. I'll see you tomorrow." His warm smile was solidly in place.

I headed directly to my new bank to make a significant deposit. Afterwards, I paid for the furniture I ordered and paid cash for Mom and Dad's new set of wheels, which would be ready and registered in their names by the end of the week. Feeling good about my day, I returned home to Mom and Dad's. They greeted me warmly and asked how everything went. I told them about everything except their new car.

"I can't wait to see your apartment, Tojo. It sounds perfect. Not too fancy, not too shabby. Like you," said Mom with one of her enigmatic smiles.

"Yes, Joe. I want to see it, too," added Dad.

"I'll have you both come to dinner once I get settled," I offered.

"That sounds nice Tojo. Maybe you could have Lisa join us, so you aren't the odd man out," said Mom.

Lisa! In all the hubbub of the moment I'd set thoughts of her aside. Now they came back at me in a torrent. "That's a great idea, Mom. I'll see if she's free for Saturday night, if that works for you."

"Oh, let me check my social calendar. Ah, it looks like Saturday night is open," she said with a warm grin.

"Do you have any conflicts, Dad?"

"Hell no! My social calendar is wide open."

"Then it's settled. Saturday night at my new digs."

"Why don't you call Lisa now, see if she's free?" said Mom.

"Now?"

"Strike when the iron is hot," she said, using an expression she'd picked up somewhere along the way.

I took out my phone, found her number in my contact list and hit the call symbol. I put my phone on speaker so Mom and Dad could hear, and the ringtone filled the room.

"Hello, Lisa's Upholstery Shop. How may I help you?" came her friendly voice.

"Hi, Lisa. It's Joe. I'm sitting here with Mom and Dad. We all want you to come to dinner Saturday night at my new apartment," I said.

"Saturday night? This Saturday night?" she said, her voice rising as she spoke.

"Is that a problem? We can always do it some other time," I said, thinking I'd put her on the spot.

"No, Joe, there isn't a problem. While you were speaking, I checked my calendar and Saturday night is wide open," she said. I could feel her smile through the phone. Mom's happy chuckle rolled out of her, filling the background.

"Is that your mother, Joe?" she asked, hearing the soft laughter.

"Uh huh. She thought it was funny when you said you checked your calendar. She said the same thing to me when I asked her if Saturday night worked for her. Seems you two have a lot in common."

"I'm looking forward to meeting her. And your dad as well. By the way, where's this new apartment of yours?" she asked.

I told her.

"Sounds easy enough. Are you the chef for Saturday night's supper?"

"I'm thinking of ordering Chinese," I said with my tongue firmly in my cheek.

"Ah, the old Chinese copout," said Lisa.

Mom's loud snicker filled the background.

"Sounds like your mother feels the same way," said Lisa.

"Oh, she'll love it. She needs a break from her traditional Japanese dishes," I said.

"We'll see. What time Saturday evening?" she asked.

"How about six-thirty? Give us all a chance to drink a lot of wine, help the Chinese go down easier," I said.

"Six-thirty it is. How many bottles of wine do you want me to bring?"

"I don't want you to bring any. This is my treat," I said.

"Okay, Joe. See you all Saturday evening. I'll wear my Chinese kimono," said Lisa.

"How does a Chinese kimono differ from a Japanese one?" I asked, puzzled.

"The Chinese ones have egg foo young on the fronts," said smarty Lisa. Mom's guffaw filled the background.

The next day I returned to Mister Whiteman's jewelry emporium at noon. No, that's not right. A glance at my watch as I pulled open his door showed it to be 11:59. I was early. Mister Whiteman looked my way, his smile of recognition warming the atmosphere. Clearly, he didn't mind my early intervention.

"Ah, Mister Roberts! Come, come. I have those sketches for you." He spread three sheets of white paper on the countertop as I approached. Each page had six designs drawn meticulously on it. The man had a flair for design, that was obvious.

"You've been busy, Mister Whiteman," I said as my eyes scanned the designs of pendants.

"It is nothing. I have arranged the designs from simple ones to more complex ones. Naturally the more complex ones employ more diamonds and more intricate workmanship," he said.

My eyes rolled over the designs, taking in the shapes and numbers of diamonds in each. Most were in the shape of crosses, some simple, others more elaborate. A question occurred to me. "Have you given a price for your labor and materials for each one?" I asked, glancing up at him as I spoke.

"I have done more than that," he said while putting three more sheets on the counter.

I saw they were labeled A, B and C, the same as the design sheets. Each one listed the diamond value as well as the labor and materials cost for each design. Smart. That showed me what I needed to pay for the construction and gave a fair appraisal for the completed pendant. I saw the totals ranged from $3900 to $79,500. The diamond value made up 75 percent or more of the cost of each. "Very impressive, Mister Whiteman. I'll show these designs to my mom and sister and let them choose the ones they want," I said.

"And if by chance they don't find a design that pleases them, you need only let me know and I will create more for them," said Mister Whiteman with an open gesture of his hands.

I left his store feeling confident that Mom and Kim would find something to their liking in the three sheets I held in my hand.

My sister Kimiko, shortened to Kim like Tojo got shortened to Joe, is two years younger than me. She got her college degree while I was off doing search and rescue without the rescue in Iraq and took a job with an accounting firm in Phoenix. She was always good with numbers. We share the gift of great memory so accounting work was a natural for her. She moved out of our parents' house and found an apartment she shares with another single girl in Phoenix. I saw her when I first got home but her work and social life keep her occupied. I called her to invite her to my apartment-christening party. Kill two birds with one stone. Show her the pendant sketches and find out what's new in her life. She accepted without hesitation. It's obvious that she keeps her social calendar in her head.

When I returned to my parents' home, I corralled Mom and showed her the sketches while I explained that I wanted to share my good fortune with her. She went through her usual, expected resistance, saying she'd made it that far in her life without a pendant so why would she need one now? I did the ten second silent stare and then said that it would be her good luck charm, plus she could look at it and think of me.

"I didn't have a pendant to remind me of you while you were halfway around the world and facing danger every day," she said with a little shake of her head.

"I know. Wouldn't it have been nice if you did?"

That set the wheels turning, I could see. She glanced down at the sketches. "If I picked one it would have to be simple. You know I've never liked gawdy," she said. She lifted her head and smiled at me as she said that.

"Do you see the letters at the top of the pages? A is least expensive, B is moderate, and C is more detailed, intricate," I explained.

"If I want simple, I should choose a design from the A page, am I right?"

"I want you to look at all of the designs and pick one you like. The jeweler said he'd draw up some more if you didn't find something you really like," I said.

"You are a very generous son, Tojo. I'll look them over carefully," she said by way of dismissal, I could tell.

I thought of one more convincer. "I invited Kim to join us at my Saturday dinner and I'm going to show her the sketches, too. Maybe you two can pick the same design and bump pendants when you hug each other."

"Oh, that's perfect! I'll hold off making a choice until Kimiko sees them and makes her decision," she said, her enigmatic smile back in place.

The next day the Ford dealer called to say that my parents' new car was all prepped and my check had cleared.

"Come get it any time, Mister Roberts," said the happy salesman.

"I'll be there within the hour," I said.

I told Dad I needed his help to pick something up and he got behind the wheel of his old Escape without complaint. I gave him directions to the Ford dealership, and he got a funny look on his face but headed out, holding his curiosity in check. When he pulled into the dealership I climbed out and the salesman spotted me at once.

"Welcome back, Mister Roberts. I have everything set up for you."

Perfect. I could sense that Dad assumed I was buying a car for myself. We followed the salesman to the new Escape Limited Edition and the salesman turned towards me with two sets of keys in his hand, the registration in the other hand, his broad face barely able to contain his smile.

"Give those to my father," I said.

The salesman turned to Dad, holding out keys and registration.

"No, no. Those are his," he managed to say.

I reached out and plucked the registration from the salesman and handed it to Dad. "Look at the name on the registration, Dad. It's yours and Mom's," I said, smiling at his confusion.

"But I have a car," he said.

"No, Dad. I'm getting your old car and you and Mom get this new one. It's the least I can do to repay you for all you and Mom have done for me."

I swear I saw a tear welling up in the salesman's eyes.

"Oh, Son, you didn't have to do this," he said, his voice shaky as the reality of it sank home to him.

"That's the beauty of it. I didn't have to, but it feels right to me. Now drive your new car home and show Mom," I said as the salesman placed the two sets of keys in his hand.

I followed him home in my new old set of wheels and stood and watched Mom's reaction. It was a wonderful, happy moment that shoved my persistent flashbacks into the background for a blessed moment.

Eight

ON THE WEDNESDAY before my gala Saturday night mixer Mom called to rescue me.

"I know your heart is in the right place, Tojo, but I think serving Chinese takeout Saturday could be a wet blanket."

I knew what she meant. And I might add, my plan seemed to be working. "What do you suggest, Mom?" I asked innocently enough.

"With my help, I think you should make a Chanko Nabe hot pot. I'll bring my Nabe pot and the ingredients over on Saturday morning and we can set it up on your dinner table. I can show you how to make it, and you'll be the life of the party. What do you think, Tojo?"

"I think that's a wonderful idea, Mom. I've always wanted to know how to make Chanko Nabe," I said as I breathed a silent sigh of relief over Mom coming to my rescue. The thought of Chinese takeout was off-putting, even for me.

True to her word, Mom arrived on Saturday morning. I was hanging pictures on the walls to make my new apartment homier, and she gave me a hand with one of the larger ones. When it was in place she said, "Come with me, Tojo, to get things from my new car," she said with emphasis on *new*.

Together we hauled the cast iron Nabe pot and the bags of ingredients into my apartment.

"Put the pot on your new table, Tojo. Do you have an extension cord?"

Of course not. Why would I need an extension cord in my new apartment?

"No, Mom. Did you happen to bring one?"

"Yes, Tojo. It's on the back seat. Here's the key."

"Dutiful Tojo went back out, got the extension cord and returned.

"We don't need it now, but you'll need it on Saturday evening," she explained, smiling sweetly.

In the kitchen she took the containers of prawns, crabmeat, tofu, mushrooms, noodles, and cabbage from the bags and placed them in my fridge. She finished by handing me a container of miso paste. "Put that in the refrigerator, too, Tojo. It keeps it fresh," she added.

Mom followed by giving me a card of instructions that detailed how to prepare it all. I looked it over and handed it back to her. "No, Tojo. You keep it," she said as she pushed it back at me. As she did so a smile appeared on her face and she said, "You and that memory of yours!"

"Thanks, Mom. I've got it," I said, acknowledging her comment by matching her smile.

By that Saturday afternoon I'd done all I could to buff my apartment into shape and get out the dishes, forks, and spoons and all the other stuff needed to make my dinner table look ready for the occasion. The centerpiece was Mom's Nabe pot, set next to my place at the table. The extension cord presented a challenge. I didn't want anyone tripping over it. I solved the problem by tucking it under a scatter rug.

I made a final walkthrough of everything. I had beer in the fridge, wine on the sideboard and a bottle of Old Leather bourbon for Dad and anyone else with an adventurous streak. An array of glasses sat on the counter, patiently waiting for my guests.

For snacks I had chips and dips, plus celery stalks imbedded with cream cheese, and a cheese ball on a plate with crackers.

I ducked into the bathroom to make sure my toothbrush and shaving gear were tucked out of sight and hand towels and a fresh soap dispenser were ready on the counter. I also installed a fresh roll of toilet paper and stowed the used roll under the sink.

I checked my bedroom, which wasn't part of the party space, but a curious sister or mother might poke a head in to check it out. My bed was made, and clothes were tucked away. I figured it should pass a cursory inspection.

When I switched on the floor lamp, I realized that I got no shock. My apartment seemed to be free of static electricity, unlike Lisa's. I wondered what the difference could be.

At six-fifteen I poured the diluted miso solution I'd mixed up earlier into Mom's Nabe pot and plugged in the extension cord. The small red light on the pot's front told me it was working. I was as ready as I'd ever be.

Let the games begin.

Kim showed up first. After we hugged and pecked, she scooted about the room, her eyes everywhere.

"It's nice, Joe. It looks like you," she said, a smile of satisfaction gracing her features.

"Thanks, Sis. I figured it was time I got independent from Mom and Dad. It suits me fine," I said. I retrieved the pendant sketches and handed them to her.

"What's this?"

"You know about the diamonds, right?"

"Yes. Mom told me you thought they were pebbles," she said with a grin.

"I did. Anyway, I want you and Mom to pick out a design and I'll have it made up for you," I said.

"Oh, for heaven's sake! You don't have to do that, Joe," she said, protesting.

"That's the beauty of it, Kim. I don't have to, but I want to," I said.

"You know Mom and I don't go in for jewelry," she argued.

"That's the great thing about a pendant. You can wear it, and nobody will see it if you don't want them to. I told Mom maybe the two of you could settle on the same design. A common bond," I added.

"Oh, that's so sweet!" she said. She glanced back at the designs as the door buzzer sounded. I crossed to the door and pushed the release without asking who was there over the intercom. If it was a party crasher, he or she would even up the numbers. Maybe a future boyfriend for Kim.

A knock on the door a short time later solved the problem. Mom and Dad breezed in, Dad clutching a vase of cut flowers for the table. He pressed them in my hands without ceremony and I set them on the table while Mom, Dad and Kim did the hug and peck thing. Formalities out of the way, Mom and Kim huddled over the pendant designs and Dad spotted the bourbon and broke the seal.

"Do you have any ice, Son?"

Ice! How could I forget ice?

"Sure, Dad. I was keeping it cold." Talk about a lame line. I opened the freezer section and pulled out the ice bin, poured a dozen or so cubes into a bowl and put the bin back in the freezer section. For a scoop I took out a large spoon and set it in the bowl. Dad smiled at the results.

"Thanks, Joe. Are you joining me?" he asked, the bourbon bottle held aloft.

"Don't mind if I do," I said. I picked up a glass, fed it with ice and bourbon and touched the rim to Dad's.

"Cheers, Son. Your place looks swell."

"Cheers, Dad. Thanks."

We sipped our chilled bourbon in a silence interrupted by the doorbell sounding. I went to the intercom as Lisa's voice came through. "Hi, Joe. It's Lisa."

"Hey, Lisa. Come on up!" I said as I pushed the door release button. Mom and Kim exchanged a look, hearing what I said. I waited by the door for Lisa's knock, unable to think of doing anything else.

I jumped when I heard the soft knock at the door, I'm not sure why. It wasn't as if I wasn't expecting it. Nerves brought on by having my first get-together, plus maybe a worry about how my family would get along with Lisa? It was time to find out. I pulled the door wide and there she stood, a warm smile lighting up her face. She wore a pale green summer dress that showed off her figure without being showy. Her dark hair was tied in the back in a ponytail with a pale green ribbon. She held a bottle of wine with its own green ribbon around the neck.

"Hi, Joe," she said while her black eyes searched the room. "It looks like I'm late."

"Not at all. Everyone else came early," I said to put her at ease.

She stepped inside and I closed the door behind her. "Hey, everyone. This is Lisa Goodweather, the girl I met at the VA," I announced to my family.

They responded by surrounding Lisa, everyone doing the hug thing, the peck thing reserved for later if they felt it was warranted. Kim went first, then Mom, then Dad. I relaxed seeing the friendly reception they gave her. She continued to clutch the bottle of wine she'd brought so I stepped in to rescue her.

"Here, Lisa, let me take the bottle from you, and many thanks for bringing it. You're so thoughtful," I said, beaming.

"It's the same wine you brought to my dinner so we're even now," she said, her smile having its effect on me. She handed me the bottle and I took it, my hand brushing hers as I did so. A noticeable spark leapt from her hand to mine. And I thought my apartment was free of static electricity. Go figure.

I took the bottle to the fridge while Mom and Kim closed in around Lisa. Dad followed me, his glass empty. "Time for a refill, Son," he said, his glass held out. I retrieved my empty glass and put ice in both. Dad picked up the Old Leather bottle and poured a respectable splash in each. We clinked glasses and took sips.

"Nice young lady there," he said with a sweeping gesture at Lisa.

I eyeballed the interaction between Lisa and my two female family members. They were having an animated conversation, all fully engaged. My anxiety level dropped into the comfort zone. I saw that none were clutching glasses, so I stepped back over to play the perfect host. "Can I get you ladies anything to drink?" I asked in a voice loud enough to cut through their chatter. Three sets of eyes turned my way, followed by three warm smiles. All three requested wine, then resumed their woman talk. I left them to fill their orders, glad that Lisa had brought a bottle. I had two in the fridge, but the way things were going I could run out. I didn't need to win the Bad Host Award for my first attempt at socializing.

I carried the three glasses back to the ladies, observing that they were all fully engaged, as before. They accepted their glasses with a smile, took a sip and returned to their deep discussion. I walked back over to join Dad who was busy putting a dent in the cheese ball.

"Here you go, Son," he said, holding a cheese-smeared cracker out to me. I took it and stuffed it in my mouth, then chewed it to an unrecognizable state of oblivion.

"Thanks, Dad." It came out sounding like Fanks, Dad, the cheese sticking to the roof of my mouth.

"Sounds like you need another shot of Old Leather," he said with a smile as he rattled the ice cubes in his glass.

Dad has an incredible tolerance for alcohol. I've seen him drink many friends under the table. Me, not so good. We never went up against each other, but I have no doubt that I'd be the loser. "I'll knock back one more with you, Dad, but I'll have to start dinner soon," I said while I went to the ice maker. On his part, Dad filled both our glasses well above the halfway point. We clinked glasses, said "cheers!" and sipped the strong, tastebud-titillating bourbon. "Ah!" we sighed as one. "That's damned good bourbon," added Dad.

A glance at my watch told me it was closing in on eight, and Mom had suggested that we eat at around half past. I'd already figured that fifteen minutes would be enough time to toss all the ingredients into the pot, so I had time to circulate amongst my guests. "Let's go see how the ladies are doing, Dad."

"From where I'm standing, they're doing just fine," he said in between sips.

"Trust but verify. I'll go check."

"Okay, Son. I'll join you," said Dad as he fell in next to me.

As we approached, the ladies turned and welcomed our arrival with their smiles. "Have you solved the problems of the world?" I asked.

"All but one," said Mom, sporting her enigmatic smile.

"What one is that?" I asked while thinking that she was setting me up.

"You, Tojo. For the life of us we can't figure you out."

"Did you come up with any suggestions? I'm open to your ideas," I said, sharing my smile with the three of them.

"No, Tojo. We decided to give you some time and space to come up with your own solutions, isn't that right, ladies?" she said with a nod to Kim and Lisa. They smiled and nodded back at Mom.

"I appreciate that. As you know, I got a degree in Life Studies from good old Southern Aurora, and then the army gave me two more years of their version of Life Studies. With all that, I'm confident that a decision is on the horizon," I said, trying my best to sound confident.

"That's my boy," said Mom. Kim and Lisa grinned at her motherly statement.

"Meanwhile, is anybody getting hungry?" I asked.

Heads nodded and Mom spoke up. "Another little splash of wine would be welcome while you prepare the dinner, Tojo."

"I'm on it!" I announced. I made a beeline for the fridge. Dad saw me coming and volunteered to be the wine steward. I thanked him, handed him the open wine bottle, and began gathering the dinner ingredients. I carried the stuff to the table and dumped the noodles into the simmering miso mixture. Step one. Check.

When I added the prawns and crabmeat to the mix, the last step in the process, the ladies' heads were turned in my direction, the rich aroma reaching out to them. I uncorked another bottle of wine and set it on the table while Dad mixed a final Old Leather bourbon. All was ready.

"Come and get it!" I announced in a voice that reached everyone. None of them needed to be asked twice. They advanced on the table. Mom and Dad sat on my right and Kim and Lisa sat on my left, Kim leaving the chair next to me for Lisa. Once we were seated, I held my hands together in front of me and my guests did likewise. Dad as elder began and we all joined in. "Itadakimasu." Thank you for this meal. Before conversation flowed again, I looked over at Mom and said, "Gochisosama." Thank you for putting so much effort into this meal. She blushed and gave me a dismissive wave of her hand.

I ladled the rich mixture into the bowls and passed them around, my parents getting theirs first, then Kim and Lisa next. I filled mine and set it down. "The moment of truth," I said as I scooped up a spoonful.

Dad spoke up. "Sorry to say, Son. This isn't very good." He wore a disappointed expression on his face. My face fell, hearing his criticism.

"What's missing, Dad?" Silence filled the room.

"Nothing's missing. It's just not very good. He paused dramatically and said, "It's excellent, Son." He beamed with the success of his joke, and everyone laughed at his wit while I remembered playing the same joke on Lisa at her dinner for us. I knew firsthand the pain she felt.

"Thanks, Dad. I could whack you on the arm and kiss you on your bald spot, but I'll save it for later." My way of letting Lisa know I understood the pain I caused her. She locked eyes with mine, her smile making me go weak in the knees. Good thing I was sitting down.

The dinner went well. Conversation flowed around the table, and Dad and I had seconds of the excellent Chanko Nabe. When everyone had finished, I got up from the table and went to my pantry where I picked up a cookie tin and carried it to the table. I pulled off the lid and set the container in the center of the table. "Oh! Sesame cookies," said Kim. She picked up the tin, took a cookie and passed the tin across the table to Mom. The tin quickly made the rounds. I held it out to Lisa and when she brushed my hand while reaching for a cookie the static electricity made its appearance again. I flinched, feeling it.

Lisa saw my reaction. "What, Joe?" she asked, her voice soft, meant for me alone.

"Didn't you feel it?" I whispered.

"Feel what?" she asked, a puzzled expression on her face.

"The static electricity. It must be the dry air," I whispered.

"What are you two so busy talking about?" Dad, ever-observant, had noticed.

"I was commenting about the static electricity, Dad."

"Must be on your side of the table. I haven't noticed any over here," he said.

Mom's facial expression looked like the cat that swallowed the canary.

I changed the subject. "So, what do you think about my apartment?" I asked with a hand-sweep at everyone.

Kim: "It's a perfect man cave for you, Joe."

Mom: "It's lovely, Son, but remember, you always have a room in our home."

Dad: "I love it, Joe. It's already my favorite place to go for a drink."

Lisa: "It's a warm and comfy place for you. You've made a great choice, Joe."

"Well, on those well-chosen notes, I'll open the last bottle of chilled wine to put the icing on the cake." I took Lisa's bottle from the fridge, extracted the cork with a satisfying pop and circled the table, pouring wine into glasses as requested. Most settled for a small splash, leaving half a bottle in reserve.

Dad took a sip from his glass and, in the silence that followed asked, "How's everything going for you two at the VA?" His eyes swept over Lisa and me as his question broke through the thin air in the room.

I didn't know what Lisa was thinking. I hadn't told her that I mentioned her PTSD issues with my parents so Dad's question could be causing her pain. Her answer caught me by surprise. She reached over and put her hand on mine, sending that now-familiar shockwave through my system, and said, "Your son Joe, or should I say Tojo, has been an enormous help to me and to many others in the group. He has shared his own issues with us and has explained what he's doing to combat his flashbacks and nightmares. I'm following his examples and it's helping me," she said while her eyes moved around the table, touching everyone.

I breathed a sigh of relief. Lisa handled the question admirably well, considering how it must have caught her off-guard. "My turn," I said, breaking the silence that followed Lisa's remarks. "I'm making progress. I don't wake up in the night with my T-shirt soaked through with sweat with my nightmare pursuing me from my dreams into reality. Most nights, anyway," I added with a grim smile.

"What do you do to reduce the nightmares?" asked Kim.

I explained how I discovered that I could build obstacles in my mind that slowed and sometimes stopped my nightmare from getting through to me. "It's not easy, and sometimes it breaks through. On nights like that the sweats return," I said.

"It must be awful having to go through that, night after night," said Kim, her sweet face radiating sympathy.

"It was, at first. To be honest, I considered ending it all on more than one occasion. But I'm beyond that now, because I can feel the progress I've made, and I firmly believe that I can eventually defeat the nightmare, put it in a sealed box forever."

"You know that we'll always be here for you, Tojo, to help you through this in any way we can," said Mom, her eyes on mine as she spoke. I could sense the worry I caused by confessing to having suicidal thoughts.

"I know, Mom. I can't begin to tell you what your love and support means to me."

Lisa found her voice. "And as Joe finds support through you, Mrs. Roberts, I find strength and support through him." She squeezed my hand, sending ripples of electricity through me.

Time to change the subject. "Who wants another splash of wine?" I asked around.

Mom responded by glancing at her watch. Her eyebrows shot skyward, and she said, "Mercy me! Look at the time. Your father and I should be heading back home."

My watch showed it to be a frog whisker past nine-thirty. "Are you sure you can't stay a little longer? The party's just getting started," I said, already knowing the response she'd give.

"Heaven's no. You know your father likes to be in bed by eleven, and he catches the late news before that. It's been a delightful evening, Tojo. You've outdone yourself on this your first social gathering," she added, embellishing her comment with her warm smile.

"She's right, Son. We'll leave you young folks to carry on. We'd be a wet blanket if we stayed any longer. Oh, and take good care of that bourbon. I'll be along for a snort or two down the road," said Dad, a sly grin spreading across his craggy face.

"All right, if you say so. I'll come by tomorrow with your Nabe pot and some leftovers, Mom."

"Bring the pot but keep the leftovers. It'll reassure me that you aren't in danger of starving," she said, adding her motherly smile I knew so well.

Everyone got up from the table and walked Mom and Dad to the door. We took turns hugging and pecking. When my turn came, Mom whispered in my ear. "You remember to treat her right, Tojo." I understood what she meant. I was pleased when Mom bestowed a peck on Lisa, which Lisa returned. I held the door open, and Mom and Dad were on their way. The three of us returned to the table, Kim taking Mom's chair. I had Lisa on my left and Kim on my right. We formed an isosceles triangle.

Kim spoke first. "I had no idea that you two suffered from such dreadful nightmares. If it was me, I don't know how I could handle it."

Lisa said, "If it wasn't for Joe's intervention that offered me a way to get a handle on my flashbacks, I'd more than likely be snowed by drugs as a way to cope."

"That would be a terrible way to have to go through life," said Kim.

"That's true, but I'd guess that close to a quarter of the people in my group opt for drugs as a solution to their issues. Problem is, once they opt for drugs, they're giving up on leading normal lives again," said Lisa. I nodded in agreement.

"So, tell me, Joe. What do you do to weaken your nightmares, your flashbacks? I know we both share an incredible memory, so anything that happens to you will be in your memory, for better or for worse," said Kim.

I picked up the wine bottle and poured a healthy dollop into each of our glasses. No objections were raised. "It'll be easier for you to understand, Kim, since you have the same kind of memory. Think about what you do when something happens to you that you'd just as soon forget. If you're like me, you build a wall around the ugly memory in your head, so it doesn't keep popping up, it isn't so accessible. I tried that with my nightmares, but they were much stronger than a simple wall could block. So I went on the offensive, building defenses that my nightmare had to face to get through to me. Some of them worked and some were failures. With each defeat, though, I learned something, and my next defenses were more effective. I'm to the point now where I get through most nights with minimal nightmares. It's a constant fight, and I think I'm winning. The alternative, a life snowed by drugs, is nothing I'd care to live with," I said.

"You two are an inspiration," said Kim. She picked up her wine glass, saluted Lisa and me and downed the pale liquid in a single gulp. She set her glass down, pushed back in her chair, and stood up.

"Where are you going?" I asked, knowing the answer.

"It's time for me to make tracks to my own digs," she said. I told my roomie I'd be home by ten, which is no longer possible. It's been great fun spending time with you, Joe, and it's a pleasure meeting you, Lisa." We hugged and pecked, and then she and Lisa hugged and pecked. A warm expression of acceptance. Lisa was no longer a stranger to my family. Something about that made me feel good, not sure why.

When I closed the door on the departing Kim, Lisa said, "I should be going, too."

"You have wine to finish," I said.

"Oh, all right. Then I should go."

We returned to the table, and I turned my chair sideways, facing her.

She stared into my eyes a moment. "I'm not sure I've figured you out, Joe. First, I saw you as you stood in front of a room of strangers and talked to us about PTSD, your PTSD, and how you were getting a handle on it. You overflowed with confidence, which spilled over into the whole room. You seemed a little cocky, even."

"Now I've seen you interact with your family. When your mother joked that she, we couldn't figure you out, you told her you were open to suggestions. She said she wasn't offering you any, that you'd come up with something on your own. You as much as said that you were still working things out. So, which of these two people is the real Joe Roberts?" she asked, a quizzical expression on her cherubic face.

I thought a moment and said, "I'm both of those people. I spoke with confidence and conviction to you and the others at the VA, and I let Mom and Kim and you know that I'm still struggling with my future. The thing that complicates it is my diamonds and gold."

"What?"

I realized that I hadn't told Lisa of my newfound wealth brought back from Iraq. I summed it up for her. At that time, I had no idea of the total value, only that it was a tidy sum.

"That explains a lot, Joe. I don't know what I'd do if I came into that kind of a windfall."

"In some ways I think that I don't deserve it, that I should give it to charity, but in other ways I think it came to me for a reason and I should use it to bring good to my corner of the world."

Lisa drained her wine glass and set it on the table. "You've helped me know you better, Joe. It explains the conflict and indecision you showed earlier. And on that note, I really must go." She got to her feet and headed for the door, me following at her side, unsure what, if anything, I should do. My Mom's guiding words echoed in my head. *You tread lightly with her, you hear me, Tojo?*

As I reached for the door handle, Lisa stepped in front of me and cupped my face with her hands, drawing my face down to hers. Our lips met, the electric current flowed between us, and she kissed me, gently at first, and more enthusiastically as she continued. I responded with equal enthusiasm. When I had thoughts of picking her up and carrying her off to the bedroom she stepped back, her eyes closed and said, "This is a test. Lisa is conducting a test of her feelings for Joe Roberts. This is only a test." It was the sweetest public service announcement I'd ever heard.

She opened her eyes, said "Good night, Joe," and was out the door before I could think of something to say. I stood there a moment, wondering if I'd imagined the whole scene. Recalling the current that flowed into me when her lips pressed against mine, I knew it had been real. Lisa was one high-voltage lady.

Nine

M Y CELL PHONE's ringtone woke me in the morning. I marveled at the fact that my T-shirt was dry as I reached to answer it. Another small victory over my nightmare. My phone face told me two things. It was eight o'clock, the latest I'd slept in a long time, and the call was from the Roberts' residence.

"Good morning," I said into the phone, my voice betraying my emergence from sleep.

"Good morning, Tojo. Are you alone?" It was Mom.

"Yes, Mom. Quite alone. Lisa left a short time after Kim did," I said.

"That's good, Tojo. You're good to respect boundaries with Lisa at this time of her life."

"I'm a good little martyr, Mom." I brushed my index finger across my lips, recalling Lisa's departing test. I wondered idly what score she gave me. Hell, I figured that if I'd failed it, I was ready to take the test again. Practice makes perfect, right?

"Yes, well, you stay being a good little martyr, Tojo. In Lisa's fragile condition there's no telling how gullible she might be, and then she has to live with it forever after," pronounced my dear Mom.

"I hear you, Mom. I've always respected other people's boundaries." *To the point of missing out on some great moments, no doubt.*

"Now, on another subject. Kimiko and I looked over all the jewelry designs that you gave us, and we both agreed on the same one. It's on page one, the second line, the one in the middle. It's a simple cross and we both thought it was a perfect fit for us. And here's something to log away in your memory. Lisa watched us as we went through the choices, and when we both chose that design, she wrapped her arms around both of us and said it was a perfect choice. If things work out between the two of you, it might make a nice gift for her."

"And then you can be a threesome," I said.

"That would be nice, Tojo. Both Kimiko and I agree that Lisa is a charming young lady."

"Thanks for all that, Mom. I'll go see the jeweler and get your pendants ordered."

"You're a sweet boy, Tojo."

"I'm twenty-four years old, Mom. I'm no longer a boy," I said.

"No matter how old you get, Tojo, you'll always be my sweet boy," she said sweetly.

I knew there was no changing her mind. It was made up. Truth be told, it was made up years ago.

I shaved, dressed, downed a bowl of cereal and headed for Whiteman's jewelry store. He brought out his copy of the sketches, I pointed to the design Mom and Kim had chosen, he smiled and said my mom and sister had excellent taste and he'd get right on it. I asked him if I could get a discount if he made three of them and he assured me that I could since he would be using the same mold to cast all three settings.

"Then three it is," I said, making a sweeping gesture with my hand. I considered for a moment if I would ever give the third cross to Lisa.

As I was turning to leave, a thought occurred to me. I had no idea how much all the diamonds locked away in my safety deposit box were worth. If I was going to use the diamonds to guide my life, do something worthwhile, I needed to know what I had for resources. If I had a number to go on, I could budget my expenses and make my wealth last longer, maybe even into my retirement years. I turned back to Mr. Whiteman and asked him if he would assess all my diamonds, not just the ones he'd already handled.

"That's what I'm in business for, Mister Roberts. And you must call me Harold from now on," he said, his smile warming the edges of his round face.

"Harold it is, and I'm Tojo, but everyone but Mom calls me Joe," I said, smiling at the thought.

"A pleasure, Joe," said Harold, extending his chubby hand. His grip was firm. Jeweler's hands are busy hands.

"I'll bring you a pouch at a time so you can keep track of all of them," I said.

"It sounds like I've got my work cut out for me," said Harold, his warm smile overspreading his cherubic face.

"I'd say you do. When you're finished, I'll have a much better idea how much I have. It will help me plan my philanthropic work."

"That sounds interesting. What do you plan to do?"

"I'm not sure yet. Whatever it is, I think I should be giving back to the less fortunate out there for the wealth of diamonds that came my way," I said.

"There's that man on a TV show who goes around finding people who are in a jam and fixing things for them, As I recall, he calls himself the Equalizer. Is that what you mean?" asked Harold.

I thought of Lisa. I'd agreed to help her get even with the man who raped her. It fit the image Harold described. Joe Roberts the Equalizer. Somehow it didn't fit the picture I was trying to develop. "I don't think so, Harold, but who knows?"

I left Harold with the task of creating the three pendants for the women in my life and made a trip to my bank and my safety deposit box. I took out a pouch of the large diamonds, might as well start with the big boys, and dropped it off with Harold. He was in the back preparing his molds when I came in. The acrid odor of molten metal, presumably gold, reached my nostrils.

"I'll be out in a minute, Joe. Thanks for your patience."

"No problem, Harold. Take your time."

He walked through the curtain a short time later, his face moist with perspiration. "I've finished one of the settings, Joe. The next two will go easier." He patted his face with a snow-white handkerchief he took from a back pocket.

"I brought a pouch of stones for you to appraise," I said, holding it out to him.

"Ah, yes. I'll get to them as soon as I finish the other two castings," he said while taking the zipper pouch from me. He turned and carried it behind the curtained doorway, and I heard him open and close a safe. I appreciated his security. It wouldn't do to have a thief stroll in and walk off with the pouch.

"Thanks, Harold!" I called out to him. "See you in a couple days."

"That will be perfect, Joe. See you then!" he called back to me.

I left his store, my thoughts occupied with the challenge of what to do with my wealth.

When I woke up the next morning my T-shirt was damp, but I couldn't for the life of me remember having a visit from my nightmare. Progress.

As I lay there in bed, reviewing my night's sleep, it struck me that I'd already set a course for my life's plan. My new-found wealth could be used to bring happiness to others, and to me as well. I'd already experienced the pleasure it gave me when I bought a new car for my parents, and I anticipated the pleasure ahead when I presented Mom and Kim with their pendants. As for Lisa and her plan to even the score with the ogre who raped her, I needed to work on that. I figured that the outcome should please me as much as it pleased Lisa. I had no problem helping her, but I knew I needed to feel good, not guilty about the outcome. One nasty nightmare is more than enough, thank you. The time had come for a planning session with Lisa. I also wanted to find out what she had to say about the test she conducted. Who knows? Maybe I failed it. That would set me back a few notches. Not a pleasant thought.

I climbed out of bed and performed my morning ablutions, nicking my chin slightly when I overdid trying to shave the whiskers from the cleft in my chin. Dressed, I brewed coffee and toasted a bagel, slathering it with jalapeno cream cheese. My day was off to a spicy start. Yum.

With my second cup of coffee poured, I checked the time. It was a decent gap past eight. I hoped Lisa was up and around as I tapped in her contact number. She picked up on the third ringy-dingy, leaving me to wonder if I'd shaken her from slumber. My fears were dispelled when she spoke.

"Lisa's upholstery. How may I help you?"

If her phone was anything like mine, caller ID would have told her it was me. Should I be thinking *uh oh?* "Hey, Lisa. It's me, Joe," I said, guessing, no hoping that she hadn't seen it was me calling.

Hi, Joe. What took you so long?"

Confusion reigned. "What do you mean?"

"I thought you might be curious about how my little test came out," she said. There was an unmistakable tease in her voice.

Time to play it cool. "Oh, that? I thought I should give you time to reach a decision. I half expected you to call me with the results," I said. I found it difficult to speak clearly with my tongue tucked solidly in my cheek.

"If it's not about my test, what prompted you to call me?" she asked, cutting to the chase.

"I think it's time we sat down and planned our trip to Schenectady."

Lisa was silent a moment. "Oh. Yes. We should do that," she said. I thought I could hear her wheels grinding through the phone.

"What's your schedule look like?" I asked.

"The only thing on my horizon is tomorrow's PTSD meeting at the VA," she said.

Thanks for the reminder, Lisa! "Right. An afternoon meeting," I said.

"Rescheduled so more PTSD clients can attend," she said.

Rescheduled by Larry so I can reach out to more of them. "I'll be there," I said, thinking how dumb that sounded when the words tumbled out.

"You'll be speaking to the group, won't you?"

"Uh huh. Larry thinks my message can be helpful."

"I know from personal experience that he's right," said Lisa, no bull coming through in her voice.

"I appreciate your vote of confidence."

"So, if it works for you, I'll have you come to my apartment after. We can talk about Schenectady, and I'll make dinner for us," said Lisa.

"It works for me. See you at tomorrow's meeting."

"Great. See you there. Oh, by the way, you passed the test. Barely," said Lisa.

"Barely?"

"I'll explain the test results when I see you tomorrow, Joe." She disconnected, ending the conversation.

I stood there a moment, transfixed by Lisa's comment. Then I shook my head to shed the questions bubbling up and focused my attention on my talk at the VA tomorrow. I considered where I sat in my own recovery. It compared favorably to a roller coaster ride, with both highs and lows. My nightmare turned out to be a quick learner. The defenses I put up worked well the first night, but often fell under my nightmare's onslaught the next night. To keep one step ahead of it I needed to shift the defenses I built in my mind every night. If I got careless and skipped a night, I paid for it with a wet T-shirt and a mostly sleepless night. The horrors of that night in Iraq came back at me night after night when I closed my eyes to sleep.

The trilling of my phone brought me back to the here and now. I thought it might be Lisa, calling back with more information about her test. I was wrong. It was Harold Whiteman, my caller ID told me.

"Hey, Harold. How's it going?" I asked into the phone.

"It's, ah, going fine, Joe. I'd like you to come to my store so we can talk about the items you brought to me," he said, his voice charged with mystery.

Now what? "Is everything all right?" I asked him.

"Yes, of course. I just have a few questions for you before we go further," said Harold.

More mystery. "Okay, Harold. I'll be there within the hour."

"Perfect, Joe. See you soon." Harold ended the call.

My mind whirled with unanswered questions. The answer that dominated all the other candidates was that my big diamonds turned out to be worthless. That would change everything. I picked up my key ring, locked the apartment door behind me and took the stairs two at a time to the ground floor. I dashed out the door and leaped into my car with disastrous thoughts filling my mind.

The little bell over Harold's door dinged my arrival and Harold looked up to see me, his face all business. He came around the corner of the counter and stepped quickly to the entry door. He flipped the sign in the window from OPEN to CLOSED, spun the deadbolt to the locked position, and brought his eyes to bear on mine. "A precaution, Joe. Come. Let's go in the back."

Puzzled, confused, I followed him behind the counter and into his back room where he did all his jewelry work. It was a compact area. A tall, formidable looking safe stood against the far wall and a large worktable sat in the middle of the room. An array of tools I was unfamiliar with were lined up in the table's center. A red enamel kiln sat near the side of the table. I guessed it was used to melt silver and gold to make Harold's settings. Two simple wood chairs with padded seats faced the table.

"Have a seat, Joe, please," said Harold, beckoning at the two chairs. I pulled one out and sat. Harold took the other one.

"What's this all about, Harold?" I asked, my eyes locked on his.

He returned my gaze and said, "Your last pouch of stones has me nervous, Joe. I felt that I needed to be discreet."

"All right. You've got good news and bad news, right? Tell me the good news first," I said.

"The good news is, that last pouch of diamonds has a wholesale market value of three point six million dollars."

I thanked God for small favors. If I hadn't been sitting down, who knows where I would have ended up? In a heap on the floor, for starters, Harold would have struggled to pick me up. I was conscious of a gasp coming out of me. "Are you sure?" I managed to ask when I'd gained a semblance of control.

"Absolutely. It is my job to be sure," he said.

"Okay, Harold, what's the bad news?"

"The bad news is, I don't feel comfortable having that kind of wealth here in my store. Jewelry stores are a prime target for clever thieves," said Harold, finishing his sentence by spreading his open hands on the table in front of him.

"But you have that big safe over there," I said with a gesture towards it.

"If a thief came in and put the muzzle of a gun against my head, I would open that safe in a heartbeat," he said, no apology in his voice.

"I get it. What do you suggest that we do?" I asked.

"I have taken the liberty to put a paper in the pouch with my certification of value on it. I have further sealed the pouch. It cannot be opened without breaking the seal. If it remains that way my certification will be valid. Do you follow me?" asked Harold.

"I do. I'll return it to my safety deposit box."

"Do you own a firearm?"

I thought back on the guns I carried and used while in the army, firearms I set aside when I mustered out. "No," I said.

"Well, I strongly recommend that you consider it. Many unsuspecting people are accosted and robbed every day. It would be a disaster if it happened while you were carrying a pouch of your diamonds," said Harold.

"I get your point, Harold. I'll put a visit to a gun shop on my priority list. Is that why you were so mysterious when you called me?" I asked.

"Yes. I'm more than a little paranoid. I was robbed a couple years ago, and it was obvious that the thieves had been watching me, watching my store, to figure out the best time to rob me. I suspected that they had somehow tapped my phone and knew from my conversations when I received a shipment of diamonds. I vowed to do everything possible to keep it from happening again. Two hundred and fifty thousand dollars of insurance didn't begin to cover it all. I was fortunate that I had cash reserves. Otherwise, I would have been out of business," he said.

"That's terrible, Harold. Now I know where you're coming from. Do you keep a gun handy in case there's another robbery?"

"Heavens no. The robbery I experienced taught me that if I had a gun and tried to use it, I would have been shot dead. The two thieves pulled out handguns and held them on me during the entire robbery. I'd rather be a live coward than a dead hero," he said.

I left Harold's store with the wildly valuable pouch of diamonds concealed under my shirt, searching everyone and everywhere for threats. My imagination had me prepared for an assault from every person I passed. Somehow, I made it to my car unscathed. I drove directly to the bank, checking the cars behind me for a tail the whole way. I pulled into the bank's parking area, and when I climbed out, I searched everywhere around me for threats as I made it to the bank's front entrance. Once inside, I relaxed. A little. When the pouch of diamonds was safely back inside my safety deposit box I relaxed even more. It occurred to me in that moment that wealth has its advantages. And disadvantages.

Conceding that Harold had made a good point, I found a gun shop and went in. An employee spotted me (my six-foot four frame is hard to miss) and offered me a welcoming smile. I strolled to the glass counters and their displays of handguns. I was overwhelmed by the selection. Revolvers and semi-automatics vied for my attention. I moved down the line and suddenly stopped dead in my tracks. My eyes locked onto an M9, the handgun issued to me in Iraq. The clerk saw me staring at it.

"You want to see that one? It's a Beretta 92FS," he said as he slid open the door on the rear of the cabinet.

"I know it as an M9," I said, eyeing the handgun as he lifted it out.

"Ex-military, right? Yeah, it's one and the same," he said, confirming my statement. He popped the mag and worked the action to show me it was clear, then passed it to me butt-first.

When my hand closed on it a flood of memories surged through me. It was like shaking hands with a long-lost friend. I'd put well over a thousand rounds through the M9 that hung at my side in Iraq. My target was paper, not human flesh. No, that's a lie. I targeted flesh in Tal Afar. Shoot or die. I shot, and I lived to fight another day.

I hefted the Beretta and, seeing that I had an unobstructed line of fire, I put the sights on a picture hanging on the wall at the other end of the store and whispered *blam!* The salesman, watching, said, "Looks like you've found a long-lost friend. I'd say it suits you."

I had to agree. "I'll take it, and a couple boxes of jacketed hollow points. Oh, and a holster," I added.

"A man who knows what he wants. I like that," said the salesman. He took out the box the Beretta came in and located two boxes of 9mm jacketed hollow point ammo, setting them on the counter. I opened the Beretta box and saw it contained a second magazine and a cleaning brush, plus a keyed lock.

"Do you want an IWB or OWB holster?" the salesman asked.

I knew what he was asking. An IWB holster is positioned inside the waistband for concealment while an OWB holster hangs on the belt outside the waistband for all the world to see. I opted for concealed carry. I'll take an IWB holster, as long as it's comfortable," I said.

"Your tall lean frame is perfect for an IWB holster. You should have no problem getting used to it," said the salesman. He took out a long form and set it on the counter in front of me, adding a pen for me to write with. I saw it was a Form 4473, a federal firearms registration application. Sixteen questions after name and address, all dealing with any past felonies, drug use, restraining orders and so forth. I was clean. I finished the form in less than ten minutes. The clerk collected my driver's license and went to a phone. I watched as he recited my information to the call center. I heard him say "Thank you," he scribbled something on the form and came back to me.

"Everything good?" I asked, unable to think of any reason why it wasn't.

"You passed with flying colors," he said, smiling.

A thought occurred to me. "Is there a range nearby where I can sight this puppy in?"

"You've come to the right place. We have an indoor range in the back of the store, open free of charge to our customers," said the clerk, a wide grin filling his face.

"Lead the way," I said.

He did.

The range had four firing lanes, all unoccupied. I took the first one. I set my gear on the ledge in front of me and strung the holster onto my belt. Then I filled both mags with hollow points and inserted one of them into the M9, worked the slide to chamber a round and fitted the loaded Beretta into the holster. While I did that, the clerk busied himself with attaching a silhouette target to the pulley. There were hearing and eye protectors provided by the store, and I put them on. "What distance do you want me to set the target?" the clerk asked.

I saw that the range was fifty yards long. "Run it out to twenty-five and let's see what I can do."

When the target settled at twenty-five yards I barked, "Ready on the firing line!" All was clear, I saw. I drew the Beretta and brought it up to the firing position in a fluid motion, then sent five rounds at the target in quick succession. My sight point was center mass. I holstered my Beretta and hollered 'clear!' then asked the clerk to bring in the target. As the target was pulleyed back, I could see five tight holes, all placed an inch left of center. I drew the Beretta from my new holster and adjusted the rear windage to compensate, then put it back in the holster. "Let's do it again," I said to the clerk. He ran the target back out.

My next five shots were tightly grouped in center mass. Satisfied, I fired my last five rounds at the silhouette's head. Then I ejected the empty mag and replaced it with the full one. I fired three shot groups, two at center mass and one at the head. The good old double-tap. I holstered my empty Beretta, said 'clear!' and had a look at the target. "Nice fuckin' shooting," said the clerk, seeing my tight groupings. His voice said he was impressed.

"Thanks." I agreed. I'd dotted the I's and crossed the T's. "Add a cleaning kit to the total and I'll give you my credit card."

He did, I did, and I was out the door with a bag in my left hand and a comfortable new friend on my right hip, all locked and loaded. Next stop: Back to the bank and my safety deposit box. Once I was securely inside one of the locked cubicles, I opened the box and did some ballpark calculations. I had two pouches of large diamonds, two pouches of medium-sized ones, and a third pouch of small diamonds. If the medium-sized ones were worth, say, a million dollars a pouch, and I added in the gold coins, I was the dumb-luck owner of over ten million dollars in diamonds and gold! *Maybe I should re-up, collect more goat skin bags and double my net worth.* Remembering the nightmares I brought home with me, I quickly dismissed that thought.

Most people would welcome a windfall of ten million dollars, but for me it created a million-dollar problem, and I needed a solution. I wanted to use it to help people who were down on their luck. I could simply donate it to a charity, or several charities for that matter, but then it would be out of my hands. If I did that, I knew I'd regret it when I came across someone in need. So, what to do? For now, my wealth was secure in my safety deposit box. I had the luxury of time to come up with a lifelong plan. It made no sense to make a hurried decision that I might live to regret later.

Ten

Larry greeted me with a warm hug when I arrived at the VA for my one o'clock session in front of the group. "How's it going, Joe? You still keeping your nightmares at bay?"

I told him of my successes, and failures, which would form the basis for my presentation.

Sounds to me like you're starting to win more than you're losing," he commented.

I hadn't thought of it like that. Larry had a point. A good one.

Larry glanced at his wristwatch and said, "Let's go give them hell. Showtime!"

I followed him to the group room. It was packed with vets suffering from PTSD. I recognized most of the faces. I spotted Lisa sitting in the back row. She didn't look at me. A queasy feeling settled in over my stomach.

Larry did his intro. "Hey, everyone. A lot of you know Joe Roberts from his earlier talks. Joe served in Iraq and, like you, he brought home his share of nightmares from his time there. He's been working hard to get those nightmares under control, and he's come to tell you how he's doing. And more important, what he's doing. Let's give him a two-hand welcome."

Everyone clapped vigorously for ten, fifteen seconds while I walked to the front of the room. I held up a hand to end it while smiling to let them know I appreciated it. I started by going over my nightmares and what caused them, and then I spoke about setting mental traps and blockades in my mind, all designed to slow or stop my nightmare from breaking through and disturbing my sleep.

"My nightmare is not only smart but it's persistent, too. If I set up defenses in my mind that work and I get a nightmare-free night out of them, I've learned that they don't work two nights in a row. My smartassed nightmare learns how to get around them the next night and I wake up soaked in sweat, the nightmare raining terror down on me.

"So, what I have is a constant battle to slow or stop my nightmare from breaking through my defenses and ruining my night. Once my nightmare learns the safe way around one of my defenses, it no longer works to stop it and I need to come up with a new one. If my defenses include explosives or pits with punji sticks or tripwires that trigger claymores, and my nightmare gets injured, it takes a night or two for the nightmare to recover from the injuries. But recover it does, no matter how bad the injury.

"Since we're all suffering in the same way, I think you know where this is going. We can gain the upper hand on our nightmares, but it takes a constant shifting of our defenses to keep ahead of them, keep them from showing up in our dreams and ruining our night's sleep. I wish I could say that I've defeated my nightmares once and for all, but that would be a lie. I *can* say that many of my defenses have worked, and I've enjoyed dreamless nights and a dry T-shirt to show for it."

Most of the vets laughed at my last statement. They knew about wet T-shirts.

"Questions?" I asked. I'd said my piece and it was time to let them speak their minds.

"Yeah, uh, Joe," began a heavyset young man in the front row, "you said that once you use a defense, it no longer works. Where do you get all your defenses? Seems like you'll run out, and then what?"

"That's a great question, Barry," I said, reading his name tag. "Every defense is built in a unique way. It might be on a hilltop, or in the woods, or with a body of water as a barrier. You can change the same defense to suit the location, and because the setting is different the defense will fool your nightmare again. But unless you change the setting, the nightmare will figure a way around it. It becomes a game of shifting scenes and defenses to stay a step ahead of your nightmares. Does that help?"

"Yeah, it does. I have to be thinking of new and different defenses if I want to gain the upper hand, for even one nightmare-free night," said Barry.

"That's right. What I'm working on now is a way to cause injury to my nightmare *every* night. I remember waking up after a Claymore went off in my dreams and seeing my nightmare with tatters of it lying on the ground. I think if I can cause that kind of injury to it every night, maybe it won't be able to recover enough to bother my dreams. That's my hope, anyway," I said.

Many questions followed, and I tried my best to answer them openly and honestly. Most of those who were present got involved in the give and take, but I spotted a half a dozen men who sat quietly, staring in my direction but giving no indication that they were taking anything in. Were their minds busy processing what I said, or were they off somewhere else, lost in a drug-induced fog? I made a mental note to ask Larry what he thought.

When a break occurred in the questioning, Larry stepped up next to me and said, "I hate to be a wet blanket but we're out of time, guys. And gals," he added, acknowledging the few women scattered in the crowd. "Thank you, Joe, for your words of encouragement. Let's all go home and see if we can use Joe's mind tricks to block our nightmares, our flashbacks."

The vets expressed their appreciation by clapping enthusiastically before filing out. Several offered me comments of thanks as they filed past me. I smiled and nodded at them. It occurred to me that if I reached even one of them with my message, my time was well spent. Lisa, last to leave, left Larry and me alone in the empty room.

The next thing I knew, Larry was bear-hugging me. He stepped away and said, "Thanks, man. That was another great presentation. In this world, if you broke through to even one of those guys, it would make every bit of your time worthwhile."

I could feel a grin stretching across my face. "Funny, Larry. I had the same exact thought seconds ago."

"In this business, I count success like the frog jumping out of the well. Three feet up, followed by it sliding back down two feet. Slow but steady progress is my hope for these vets. And that includes you," he said pointedly.

"You're right there. Just when I think I've jumped out of the well my nightmare comes storming back and I slide back down. Every victory is a milestone for me."

"You're my best success story, Joe. You keep on jumping and one of those jumps will have you clear of the well," said Larry, his three-fingered hand giving my upper arm a squeeze.

"What about those guys who sat and stared? Are they beyond hope?"

"I'd never count anyone out. You never know when they might catch a word or a phrase that starts their wheels turning," he said.

Fortified by my presentation and Larry's thoughtful words, I made my way to the entrance. I pushed through to find Lisa waiting, a warm smile pulling me in. "You did it again, Joe. I glanced around the room as you spoke, and you captured everyone's attention. Well, almost everyone," she added as she encircled my arm with hers. I felt the familiar shock of static electricity move up my arm.

"Yeah, I spotted a couple guys staring off into space. Seems like the medication they're on keeps them from concentrating. It's too bad they can't come off their meds for the class, maybe focus on gaining the upper hand over their flashbacks and nightmares. I asked Larry about them, and he said they might catch a word or a phrase that gets them thinking," I said as Lisa led the way to the parking lot.

"Why don't you ask Larry if there's a way that they could come drug free for the next meeting? Maybe he could make it happen," said Lisa, her eyes searching mine as she spoke.

"That's a great idea, Lisa. I like it. I'll see what he has to say."

We reached our cars. Lisa had spotted mine and parked next to it. Convenient. She opened hers and climbed in while I slid behind the wheel of mine, and I followed her to her apartment. It had its own parking area, and I took the space next to hers. We walked together to the entrance, she used her key to open the door and we went directly to her apartment. "Excuse the mess," she said with a sweep of her hand as she closed the door behind us.

I glanced around. Everything was neat, orderly. I thought of my apartment. If Lisa's was a mess, mine was a pigpen by comparison. "How can you live in such a messy apartment?" I asked as I worked my tongue into my cheek.

Lisa searched my face, then broke out in a soft, low chuckle. She put her hand on my arm and said, "Oh, my, Joe. You had me going for a second there." The wave of electric current flowed up my arm, sending a comforting warmth through me.

"You want a cup of coffee? I know I can use one," she said.

"Sounds good. Can I help?"

"No need. I put water and coffee in the machine before I left. All I have to do is turn it on and let it do its thing," she said.

I glanced at the counter and confirmed what she'd said. Two mugs sat waiting to be filled. The coffee maker began sending out its unique brewing sounds. *Blurk-blurk,* it said. *Blurk-blurk.* I turned and made my way to Lisa's sofa, taking in the bold fabric and careful workmanship. "Did you do your upholstery thing on this sofa?" I asked, my eyes finding hers.

"Guilty," she said, smiling.

"It looks very professional," I said as I ran my hand along the fabric of the arm.

"You should've seen it when I bought it at the thrift store. It cost me more to get it to my shop than I paid for it," she said. The *blurking* had stopped and she poured coffee into the two mugs.

"It looks brand new. You definitely know how to wield a tack hammer," I said, recalling her fantasy of tacking her attacker.

She smiled at me, aware that I remembered her fantasy. "Come do the milk and sugar thing with your coffee," she said with a sweeping gesture.

"I drink it the way it comes out of the pot," I said.

"Then sit tight and I'll bring it to you. Two black coffees, coming up." She closed the distance between us and passed me a steaming mug. Fingers touched and an electric surge made me flinch, jiggling my mug.

"Oh, careful, Joe. Are you okay?" said Lisa, concern showing.

"I'm good. It's just that there's a lot of static electricity in the room."

Lisa contemplated my face for a long moment before she sat in the upholstered chair facing me. She took an exploratory sip from her mug and said, "Where do we go from here?"

Her question was charged with meaning. *You tread lightly with her, you hear me, Tojo?* My mother's words echoed in my ears. I ignored the implications of Lisa's question and stayed with what we came together to discuss. "Tell me what you know about your attacker, Lisa," I said while watching her for a reaction. Her facial expression never changed as she launched into name, address, rank, and the timetable she'd gleaned from his army records. She spoke in a flat, neutral voice, her emotions held in check.

"His name is George Lawrence Wittingly, Captain, U.S. Army. When he's on leave he goes home to his parents' home in Schenectady, New York. He is single, never married. He is due up for a three-week leave which begins on July 8th. That's three weeks from now," recited Lisa.

"Do you still want to drive an upholstery tack through his offending member?"

"Yes. That would be poetic justice, in my mind," said Lisa, her face a blank slate, unreadable.

"What do you know of his parents? What's around his house?" I asked.

"I've looked at it on Google Earth. It's a two-story colonial-style house in a suburban neighborhood of similar homes. Middle class, not high end," Lisa added.

"What's Google Earth? I've never heard of it," I said.

"It's a new app from Google. Using satellite technology, they have images of most of the world. The cool thing is, they can magnify the images so you're looking at houses and streets from just above the ground," said Lisa.

"What'll they think of next? That's incredible," I said.

"It is. Now you can look at houses and towns anywhere in the world from the comfort of your home."

"So, with Google Earth, can you see stores, restaurants and bars within walking distance of the Wittingly house?"

"I'd say yes but let me check it out and identify everything he could walk to," said Lisa.

"Can you see trees, bushes around his house and around the surrounding houses?"

"I get it. We'll need cover, concealment to pull this off. Let me make a list," said Lisa as she stood up and walked briskly to the kitchen counter to get pen and paper. Seeing the coffee pot, she asked me if I wanted a refill.

"Sure, but let me help," I said, getting to my feet and striding to her side, cup in hand. Lisa picked up the pot and I held my cup out. She placed her left hand on my wrist as she poured the coffee into my mug, and I felt a jolt followed by a flow of warm energy from my wrist through the rest of my body. All at once it dawned on me what was going on. It wasn't static electricity jumping from Lisa to me. All those small occurrences I thought were caused by sparks of electricity jumping between us were nothing more than magnetic attraction. When I spoke about the static electricity with Lisa, she acted puzzled, so maybe it was my magnetic attraction to Lisa, not vice versa. I remembered her comment about explaining the results of her exploratory kiss. Did I fail her test?

I set my mug on the counter, cupped her face with my hands and drew her to me. As I gazed into her eyes, I could see surprise but not fear, not revulsion, shining back at me. I brought my lips to hers and kissed her, slowly, exploring gently, then more firmly. I found myself enveloped in a warmth I'd never felt before, and pushed back, gently breaking contact before the rush carried me over the edge and into a place that I knew I'd never been before.

Lisa held my eyes with hers, her expression questioning me. I stared into her dark eyes while I struggled to regain my composure. At length I found my voice. "That was a test," I managed to say. A warm smile enveloped her beautiful face. She punched me hard on my upper arm. The spell was broken.

"Come on, you big lug. Let's get our list together." Pen and paper in hand, she walked back to the chair while I reclaimed my place on the sofa.

I sat and contemplated Lisa's soft, gentle, warm, beautiful face while she scribbled on her pad of paper. "Stores. Restaurants. Bars. Trees. Bushes. Places for concealment. What else?" she asked, looking up from the pad in her hand and into my eyes.

"If you find a restaurant or a bar, how far is it from his house and what is it like between the two? Are there trees and bushes to hide behind? Are there vacant lots? Is the space between houses big or small? Is the street flat or hilly? We need to know all of that so we can put together a successful plan of attack. Oh, here's a big one. Are there any wood picket fences in front of his house, or in front of other houses along the way? If you plan to nail him to a wood picket fence, we need to know where they are," I said, a silly grin punctuating my statement.

I could swear I saw a slight blush on Lisa's face as she turned back to her pad of paper. As she wrote, I had a thought. "Do you know if Wittingly drinks?"

"I remember him bragging about drinking friends under the table, so I'd say yes," said Lisa.

"We should look for a bar or a tavern, even a restaurant that serves alcohol somewhere near his parents' house. He's more likely than not to go out for drinks, especially in the evening," I said. Lisa wrote on her pad.

"This isn't going to be easy, is it?" she asked, looking up from writing.

"Nothing worth doing ever is," I said.

"I'll get going on these questions, but right now I should work on our dinner.

I glanced at my phone clock and was surprised to see that it was after five. *Time flies when you're having fun.* "What can I do to help?" I asked as she stood up.

"Come with me to the kitchen while I get everything set up. That way we won't need to shout back and forth," said Lisa, her warm smile drawing me to her like a moth to a flame.

What was it about her that attracted me? I reflected on past girlfriends, and my thoughts hovered over Priscilla. A sophomore at Southern Aurora when I was a junior, she knew her way around a bed, I found out. Life was great. She joined me every day after classes, and she never tired of sexual experimentation. *I'm sorry, I'm not in the mood* never came from her pretty little mouth. I thought I'd died and made it through the Pearly Gates. Life was perfect. For a while.

One morning while I showered and shaved, and Priscilla languished in bed it dawned on me that we hadn't shared a meaningful thought between us in weeks. Our life together had become a sexual marathon, but we shared nothing else. Would I be content spending my life with a woman whose only original thoughts were variations from a book she kept that bore the title *100 Sexual Positions?* I knew in that instant that I wanted, needed more from a life partner. Priscilla had taught me close to the one hundred variations in her book, and I thanked her for that education when we parted ways. If I had to guess, Priscilla will publish her own book, listing positions never dreamed of by the author of *100 Sexual Positions*.

I graduated from Priscilla to Amanda, who screwed with enthusiasm when our relationship began, but as time went by, she talked more than she screwed, which I took as a good sign, remembering Priscilla. It soon became obvious to me, sad to say, that what she had to say was a waste of good air space. I don't know why she thought I was interested in shades of lipstick or the pros and cons of false eyelashes, and when I tried to steer the conversation to more thoughtful issues, she'd throw up her hands and say, "Why do we have to talk about stuff like that now?" Amanda went one way, and I went the other.

"A penny for your thoughts." It was Lisa, breaking through my reveries. I turned to find her staring at me, a quizzical expression on her sweet, round face. She transfixed me in her crosshairs as I remembered Mom's admonition that honesty is the best policy. What to say?

"I was thinking back on my college days," I said, trying to sound nonchalant but failing miserably. I hoped Lisa hadn't noticed. She had.

"Which college days?"

Honesty is the best policy, Tojo.

Yeah, Mom, but what if it blows up a relationship before it has a chance to succeed?

Then I'd say it was never meant to be.

I thought that's what she'd say. Damn the torpedoes, full speed ahead!

"I was thinking back on old girlfriends," I said, wishing there was a simple way out of this situation.

"What triggered that?" pursued Lisa.

"You did," I said, wondering as I spoke where those stupid words came from.

"I did? What in the world are you talking about? The last I knew, we were discussing how I was going to skewer Captain Wittingly to a picket fence," she said with a shake of her head that set her ponytail in motion.

I knew that what I said next would either send me home without dinner or add dessert to my meal. I struggled to choose my words carefully, but it was like staring into a bowl of alphabet soup. All the letters were there, ready to be joined together into words, but something was stirring them. My thoughts swirled with the stirred soup, gibberish the result.

Lisa, watching my face, recognized my struggle. "What is it, Joe?" Her voice carried with it a concern I hadn't seen from her before. When she placed her hand on my arm, I had my answer as the current flowed through me.

"There's something strange going on between us, Lisa. When we first touched, I felt a shock. I thought it was static electricity. The air here in Arizona is dry, and there's plenty of static electricity to go around so I thought I had my answer. We touched, I felt a shock and I passed it off as the dry air.

"Recently, though, the jolt when we touch has changed. It's mutated to something different. It's no longer a static spark. Now it's a feeling of warmth flowing between us. I don't know how else to describe it. I know it's something I've never experienced before.

"When I kissed you earlier, I wanted to see what it might do to all the static electricity, all the warmth I feel when we touch. I got my answer quickly, and I had to back off. A blissful abyss opened before me, urging me to continue. Then my mom's voice reached out to me, and I managed to break free."

"What did your mother say?" asked Lisa as the pause between us lengthened.

"She said, 'You tread lightly with her, you hear me, Tojo?'" I said, remembering her words verbatim.

Lisa paused, taking my words in, before she said, "I knew from meeting her that you have a smart mom, Joe. Those words confirm it. She has great insight."

"I get along with her well enough," I said, doing my best to lighten the mood.

"My turn," said Lisa, smiling as she swept a strand of black hair behind her right ear.

"I'm all ears. Well, maybe not all, but close enough," I said, returning her smile.

"When you first spoke at the VA to the PTSD group, I sensed that you were an unusual person. You spoke openly and with energy and enthusiasm as you offered your way of fighting the nightmares, the flashbacks to the group. You offered a new pathway to everyone, and I embraced it with enthusiasm.

"When we talked after and shared the causes of our PTSD, I didn't feel threatened or exposed when I told you what happened to me. What I mean is, in the past whenever I've shared that dirty little secret, I've felt vulnerable afterwards, a feeling that the person that I've exposed my soul to, could turn around and blat the story to the world, bringing me shame. Or worse yet, he could sense my vulnerability and think he could take advantage of me. Sexually.

"Later, when we sat down to share miso in my apartment and you played your joke about my miso being not good and then said it was excellent, and I came around to you and thumped your shoulder and bent over to kiss you, I got a shock of my own. That gentle little kiss sent a surge of warmth through me that left me confused. I blew it off, blaming it on the wine I'd drunk.

"When I surprised you by kissing you when I was leaving your apartment, it really was a test. I was curious to find out if that warm feeling I'd felt was caused by the wine I drank or by something else. I found out quickly enough. It wasn't the wine. It was something else. I think you and I are struggling with the same emotion."

"I think you're right. Correct that. I know you're right," I said.

"Unfortunately, there's one huge obstacle standing in the way of any of this going any farther," said Lisa, a sadness in her voice that I hadn't heard before.

"What?" I asked, afraid of the answer but needing to know.

"I don't know how, but your mother sensed it right from the start. You and I have come to share an emotional connection. Most normal couples would proceed to the next step and become intimate. I can't, or I know I shouldn't. Not now, anyway. Maybe in time. Being raped by that creep captain has changed me, changed how I look at men. To my warped way of thinking, every man I meet has one thing on his mind, and that thing is repulsive to me. Now you know how much getting even with Captain Wittingly means to me. By doing so, I hope to get my life back, and with it, a life with you."

As she spoke, she reached out and placed her hand on mine. A warm surge of energy flowed through me. I knew I faced a long, uphill climb. I also knew that the obstacles and the struggles ahead were no different than the nightmares I fought with nearly every night. Lisa is a fighter. I'm a fighter. Together, we can overcome our demons. I placed both my hands on the sides of her beautiful face and drew her to me, kissing her gently. She kissed me back, gently. I moved back from her, my eyes on hers, my head reeling from the emotion that enveloped me. "No matter how long it takes, the effort will be worth every bit of it," I said, my voice trembling.

Lisa responded by drawing me to her and kissing me, her eyes wide, taking me in. One of my mother's favorite expressions came to mind: *Anything worth having is worth the wait.*

Eleven

I GOT A call the next morning from Harold Whiteman. He finished the pendants and they were ready to be picked up. I made a stop at his jewelry store a top priority. It was just past ten when I made the bell over his door ring. He looked up from his desk behind the counter, saw me and gave me a warm smile. "Ah, Joe. Good to see you. Come see what I've done," he said with a sweep of his hand.

I stepped to the counter while Harold positioned three grey felt boxes on it. Inside each box sat a gold cross with diamonds set along each branch. The diamonds at the four ends were round and larger while the ones along each branch were rectangular. They matched perfectly in size and sparkle. One item was missing.

"They're beautiful, Harold. You do fantastic work. But what about chains?" I asked.

"We hadn't discussed them. I didn't know if your ladies had chains already, but I certainly can supply them," he said while he slid open one of the glass cases and lifted out a large tray containing a selection of gold chains. He picked up one and held it, dangling, in front of him.

"I haven't a clue what length to get," I said as I slowly shook my head.

"For a pendant such as these, most women want them to fall at the top of their cleavage. Are the ladies thin, or average, or perhaps buxom?" asked Harold, his eyebrows arching with the question.

"I'd say they all fall into the average category."

"And what of their heights? Short, medium, tall," he offered.

I hadn't thought of it, but all three were well above average in height for women. Mom's Hokkaido genes had passed on to both Kim and me, and Lisa's Hokkaido mom had done the same for her. "They're all three tall women. I'd say they're all five ten, maybe a little taller," I said.

Harold smiled and sorted through the chains, withdrawing three of his longer ones and spreading them on a felt pad for me to see. All the same length, they ranged from thin, medium, and thick in diameter. "I think this length will work well. You only have to choose the thickness," he said.

The thin one looked too fragile to me, and the thick one looked like it'd dominate the crosses. "Let's go with the medium thickness ones," I said, looking up at Harold.

"Ah, you have chosen well. It is the choice I would have made, had you asked me." He sorted through his selection of chains until he found two others that matched my choice, then set to work attaching a chain to each pendant. Finished, he positioned each of them in a grey felt box with the chain clustered at the top and closed the lids.

"What do I owe you, Harold?" The moment of truth had arrived.

"My labor and the gold to make the pendants comes to fifteen hundred dollars. There's no charge for your diamonds that I set in them," he said, smiling at his little joke.

"Do you want to be paid in cash or in diamonds?"

"Oh, I definitely prefer to be paid in diamonds, especially near-perfect ones like yours," he said.

"That works for me. I trust you to select out diamonds worth fifteen hundred dollars, and we can skip receipts, too. One less thing to tell the IRS about, come tax time," I said, offering up a sly grin to top things off.

"I like the way you think, Joe," said Harold, returning a grin of his own. He placed the three grey felt boxes into a small, discreet paper bag, passed it over to me, and I was out the door, my M9 pistol a comfortable weight at my side. I made it back to my car without a problem.

I pulled into Mom and Dad's driveway a short time later. Dad heard me arrive and came out to greet me. "To what do we owe this unexpected visit, Son?" Dad loved to use highfalutin language from time to time.

"It's great to see you, Dad, but I'm here to give Mom that pendant we talked about," I said while wrapping my arm around his shoulder and giving him a hug.

"She's inside. Let's go see if she likes it," he said, his thin lips turning up in a smile.

Mom was in the kitchen, her favorite room. She looked up when Dad and I came in, smiled when she saw me. We hugged and pecked, and I stepped back and held out the grey felt box to her.

"For me?" she asked, all coy.

"For you, my wonderful mother," I said.

She lifted the lid of the box and stared at the pendant, her eyes going wide at the sight of it. I heard her sharp intake of breath. She took it from the box and set it on the palm of her hand, turning it about to see all its sides, all its sparkle. She looked up at me, her eyes misty. "It's absolutely beautiful, Tojo. You shouldn't have done this," she said, her voice hushed.

"Oh, I definitely should have, Mom. It's an insignificant gift compared to all you've done for me," I said.

"That's what moms do, Tojo. You owe me nothing," she said, a smile taking over her face.

"Let's put it on you, see if it fits right," I said while holding my hand out. When she placed it in my open palm, I realized that this was a first for me. I'd never done the chain-around-the-neck thing before.

Dad sensed my hesitation and came to the rescue. "Let me do it for you, Tojo," he offered while extending his hand. I dropped the pendant and chain onto his palm as relief flowed through me. I watched him carefully as he found the clasp, unhooked it, and stepped behind Mom. With the chain around her neck, the pendant hanging on it, he worked the clasp together and stepped back. Mom found the cross with her hand and positioned it at the top of her cleavage, a pleased expression on her rosy face. She turned to me and gave me a long, warm hug.

"Does that mean you like it, Mom?" I asked.

"No, Tojo. It means that I love it," she said, beaming widely.

"It looks great on you, Mom."

"Did you get one for Kimiko, too?"

"I did. I also had one made for Lisa, but I'm not giving it to her now," I said.

"Why, Tojo? Did something bad happen between you?" she asked, concern filling her voice.

"No, Mom. Something good happened. But you were right when you told me to tread lightly with her."

My mother smiled her Cheshire cat smile and said nothing.

"How did you know that I should tread lightly with Lisa? Are you psychic?" I asked.

"No, not psychic. Let's just say that I have walked in her shoes," she said, leaving me puzzled.

"I hope you plan to explain that to me," I pursued.

Mom paused a moment, mulling something over. At length she said, "I guess you're old enough to hear this, Tojo. When I was barely thirteen, my uncle tried to do something sexual with me. I fought him and screamed. My father heard the ruckus and burst in on him, on us. When he saw what was happening, he struck my uncle in the face with his fist, sending his front teeth flying. With blood everywhere, he marched my uncle to the front door and threw him out. I heard him shout, 'Do not *ever* come back!' I never saw him again.

"As I grew into a woman, the fear and loathing from that incident clung to me like an enveloping blanket. I suspected any man who entered my space. The older boys in high school were the worst. Later, when I met your father, he sensed that something held me back and he made no effort to advance his feelings towards me. As my emotional attachment for him grew, my fear and loathing began to lessen, until one day I awoke and knew that my love for your father had neutralized all my bad memories. So now you know how I sensed the same pain, the same fear and loathing in Lisa."

Hearing this, I stepped up to Mom and enveloped her in my arms, holding her tight to me. "You may think that you're just my mom, but I'm blessed to have you as my mother," I told her. She did the peck thing, and I gave her one of my own.

After eyes were blotted and throats cleared, I called Kim at work and arranged to meet her at five-thirty at a tavern we both knew. "What's the occasion?" she asked.

"We've got some catching up to do," I said.'

"That sounds mysterious. Are you engaged or something?"

"No. Are you?" I countered.

"Heavens no! All right, Mystery Man, I'll see you at five-thirty."

"Sounds good. See you then, Kim."

I spent the rest of the time until five shooting the bull with Dad in the garage. He'd made a small lair in one corner, complete with two easy chairs, a coffee table, and a small fridge. He'd even built a sink and counter on the back wall and decorated the wall with a wide variety of signs he'd found along the way. My favorite? "Don't throw cigarette butts in the urinal. We don't pee in your ash trays." God knows where he found it. Sometime down the road in the future I'd ask him for it. That is, if he ever tired of it.

My eyes fell on a small glass box hanging on the wall. I hadn't noticed it before, so I walked over to examine it more closely. Inside were two medals. I recognized them immediately. A Bronze Star and a Purple Heart. I turned to face Dad. "I didn't know you got medals, Dad. Tell me about them," I said.

Dad moved up alongside me and rested his hand on my shoulder. "Those aren't my medals, Son. They're yours. The army said you turned them down and did I want them. I told them I did," said Dad, his gaze steady on me.

I stared at that box and the medals inside, and the pain and horror of that night came back at me, but I realized that the intensity had lessened. It struck me that maybe the medals served a purpose. By looking at them repeatedly, my painful memories would begin to fade, lose the bitter effect they held over me. I felt hot tears run down my cheek. "Thanks for accepting them, Dad."

He saw my tears and said, "They're part of who you are, Joe. They're there for you to take whenever you're ready." I wrapped my arms around him and hugged him to me.

When we'd both recovered, Dad changed the subject. "Have you thought any more about what to do with all those diamonds?" he asked.

"I've thought plenty about it, but I haven't settled on one idea yet. I know in my heart that the best I could do is set up a plan that benefits people in need, but how do you identify people who are genuinely in need? I mean, there are loads of homeless people out there but not all of them are there because they have no other place to go," I said, my eyes on Dad,

"That's true. If you decide to help homeless people, you'll need to come up with a screening process that eliminates those who aren't truly down and out," said Dad.

"And then there's that whole group of mentally ill people floating around the streets everywhere in the country. When the mental institutions closed and sent all those patients out to fend for themselves, the creative ones committed simple, non-violent crimes that landed them in jail or prison. It guaranteed that they'd be taken care of. The less creative ones struggle daily to find food and shelter out there."

"You know, Joe, the list is endless. In addition to the homeless and the mentally ill, there's the disabled, the misfits who can't hold down a job, the sick and dying, and don't forget the men and women who are beaten and abused in relationships gone bad."

"I know. It's a huge challenge to come up with a plan that will have my assets providing the maximum benefit for the most people. The easy way out is to gift it all to charities and let them figure out how to spend it," I said.

"Yeah, but you're a fighter, not a quitter, Joe. I know you wouldn't get any pleasure from passing it on to others to spend the way they want to, maybe after lining their own pockets with a fair share of your gift," said Dad.

"You're right. If I'm going to get any pleasure from the way my wealth gets distributed, I've got to do it myself. So here we are, back at square one. Who best deserves a boost of money from me?"

"There's no easy solution, that's for sure. Remember, I'm here to talk over any ideas you may have, and I wish you the best in reaching a decision that's right for you. So now you know how the Rockefellers and the Carnegies felt when it came time for them to help the needy. They may have had more money, but the problem is the same," said Dad.

"Guess I'm in good company, Dad."

As I turned into the tavern's parking lot, I spotted Kim's car pulling in, so I took the spot next to hers. With the grey felt box tucked into my trousers pocket I stepped from the car and went around to open Kim's door. It was locked. She looked out and saw me, then unlocked her door and stepped out, a warm smile leading the way. We hugged and pecked. "Why was your door locked?" I asked, puzzled.

"It's a defensive thing, Joe. I've heard plenty of stories about women being accosted in their cars when they pull into a parking lot," said Kim.

"I get it. It's a nasty world we live in," I said, my right hand reflexively dropping to the handgun holstered at my side.

"Right you are, Joe. An ounce of prevention is worth a pound of cure," said Kim, the smile still there.

We walked together to the tavern entrance, chatting about everything and nothing. Inside, I spotted a vacant table along the right wall and steered Kim to it. We sat facing each other.

"Okay, Joe, tell me. What's the big mystery? I don't see any bandages on you, so you haven't been in an accident. Or a fight," said Kim.

A waitress appeared at our table, all smiles, identified herself as Molly and said she was ready to take our drink orders. The questioning could wait. Kim ordered a margarita on ice, no salt, and I opted for a local dark beer from the tap. Molly went off to get our drinks and Kim wasted no time getting back to quizzing me.

"Is it animal, vegetable or mineral?" she asked.

"Oh, it's definitely mineral," I said, my hands resting on the table between us.

"You're not making this any easier," she said, adding a hint of frustration to her words.

"I'll explain as soon as our drinks get here," I said while I bobbed my eyebrows in a way that I hoped made my words even more mysterious. It was obvious that Kim had forgotten about picking out a pendant with Mom.

Kim shook her head and glanced about, our waitress Molly the target of her search. Her face lit up and I turned to see Molly headed our way with our drink order. She set Kim's margarita in front of her and my beer down in front of me. While Molly asked if there was anything else and Kim told her no, I fished the grey felt box from my front pocket and set it on my lap. Molly gone, I raised my beer glass to Kim, and she did the same with her iced margarita. We touched glasses, said *cheers!* and took a sip.

"All right, Mystery Man, what's this all about?"

"This," I said as I set the grey felt box in front of her.

"What? Oh. Is this what I think it is?" she whispered, her eyebrows lifting.

"Open it, Kim."

She did, and stared speechless at the pendant for a moment, her mouth gaping. Finally, she found her voice. "Oh my God, Joe. It's beautiful. The picture Mom and I chose didn't begin to give it justice. You shouldn't have," she gushed.

"Let's put it on, see how it looks on you," I said.

Kim lifted it from the box and opened the clasp while I stood and moved behind her. She handed it off to me and I placed it around her neck and united the clasp with the loop on the chain. "There," I said as I stepped back. The cross rested perfectly at the top of her cleavage, revealed by her V-front print blouse.

She patted the pendant with her long fingers, sensing its position on her chest. "How did you pick the right chain length? It rests precisely where I want it to be, Joe."

"The jeweler had a lot to do with that. He asked me questions about you and Mom and Lisa, how tall you are and all, and he picked out chains that fit you all," I said.

"You had one made for Lisa, too?" she asked, a quizzical expression flooding her face.

"I did, yes, but I haven't given it to her," I said.

"You really like her, don't you?"

"What's not to like," I said, trying to sound non-committal.

"Oh, I think she's perfect for you, Joe. She's charming, she's intelligent, she's beautiful, and you and she share PTSD together. What more could you ask for?" said Lisa. She lifted her ice-frosted glass and took a sip while she examined my face for a reaction.

"There is a certain magnetic connection between us. At first, I thought it was good old static electricity but as time went on it grew into a warm feeling I get when we touch," I said.

"Okay, so ask yourself how you'd feel if she moved away and left no forwarding address. Would you move on and forget about her, or would you do everything in your power to find her?"

"I'll have to think about that," I said, dodging her question. "Meanwhile, how's your job going? Still love it, or is it starting to get boring?"

"Oh, I love my work. As you know, I've always loved crunching numbers, and I get to do that all day, every day. It's a perfect fit for me," she said with a gentle toss of her head.

"I'm happy for you. Did you hear that I have a big problem?"

"No. What?"

"I recently found out that all those diamonds are worth a huge sum of money. And then there's the gold, too," I said. I took a healthy sip of my beer in the silence that followed.

"What's huge?" Kim asked, her eyebrows lifting with the question.

"Huge is like, ten million dollars," I said.

"Holy jumping catfish! That *is* huge. Your stint in Iraq paid you well."

"Yeah, but I'd gladly exchange it for a PTSD-free life," I said.

"I thought you were getting a handle on those nightmares."

"True, but they're persistent. They come back when I least expect them."

"So, any thoughts on what to do with all that wealth?" asked Kim.

"I want to use it to help the needy."

"That's a big generalization. Can you be more specific?"

"I wish I could. Donating it all to a bunch of charities wouldn't give me any satisfaction. I'm trying to come up with a way that I can be personally involved in lifting people up, give them a fresh chance in life," I said.

"The next John Beresford Tipton," said Kim as she set her half-empty glass down.

"Maybe, but he handed out a million dollars at a whack. I'd be all done, all through in no time if I passed out that kind of money."

"True. I'll think about it while you think about it. Meanwhile, I've got to get going," said Kim as she gathered up her purse and car keys.

I downed the rest of my beer, took two twenties from my wallet, and dropped them on the table before getting to my feet. Kim pushed back, stood up and gave me a huge hug and a peck on my cheek. She said, "Thank you so very, very much for the lovely cross, Joe. It will rest here forever." She patted the top of her cleavage for emphasis.

"I'm glad you like it. It looks like it belongs there," I said. We walked together to our cars and said goodnight. I drove out onto the street, no closer to figuring out how to spend my windfall. Then it hit me. Maybe I was.

Twelve

"**G**ood morning, Joe. I've got information to share with you about Captain Wittingly."

It was Lisa, brightening my new day with her warm, soft voice. "You work fast, Lisa."

"I have my best interests at heart. Between you and me, I can't wait to nail the creep."

"Nice double entendre. Let's hope your nailing goes off without a hitch," I said, grinning at the repartee.

"Careful planning will win the day. Do you want me to email the info to you, or do you want to hear it from me face to face?"

"Face to face wins every time. Where are you?"

"I'm at my upholstery shop."

"I'm on my way."

As I drove, I reviewed my feelings I had for Lisa. Kim had made a good point. If Lisa left without a forwarding address, what would I do? For a moment I pictured that scenario. I wake up to find she's gone without any warning or note to explain why. I'm dumbfounded, but it's more than that. She's taken part of me with her. It's a big chunk that leaves me in tatters, like my nightmare after the Claymore ripped into it. *Yes, Kim, I'd go after her.*

I parallel parked outside Lisa's shop, leaving two spaces for any customers coming her way, and walked briskly to the entrance, the morning heat already building. I pushed open the door and stepped inside. Cool air bombarded my open pores. Since it was my first visit, I looked around. Ten feet in front of me sat a three-foot long polished wood counter. There were wide openings on either side that led to her work area, the center of the room. I saw a jumble of furniture grouped along the walls waiting for her skilled hands, and a large sofa sat in the middle of the space, perched on a raised platform. Lisa was working on it. She looked at me when I walked in.

"Hey, Joe. That was fast. Traffic must be light," she said. She held a small tack hammer in her right hand.

"It was." I stopped short of telling her that it gave me time to think about her.

"Thanks for coming right over. This won't take long," she said. She set her hammer on a small worktable and turned to face me.

"I had a break in my busy schedule, so no problem," I said, showing her a silly smile.

Let's sit down and I'll tell you what I've learned," she said with a sweep of her hand at two beautifully upholstered easy chairs set on either side of a small, polished wood coffee table.

"Did you reupholster these chairs?" I asked as we sat.

"I cannot tell a lie. I like my nose at its present length. Yes," she said. It was her turn for a silly smile.

"You do impressive work," I said while I ran my hand along the padded arm.

"Thank you. I had a good teacher."

"A teacher taught you how to do all this?" I asked, my arm making a sweep across the room.

"Yes. I was an apprentice to an older man in the valley. He was getting close to the end of his career, and he enjoyed teaching others the tricks of the trade. His version of passing it forward. He taught me well, and one day he came up to me and said it was time for me to start my own business, he'd taught me everything he knew. So, I took his advice, and here I am," she said.

"Nice story, and with a happy ending. I like it. So, time to change the subject. Tell me what more you learned about the evil captain and his haunts," I said.

Lisa leaned forward and retrieved a pad of yellow paper from the table, then sat back while her eyes swept over her notes. Her review done, she turned to me and began her summary. "I started by searching the area within two miles of his parents' house, using Google Earth and the Schenectady Chamber of Commerce website to do it. There's a small strip mall less than a mile away. It has a deli, a gift shop, a shoe store, a discount store, and a restaurant. The restaurant has a full bar, by the way. I also found a tavern less than a mile from his parents' house. The terrain is fairly flat, so walking there is a piece of cake," she added, tapping her index finger on the notepad for emphasis.

"All good information," I said.

"So, armed with all that, I made two phone calls, one to the restaurant and one to the tavern. I told the person who answered that I was trying to get in touch with Captain Wittingly who lived nearby, and did he know if Captain Wittingly ever came there? Guess what they told me?"

"You've got me on the edge of my seat," I said. I slid forward to emphasize the point.

"They said, 'Who's Captain Wittingly?' To which I replied, 'George Wittingly. He's a captain in the army and when he comes home on leave, he stays with his parents.'"

"Did either of them know him?" I asked Lisa, still perched forward, expectant.

"Surprise of surprises! They both knew who he was, and they went on to say that he stopped in when he was staying at his parents' home," said Lisa, smiling like the cat that swallowed the canary.

"Did they say whether he came alone or with his parents?" I asked.

"Ah, good question. I asked that myself. Turns out, he goes to the restaurant with his parents but goes to the tavern alone."

"Did the tavernkeeper say what days of the week he came in?"

"Yes, he did, and you can pass go and collect two hundred dollars for your keen questioning. He goes there every Saturday night when he's at his parents' home, and sometimes drops in on Wednesday nights. And one more big nugget. He walks there and back so he doesn't have to worry about driving home with a few shots under his belt," said Lisa.

"I think you're on to something. Have you studied the terrain between the tavern and his parents' house?"

"I have indeed, and thanks for asking. For half the distance, all of which is level going, the path takes him by many similar homes, most of which are set well back from the road. Three homes have white wood fences along the sidewalk, and trees and bushes grow thick along the way. There's lots of cover to shield our shenanigans," she said, a satisfied smile overspreading her beautiful face.

"Congratulations on a job well done, Lisa. The next step is for us to go to Schenectady and get to know George's neighborhood firsthand."

"I'm ready when you are," she said, knocking me off-kilter with her happy smile.

I'd been mulling over when to tell Lisa how much my wealthy windfall was worth, and now seemed to be as good a time as ever. "There's something I've been holding off telling you, Lisa," I began.

She reached out and placed her hand on my arm, sending a surge of warmth through me. "What is it, Joe?" she asked, her eyebrows peaking, worry coming over in her words.

"You know I came home with bags of diamonds and a bag of gold Krugerrands. The jeweler who appraised the first pouch had a look at a second pouch. The first pouch contained small diamonds, but the second one had large ones. He shocked me when he told me the pouch of large diamonds is worth three point six million dollars. I have a second pouch of large diamonds, plus two pouches of medium-sized ones and another of the smaller stones," I said.

I watched Lisa's mouth drop open in surprise. "I'm as shocked as you are, Joe. What are you thinking of doing with them?"

"That's the big WHAT. It's in my nature to do something to help people who are down and out, but if I'm going to get any personal satisfaction from it, I need to come up with some sort of plan that works for me. Simply donating all that to charities wouldn't give me any satisfaction," I said.

"You're asking me for suggestions, am I right?"

"You've nailed it, no pun intended," I said, offering her a sly smile and a glance at her tack hammer.

"That's going to take some thought, okay? I'll put my thinking cap on, and if I come up with any ideas, I'll let you know" she said.

"Thanks. Meanwhile, how much time do we have before Captain George returns to Schenectady?"

"Eighteen days from today," said Lisa, reciting from memory.

"We should go to Schenectady in the next week and do some reconnoitering. What's your schedule look like?"

"Your schedule is my schedule. How long do you think we'll be gone?" she asked.

"Flying there and back will take two days, and a day to reconnoiter, for a total of three days. I think that should work. If we go on a Friday and come back on a Sunday, you'll miss two workdays," I said.

"That's not a problem. I'll tell customers waiting for their stuff that there's going to be a two-day delay," said Lisa.

"Okay. I'll make the reservations and let you know when everything's scheduled," I said.

"I can't wait. Meanwhile, do you want to see a demonstration of my hammer skills?" she asked, a coy smile overspreading her lovely face.

"I'm all eyes," I said. She walked over to the sofa she'd been working on. A closer look showed that she was covering it in red leather, and she was putting the finishing touches on it. That involved placing those decorative round brass nails in a neat row along all the seams.

Lisa picked up her tack hammer and a container of those brass nails, turned to give me a confident smile, and went to work. She put the hammer head into the nail container and brought it out with a nail held magnetically to its head. With her eyes on the line of nails that she'd already set, she brought the hammer down, driving the nail through the leather and into the wood frame of the sofa. Back to the nail container for another nail. Down on the sofa. Back for another nail. Down on the sofa. Five times she did this before turning back to me, the smile still there.

I walked over to inspect the results. The line of decorative nails was perfectly aligned. If I'd been called upon to do that, I'd still be pounding the first nail. "That was impressive. Lisa. You've got the touch," I said, nodding my head at the straight line of brass tacks she'd hammered.

"I had a great instructor," she said, her way of deflecting my praise.

"Maybe so, but your eye-hand coordination plays a big part. Looks like you're ready to nail the disgusting Captain Wittingly," I said as I watched Lisa for a reaction.

"You have no idea," she said with a shake of her beautiful head that made her ponytail do the tango.

At the door, as I was leaving, Lisa placed her hand on my arm and thanked me for coming by. "Let me know when you've made the reservations so I can tell my customers, okay?" she said, her voice soft to my ears. I struggled to hear her as the energy flowed from her hand and into me, leaving me breathless.

Thirteen

As I DROVE back to my apartment, I mulled over ways to spend my newfound wealth in a way that benefitted the neediest people. I knew that many federal and state programs helped the needy, so it made no sense to duplicate any of those. My niche would be in an area where people could benefit from a leg up when my help was their only way out. My head spun with crazy thoughts, but none felt like the right fit for me.

I drove past a small city park and spotted three disheveled-looking bodies stretched out on benches. That gave me an idea. I parked and walked back to them, eyeing them as I approached. I guessed that two were men and one was a woman. Their disheveled appearance made it difficult to tell for certain. I weighed the possibilities. If they were druggies, they were targets for other helping hands. If they were mentally ill, ditto. If they were here because they enjoyed this lifestyle, sleeping in shelters and getting free meals for the rest of their days, any help I offered wouldn't change anything. The one situation I might be able to turn around was men or women down on their luck, not wanting to live like this but having no other option. I decided to ask each of them a few questions, maybe get some answers.

I sat opposite the body on bench number one, cleared my throat noisily and said, "Hey, how's it going?"

No response.

I tried again. "Hey, guy, how're you doing?"

While I waited for a response, my eyes swept the area around the benched body and spotted a used syringe lying on the ground, the dirty needle threatening me by its very presence.

Uh huh.

Time to move on to bench two.

I sat once again on the bench opposite the reclined, immobile body and asked the same question. Might as well be consistent. "Hey, how's it going?"

"Fuck off!" mumbled the body, its voice betraying it as a male.

"That wasn't very nice. I came to see if I can help you," I said, maintaining a calm voice despite the negative odds coming at me.

"I don't want your help. Fuck off!"

"You must want something," I said.

"Yeah. I want you to fuck off!"

I couldn't think of a suitable response to his persistent crudity, so I stood and made my way to bench three and sat opposite the prone body. I coughed with enthusiasm and said, "Hey, how's it going?"

A head was raised, and two dark eyes peered suspiciously at me. "I don't know you," came a high, thin voice. I was right. This body belonged to a female if the high voice was any indication.

"No, you don't know me. I'm here to see if you're getting the help you need." Nice open statement, general enough to pass the muster.

The head brought the upper torso to an upright position and pivoted to face me. The dark eyes searched my face for clues that explained what I was up to. Possibilities came to mind. Pervert. Rapist. Thief. I waited, silent, returning the woman's searching gaze. At last, the dirty, disheveled female broke the silence. "What could you possibly do to help me?" the woman asked, suspicion dominating her voice.

"That depends a lot on you. If you need help but haven't been able to get it, maybe I can help." As I spoke, I searched the woman's face. Under the layers of grime, I could make out many appealing features. It was long and narrow. A thin nose divided it, and a narrow, thin mouth completed the image. Her dark hair was tangled and matted, giving her the appearance of some wild thing. While I wondered why she didn't go to a shelter and wash it, it occurred to me that it could be a defensive move on her part: maintain a dirty, disheveled appearance as a barrier that put off men wanting to have their way with her. With all the camouflage she presented, determining her age was a challenge. I guessed she was somewhere between twenty and forty, give or take a few years either side of that.

"You think I like living this way?" she said, her voice coming out strong.

"Why *are* you living like this?" I countered.

In answer the woman brought her hands to the sides of her face and rocked back and forth. My first response was that she had a mental illness, but when she spoke again, she dispelled that thought. "I'm hiding from my husband," she said, her voice charged with fear.

"Tell me about it," I said.

"Please tell me that he hasn't hired you to find me."

"I don't know him, and I don't know you, so no, nobody hired me to find you," I said.

The woman eyed me with suspicion for a moment. I could see her eyes clearly. They were dark green. She gave a little shake of her head, a decision made. I watched her relax. She sat back and told me her story. When she finished, I knew I was onto something.

She was a victim of spousal abuse, plain and simple. She'd been working as a seamstress, making beautiful dresses in an upscale shop when she met her future husband. She found his wild nature alluring. He had his own auto body shop that did well. Married, all went smoothly for the first six months. One evening she came home late after a visit with a girlfriend, and he accused her of being with another man. She denied it. He hit her in the face and in the stomach. She doubled over, crying. He said he was sorry and held her close. She forgave him.

That was the start. He found many reasons, or no reason at all, for striking her, but always apologized and held her close after, saying it wouldn't happen again. She took his abuse for a year, hoping she could change him, make him stop. Finally, she came to her senses, realizing the truth. When he left for work, she quietly packed a bag and closed the apartment door behind her, praying that it was for the last time.

She made her first stop at a woman's shelter. They took her in and sympathized with her terrible situation. Less than a week later she heard her husband pounding at the door, demanding to be allowed in to see her. The woman in charge told him that no such person was there. He shouted that he didn't believe her, and he would be back to get his wife. She knew he would. That evening, when all was quiet, she packed up and left the shelter behind. She took up a life on the streets, staying in areas her husband was unlikely to travel through. She allowed her personal appearance to deteriorate, making it harder for him, or anyone else she knew, to identify her. She learned the ways of the homeless, eating in soup kitchens and sleeping in alleyways and using gas station bathrooms for washing and relieving herself. The fear that her husband would find her drove her, ate at her, consumed her thoughts.

After hearing her story, I knew I had to help her. But how? What could I do to change her desperate situation? I needed more information from her.

"Do you have anywhere that you can go, that your husband doesn't know about, maybe out of the city, out of the state?" I asked.

"No. I talked too much about my friends and my family with him. He knows every friend, every relative I have. He's called them all, asking them if they know where I am. When I call them, I must lie about where I am. It would take only one of them to betray me, tell him I'm homeless, living on the streets, thinking that they were doing me a favor by telling him," she said.

"Is there anywhere you can think of that you'd like to move to, somewhere that you'd be safe from your husband?" I asked.

"Maybe the far side of the moon, if I could get there," she said, dead serious.

"What about going to the police, get a restraining order against him?"

"I had a girl friend who got a restraining order against her abusive husband. He killed her. Took his own life after, but that didn't help my friend," she said, her voice devoid of emotion.

I knew this wasn't going to be an easy fix, but I've never shied away from a challenge.

"Can I help you get a divorce?" I asked.

"I can't see how that could be possible. He'd deny anything I had to say."

"Do you have anything that shows what he's done to you?"

A smile broke out across her dirt-smudged face. It displayed her charm, attractiveness despite the grime on it. She pulled out a cell phone and held it up. "I have selfies I took of the bruises on my body that were made by him. Every time he hit me. Would those be any help?" she asked.

"I think they'd be an enormous help. I'm no lawyer, but I think photographic evidence like that could help convince a judge to grant you a divorce," I said.

"I feel something strange, something I've been missing for a very long time," she said.

"What's that?" I asked.

"Hope. It's been absent from my life forever, it seems. Now you've brought it back."

I was on a first-name basis with hope. It reared its happy head every time I gained an inch against my nightmare. If anyone deserved hope, it was this woman. It struck me that we'd been talking for close to an hour and I didn't know her name. "I'm glad I've brought you hope. Everything I've said to you has been open and honest. Are you willing to share your name with me?" I asked her while I held her eyes with mine.

She hesitated a moment, her dark green eyes busy searching mine. At length she said, "I think I can trust you. No, it's more than that. I need to trust you. My name is Rachel. Rachel Bonner. Bonner's my husband's last name. My born name is Hartack," she said.

"I'm Joe Roberts and I'm going to help you get through all this," I said.

"Why would you want to do that?" she asked, suspicious.

"I don't blame you for being suspicious, Rachel. It's simple, really. I have the resources to help you, and I'm deeply touched by your story. I have no other motive than to see you safe and happy again."

"I find you hard to believe, Joe Roberts, but I'm beginning to think that maybe I can."

"You can, Rachel. Now let's get you off the streets and to a place where you can be safe. Any thoughts?"

"None that I can afford," she said glumly.

"Forget afford. Like I said, I have deep pockets."

"How can I ever repay you?" she asked.

I thought a moment. "You're a seamstress, right? You could make some special clothes for me. I could take them as payment. How does that sound?" I asked her.

"It sounds all too easy, but I agree," she said, smiling through the grime that covered her long face.

"Good. We have a deal. Where can you go where you'll feel safe, never mind the cost?" I asked.

"I don't think Bill, that's my husband's first name, would ever think to look for me in a hotel or a motel that costs more than sixty dollars a night," said Rachel.

"That makes sense since he thinks you're down and out. If you'll come with me, I'll take you to a woman's clothing store I've passed many times." As I spoke, I pulled my wallet out. I took out three one-hundred-dollar bills and handed them to Rachel.

"I can't take this," she protested.

"Consider it a loan against the beautiful clothes you're going to make for me. It will buy you some nice fresh clothes. While you're shopping, oh and get a bathing suit for the motel pool, I'll make a reservation for you in a high-end motel, and when you come out of the store I'll take you there, okay?"

Rachel shook her head and sighed. She fell short of pinching herself. She nodded, tucked the money in a pocket she found somewhere and picked up her modest, soiled suitcase. I led the way to my Ford Edge. On the way I noticed that the two other bench occupants were still stretched out. *One out of three isn't bad.* I tucked her suitcase in back and held the passenger door for her. She climbed in and pulled the door closed behind her. When I got behind the wheel, she looked searchingly at me for a moment. "Tell me I'm not dreaming all this," she said.

"It's no dream, Rachel. I hope it's the start of a new life for you."

She went into the dress store while I made a reservation for her under an alias. I thought she could pass for Rachelle Banner, close enough to her real name to pass the registration desk scrutiny.

I was waiting for Rachel to emerge from the shop when I spotted a blonde strolling my way, her hands holding shopping bags. She walked right for my car. I thought she must be an absent-minded person daydreaming until she grasped the passenger side door and swung it open. I opened my mouth to shout at her when she glanced at me and smiled. Recognition flooded through me. It was Rachel. She was wearing a blonde wig she'd bought with the clothes.

"I didn't recognize you," I said in my normal voice.

"That's the idea. I don't think Bill will be looking for a blonde," she said.

"It fooled me, so I have to agree," I said with a shake of my head.

As I drove to the motel, I told Rachel I'd registered her under the name Rachelle Banner. She got it at once, confirming it with a happy smile.

I pulled up to the motel entrance and Rachel climbed out, collected her bulging bags, and gave me a wave before turning and going inside. I pulled out and headed for my apartment. As I drove, I went over what I needed to do to get Rachel's life back together.

Once I got home, I called Lisa to tell her what I'd done. She listened without interruption. When I finished, she told me she wanted to meet her. "We have a lot in common. I'm not in a terrible marriage, but we share the common bond of abuse by a man," she explained.

I got it.

"I'll arrange for us to meet Rachel at the motel tomorrow morning, say ten o'clock?"

"Ten works for me. See you tomorrow," she said. I could feel a surge of warmth come through the phone to me.

I let two hours pass before calling Rachel. I pictured her luxuriating in a soapy bathtub and I didn't want to disturb her. She had a pile of grime to wash away. When I called, she answered, her voice charged with suspicion until she heard my voice. "Oh, Joe. What a relief," she said, the tenseness in her voice draining away.

"How's your room? Any problems?" I asked.

It's beautiful. It's like I've died and gone to heaven. I used three of those little shampoo bottles, getting my hair clean," she said.

"You must be feeling better," I said.

"A thousand percent better," she said. "You're an angel sent from heaven."

That simple statement made everything worthwhile. "Can we meet in your room tomorrow morning at, say, ten? I've got a lady friend I want you to meet."

"Who is she?" The suspicion was back in her voice.

"She's a friend who shares a lot in common with you. I think you could help each other," I said.

"I'm beginning to think that I can trust you, Joe. So, yes, I'll see you both tomorrow at ten."

I met Lisa in the motel parking lot the next morning. She greeted me with a warm hand on my arm that sent a shivering warmth through me. I knew that she knew what she was doing to me. We walked side by side into the motel lobby. Rachel sat waiting for us, the blonde wig in place. *Smart move. Much easier to run from a threat in the lobby than from her room.* She stood when she saw us and came over, her eyes moving from Lisa to me and back again. "Good morning, Rachelle. Meet Lisa," I said.

Rachel extended her hand and Lisa took it in both of hers. "It's so good to meet a fellow sufferer," said Lisa as she nodded her head at Rachel.

"Let's go to my room where we can speak freely," said Rachel. She'd made the decision that Lisa presented no threats. She led the way to the elevators and pushed the button for the third floor.

"You look like a different person, Rachel," I said, eyeing her clean skin and fresh clothing. She had on a loose-fitting pink blouse and black pants that came just below her knees, I forget what they're called. Gone was the body odor she'd exuded the day before. She smelled clean, fresh.

"It's amazing what a little water can do," she said, her eyebrows lifting with her smile.

The elevator door opened, and we followed Rachel to her room. Her key opened upon a large living area. A blue sofa and two upholstered chairs surrounded a metal coffee table topped with blue tiles. A large coffee carafe and three cups sat waiting for us. Lisa and Rachel sat together on the sofa while my 240-pound frame filled one of the easy chairs. "Shall I pour?" asked Rachel, her hand on the carafe.

"Please do," Lisa and I said with one voice.

She set to work, and quickly put together three coffees, black, no sugar. Easy-peasy. We all took sips, and Lisa broke the brief silence.

"It sounds like we share a common bond, Rachel, or do you prefer Rachelle?" she asked, looking over the cup she held.

"Rachel has always worked for me," she said, a gentle smile gracing her warm face.

"Please. Tell me your story, and I'll tell you mine," said Lisa.

Rachel took a sip of her coffee and set down the cup. She told Lisa the same story she'd told me yesterday, leaving nothing out.

When she finished, Lisa sat silent a moment before she told Rachel her story of rape and abuse in Iraq.

I listened as each of them bared their souls, shocked once more that human beings could be so cruel to each other.

When Lisa ended her story, Rachel moved against her and hugged her close. Lisa returned the hug. Their mutual hug said it all: two pained souls finding solace with each other. When at last they separated, they both wiped moisture from their eyes. I was at a loss for words. Moisture filled my eyes, too.

Rachel broke the silence by saying, "Oh, my. What a bad hostess I am. Let me warm your coffee." She picked up the carafe. Lisa and I held our cups out for more. Then Rachel filled her own cup and set down the carafe.

As I settled back in my chair, Rachel turned my way and said, "Thank you, Joe, for bringing Lisa. You were right. We share a lot."

"When Joe told me about meeting you and what you've been through, I knew I had to meet you," said Lisa, her hand reaching for Rachel's arm. I wondered if the same electric warmth flowed into Rachel with her touch.

I took a long sip of my cooling coffee and set the cup on the arm of my chair, balancing it carefully. "I think our next step is to get you a good divorce lawyer, Rachel." It came out sounding like a major shift in the conversation but neither Rachel nor Lisa acted surprised.

Rachel looked at me, blinking away the lingering tears and said, "I'm ready. Truth be known, I've been ready for a very long time."

"I'll do my homework and ask around, get some recommendations. I'm thinking we should get someone far enough away from where you lived with Bill so there's no chance of a connection with your husband. I want *him* to be surprised, not you."

"I'm not going anywhere, so whoever you find is fine with me," said Rachel as she twisted a finger around one of her unfamiliar blonde wig braids.

We chatted some more and polished off the coffee before Lisa and I said our goodbyes to Rachel. I didn't envy her having to sit around a motel room while I searched for a good divorce attorney, but I knew it was a huge step up for her. I'd helped lift her from squalor only twenty-four hours before. I liked the feeling of helping her. I thought it could grow into a habit. A deeply satisfying one.

As Lisa and I walked out to our cars she asked me if we were still on for a reconnaissance trip to Schenectady.

"Absolutely. Nothing will stand in the way of our recon trip, and nothing will stand in the way of our follow-up trip to nail Captain Wittingly," I said.

"You don't think helping Rachel will complicate things?" asked Lisa. I heard the concern in her voice.

"No, I don't. Once I get her connected with a divorce attorney, she'll be busy preparing for her day in court. She can stay in my apartment while we're gone, get her out of the motel and let her cook for herself," I said.

"For that matter, she could stay in my apartment," said Lisa.

"Thanks for offering. We'll let her decide, depending on where the lawyer's office is."

"Okay. Thanks for including me in your meeting with Rachel. She deserves everything you, we can do for her," said Lisa, including herself in the rescue.

"My feelings exactly," I said. Lisa brushed my arm before getting into her car and driving off, leaving me electrified, standing alone at the side of my car.

Back in my apartment, I did a search for divorce attorneys in the area and came up with a recommended firm in Scottsdale. It seemed appropriate because it was well away from her husband Bill Bonner's neighborhood, and it was an upscale community, an area Bill was less likely to go to search for her.

I called the number and was connected to Michael Harbinger, one of the attorneys. I explained that I was researching divorce attorneys for a friend who was in a terribly abusive situation, and what kind of time frame could she expect, from the initial meeting to the divorce decree. Michael told me the average time was anywhere from six weeks to six months. It had everything to do with the response of the second party.

"So, if the second party doesn't object, the divorce can be completed in six weeks, but if he puts up a fight it could take six months," I said by way of summarizing.

"Exactly. It all depends on how the second party reacts to the filing of the divorce," said Michael.

"My friend has taken selfies over the past year, showing the cuts and bruises she's sustained from attacks by her husband. Could those help her case?" I asked.

"Indeed, they could. Evidence like that speaks volumes to any judge hearing the case."

"All right then. I'll have her call you for your earliest time slot. Her name is Rachelle Banner," I said.

"Very well, sir. I await her call."

I hung up and called Rachel. She was surprised to hear from me so soon. I gave her the attorney's name, address and phone number and told her what he'd said. "Call him as soon as you can," I said.

"I'll call him right now. Bye, Joe." I heard the line go dead. Rachel was on it.

The ball was rolling. I said a silent prayer that William Bonner wouldn't contest the divorce, but my doubts overrode my optimism. Bonner didn't seem like the sort of asshole who would go down without a fight. I formed a picture in my mind of the surprise on his face when he learns that Rachel has selfies, photos she took of the injuries he caused each time he hit her.

Fourteen

NEXT ON MY agenda was making reservations for our trip to Schenectady. I found a flight leaving Phoenix at 11:30 in the morning and arriving in Albany, New York at 9 P.M. In all it was six and a half hours of travel time, but with the time change it grew another three hours. It would be six o'clock for our bodies but nine Albany time when we landed. Nothing we could do about it. I rented a popular nondescript sedan for the twenty-minute drive to Schenectady and our stay there, and booked us two rooms, side by side, at a modestly priced motel. I called Lisa to give her the news and filled her in on the date and times.

"My, my, Joe, you work fast," she said.

"Not only did I make our reservations, but I also found a divorce attorney for Rachel. He told me the process could take anywhere from six weeks to six months. It all hinges on whether her husband cooperates or not," I said.

"No matter how it works out, it gives you and me plenty of time for our Schenectady caper," she said. I could hear relief in her voice. One less thing to worry over. We'd be leaving in four days for our recon mission to Schenectady.

My phone announced an incoming call an hour later. It was Rachel. She had an appointment with Attorney Michael Harbinger the next day at ten.

"That was fast work," I said.

"He told me he loved handling divorces where physical abuse is involved so he moved me to the head of the line," said Rachel. Her voice told me she was happy.

"That's good to hear. Maybe you'll be through all this ahead of schedule," I said.

"Maybe, but Bill Bonner isn't the sort of man to throw up his hands without a fight," she said.

"Time will tell. Wait till he hears you have pictures."

"I'd love to see his face when he finds out," said Rachel. Her broad smile came right through with her words.

"Me, too, Rachel. Call me when you get back from seeing Attorney Harbinger. Wait, do you want a ride there?" I asked, remembering her circumstance.

"There's no need to trouble yourself. I'll grab a cab," she said. "Bill would never look for me in a taxi."

"Okay. Stay safe. I look forward to hearing from you tomorrow," I said.

I had a lot of news to share with Mom and Dad, my two biggest supporters, so I called them to be sure they'd be home when I stopped by. They welcomed my visit, though they had no idea what I was getting myself involved in. Mom said she'd set another place for dinner. I checked the time. It was already five. I was surprised to find the day nearly gone. "See you at six," I told Mom. I had a half an hour to wash up and change clothes.

When I pulled into my parents' driveway, I was surprised to see Kim's car there. I hoped I hadn't interrupted something. As I neared the front door it swung open and all three of my family members stood smiling at me. "Welcome, Son," "Come in and tell us the news, Tojo," and "I can't wait to hear what's up, Joe," came from the three of them in a rush of words. I wondered how they already knew what I'd been up to. I stepped inside, Dad closed the door and Mom and Kim ushered me into the living room. Mom spoke first. "Have you set the date?" she asked, a coy smile flooding her face. Dad and Kim waited in silence.

"What?" I managed to say.

"You've come to tell us you're engaged. Am I right?" It was Mom speaking.

"Now there you go, Mom, jumping to conclusions," I said.

Disappointment replaced the smile on her face. Well, if that's not the news, what is?" she asked.

I spoke of wanting to use the wealth I'd brought back from Iraq to help other people in need and told them of seeing the three people stretched out on park benches as I drove home. I went on to say that I left my car and walked into the park and spoke to the three disheveled people there. "The one who responded favorably to my inquiries turned out to be a woman running from her physically abusive husband. She told me her story and it touched my heart. She's now in a motel under a different name and she's seeing a divorce lawyer, all thanks to me. I can't begin to tell you how much helping her has meant to me. The thought of seeing her free of her abusive husband and living a normal life, knowing that my help has made her happy again, is all the thanks I need," I said.

I could have cut the silence that followed my words with a dull knife. Dad was first to break it. "I'm proud of you, Son. Helping that woman in her time of need is something you'll always remember," he said.

Mom and Kim began speaking at the same time, but Kim backed off, showing Mom the respect that she deserved. "Tojo, you make me proud to be your mother. What you're doing to help that poor woman is nothing short of a miracle," she said, her smile returning to its proper place.

Kim put the finishing touches on everything when she said, "It looks like you've found your mission in life, Joe. I think it's wonderful."

"Thanks. Your support means more than I can say," I said. I eyed each of them as I spoke to emphasize my feelings. "Now, about Lisa."

"Yes, yes! What about Lisa?" asked Mom, struggling to contain herself.

"As you know, she continues to struggle with PTSD. I can't imagine the pain and humiliation she's coping with, all the result of the sexual assault by her commanding officer," I said.

"No, Tojo, you are quite correct. It takes another woman to fully understand what she has gone through. Being overpowered by a man who forces himself on her against her will takes something from her, leaves her feeling less of a woman," said Mom.

"She's so right, Joe," said Kim with a nod of her head.

"I'm lucky to have you two to help me understand what she's gone through," I said.

"We both speak from experience," said Mom, catching me by surprise by her flat statement.

Mom had already told me about being sexually assaulted by her uncle, a man who she'd grown up thinking she could trust, but I had no idea Kim shared a similar experience.

Kim's story echoed that of Mom's. A date who had too much to drink tried to force himself on her. She planted her knee in his crotch, a maneuver Dad had taught her when she was growing up. When he was able to stand up again, he called her a nasty bitch and a cock teaser before stumbling out of her life. Kim was left with a healthy dose of suspicion towards men.

"I didn't know you both had those things happen to you. Do either of you have nightmares or flashbacks from it?" I asked.

"No," said Mom and Kim together.

"In my case, my father brought an end to it, and it made me feel protected, safe," said Mom.

"And in my case Dad's lessons in self-defense left me feeling in control again," said Kim, adding her impish smile as an exclamation point.

"Sadly, in Lisa's case she still hasn't been able to close out that dark episode of her life. I plan to help her get closure on it," I said.

"How will you do that?" asked Mom. Kim bobbed her head, curious to know as well.

I told them about Lisa's research into her commanding officer's background and finding out that he returns to his parents' home in Schenectady, New York when he goes on leave. I told them of his upcoming leave and Lisa's plan to ambush him there, her way of getting closure, or maybe more to the point, getting revenge.

"I'm going there with her. I'll help her in any way I can," I said.

"Oh, my! Does she want to kill him? Not that I'd blame her," said Mom.

"No, killing him isn't in her plan. She wants to cause him pain, humiliate him, pay him back for what he took from her," I said, secretly hoping I wouldn't have to go into more detail.

"When are you going?" asked Kim.

"The end of the week, for a reconnaissance trip, to learn the area around his parents' house and the area nearby. Maybe we'll ask around to see if anyone knows him, knows his habits. When he comes home on leave, we hope we'll be prepared to catch him off guard, surprise him."

"You two need to be careful up there. It wouldn't be good to have anyone get suspicious about what you might be planning," said Mom.

"The military taught me well. It taught Lisa well, too," I added.

"All right, Tojo. I'll say a prayer that you and Lisa stay safe. Now, we'd really like to know what feelings you have for Lisa. I know you all too well. You hold your emotions in check. Do you like her, or what?" asked Mom, mincing no words, her dark eyes leveled on mine as she spoke.

"She does things to me that no other woman has," I blurted.

"Are you saying that you two are intimate?" asked Kim.

"No, no. Nothing like that. It's just that when we touch, whether it's accidental or planned, she sends shockwaves through me. When it first happened, I thought it was static electricity in the air, but over time I came to realize that it was something different. It's more a surge of energy that fills me with warmth and a sense of well-being. Hell, I don't know how to explain it," I said.

Mom and Kim shared a smile before turning back to me. Mom said, "It's nice that you have a connection to Lisa, Tojo, but remember what I said. You tread lightly with her. You treat her right. Am I clear?"

"You're crystal clear, Mom, and I'm following your advice," I said. *So far.*

"You're a good boy, Tojo. I'm proud of the man you've become."

My phone announced an incoming call the next day as I was enjoying a sandwich I'd thrown together. It was Rachel, my caller ID told me.

"Hey, Rachel. How's it going?"

"I just got back from my meeting with Michael Harbinger, the lawyer. He listened to my story, asked me a few questions about my husband, Bill, and took my phone to copy the photographs I'd taken of the injuries Bill gave me. He said he would prepare the divorce papers and arrange to have them served on Bill. He said he was pleased that

I came to him, and he will do everything in his power to get me the divorce I deserve," said Rachel, summarizing her visit.

"Did he give you a timetable for serving the papers on your husband?" I asked.

"Three days. He said he'll write it up today, his secretary will type it up all legal-like and he'll check it over tomorrow, and then it'll go to the sheriff, to be served on Bill on day three," said Rachel.

"That's great news, Rachel. We're making progress," I said.

"No, Joe. *You're* making progress. I'm simply going along for the ride."

"Are you getting cold feet, Rachel?"

"Cold feet? Hell, no, excuse my French! I wish I could be there when the sheriff serves the papers on Bill, to see the look on his face," she said.

"The sheriff reports back to the lawyer about how everything goes down, so we'll find out," I said.

"I can't wait. Sometimes I pinch myself to reassure myself that I'm not dreaming. You're a life saver, Joe."

"Aw shucks, Rachel. It's no big deal," I said, my way of minimizing my part.

"I *don't* stand corrected," said Rachel, her way of telling me to take some credit.

I called Lisa to fill her in on Rachel's session with her lawyer. After, we discussed our fast-approaching trip to Schenectady. Lisa told me she had an idea after seeing Rachel in the blonde wig and did I know where she bought it? I remembered taking her to the woman's shop for clothes. I gave Lisa the name and address of the store. "What do you want with a wig?" I asked.

"You'll see," she said, her voice charged with mystery.

I didn't think she was going to tell me more, so I changed the subject. "When we go to Schenectady, do you think you could let Rachel stay in your apartment? It would only be for those three days that we'll be gone."

"I would love to have her stay here. That's such a sweet idea, Joe. She'll be much more at home here than she's been in a motel room," said Lisa.

"You're the sweet one, Lisa. I'll tell Rachel the next time I talk to her."

"When you do, tell her I think she's sweet, too," said Lisa.

Sweetness seemed to be going around.

The next important call came three days later when Rachel updated me on her legal progress. "Joe, it's Rachel! The divorce papers were served on Bill and wait till you hear!" she exclaimed.

"Is it good news or bad news?" I asked, cutting to the chase.

"It started out bad but ended up good, I think," she said.

"I'm all ears," I said by way of opening the floodgates.

"This is all second-hand, from the sheriff who served the papers, but Mike said it all sounded on the up and up to him."

"Mike, huh? You're on a first-name basis with your attorney?"

"Oh. Yes, he insisted that I call him by his first name," she said.

"That's a good sign," I said while I wondered if there were ulterior motives involved.

"He's nice. Anyway, he gave me a running commentary on the conversation between the sheriff and Bill. Do you want to hear it?"

"What makes you think I want to hear it?"

"I. Oh, you're fooling with me!"

"I knew you were one sharp lady, Rachel. Tell me," I said.

"Okay, well, the sheriff found him at his shop and handed him the papers. Bill said, 'What's this?' and the sheriff said divorce papers from your wife, and Bill said 'That fuckin' bitch! I'll never divorce her,' and the sheriff said he smiled at Bill and told him that his wife had pictures she took of the injuries he did to her over the years and Bill got a blank look on his face and said, 'That fuckin' bitch!' again, this time with much less force. That was it," said Rachel.

"It sounds like old Bill got a good glimpse of the writing on the wall," I said.

"Mike said the same thing. He thinks that Bill will have a very hard time convincing a judge that he's innocent, what with all the pictures Mike will show the judge in court," said Rachel.

"That's great news, Rachel. What's the next step?" I asked.

"I have to do something called a deposition. Mike said he would be asking me a lot of questions that will be recorded, questions like descriptions of Bill's attacks on me with the photographs tagged to show the damage he did to me on each occasion. He said my pictures had a date and time stamp on them that will help me remember each incident," said Rachel.

"When does that happen?" I asked.

"I'm going to Mike's office tomorrow and he will go over the whole thing with me, so I'll be prepared when the actual deposition happens. He said that Bill has to do a deposition with his lawyer, too, so the judge can read both sides before making a decision," said Rachel.

"So, if at any time along the way, Bill decides not to contest the divorce, a judge can declare the divorce final, right?"

"Yes, that's right. Mike asked me how much I wanted Bill to pay me as a settlement, that the pain and suffering I've gone through could be worth a lot in the judge's eyes. I told him I needed to think about that. I know Bill has his own business that's doing well, but I don't know what a reasonable amount to ask for would be."

"How will you decide?" I asked.

"Mike said that part of Bill's deposition will be an accounting of his assets and liabilities. The summary will help me to decide how much to ask for."

"You're well on your way to getting the divorce you deserve, Rachel. Would you like to stay in Lisa's apartment for a few days?" I asked her.

"She wants me to stay with her?"

"She and I are going out of town for three days and her apartment will be empty. She wants you to stay there. You can cook meals instead of going out or ordering in, and it'll be more like a home than a motel room. What do you say?"

"I say yes!" said Rachel with obvious enthusiasm.

"I'll call and tell Lisa. I know she will be happy to hear you like the idea," I said.

Like the idea? I *love* it! Motel life isn't my cup of tea," said Rachel.

"I know what you're saying. Keep me posted on your meetings with Mike. I'll call you with more information on Lisa's apartment, okay?"

"Okay!" said Rachel, her voice bubbling over with energy.

I called Lisa. She was delighted to hear that Rachel wanted to stay in her apartment while we were gone to Schenectady. "Hey, I just had a thought," she said.

"Thoughts are good," I said back.

"Smarty! No, why don't I offer her my car to use, too? That's if I'll be riding with you to and from the airport," she said.

"You know you will. That way we'll only have my car to pay and park at the airport," I said.

"See, I'm saving you money already," she said, her coy smile coming through the phone line to me.

"I'll keep tabs on it all, get you a nice gift for your trouble when this is all behind us."

"Oh, Joe! You say the sweetest things," she said, a dash of sarcasm added to her words.

"Are your bags all packed and ready to go?" I asked.

"How did you guess? I've packed and repacked my suitcase a dozen times already. I want everything to go off without a hitch."

"This is a recon run. The main event is still weeks away," I said.

"It's not that far away, and besides, if we screw up on the recon run it could mess up my plans for the main event," she said.

"You're right. I'll call Rachel and make sure she has a driver's license and tell her about using your car if she does."

After ending my call to Lisa, I called Rachel. She does, and she squealed, hearing she could use Lisa's car. Everything was moving forward, smooth as silk. I hoped Schenectady went off as smoothly, too.

Fifteen

THREE DAYS LATER I got the surprise of my life when I went to pick Lisa up and a blonde opened Lisa's apartment door. Lisa had followed up by getting a wig at the store where Rachel found hers. It was flashy blonde and had two pigtails, one on each side. She'd tied a bright pink ribbon around each one. My face must have dropped, causing Lisa to smile at me. Her smile and her dark eyelashes gave her away. I chuckled and told her I liked her camouflage. I drove to Sky Harbor airport with her seated next to me.

We parked, checked in and made it through security with time to spare. I'd made the decision to leave my handgun at home. If security found it, I knew that'd be the last I'd see of it. I missed the weight of it on my hip, but so be it. When I handed Lisa her ticket, her eyes grew large, seeing it. "We're flying first class?" she said, her dark eyebrows raised in surprise.

"Why not? It's a long flight and we'll be much more comfortable," I said. I knew from memory that my long legs cried out to me when they were forced into tight quarters.

She gripped my arm, sending her usual charge of warmth through me. It was all the thanks I needed.

The flight was long but without incident. All the screaming babies were confined to cattle class. We changed planes and landed at the Albany airport in the dark, nine P.M. their time. To us it was six P.M.,

Arizona time. We debarked, picked up our rental car and headed to Schenectady, the car's GPS guiding us to our motel. We spotted an attractive-looking Italian restaurant on the way and pulled in to get a bite to eat. It was crowding ten, Schenectady time, and they were minutes from closing for the night, but we were warmly greeted and led to a table. They apologized for their depleted selections and provided us a carafe of red wine as a peace offering, which we accepted with thanks. I secured chicken alfredo and Lisa landed an order of chicken cacciatore. I poured the wine into the high-end glasses and Lisa raised hers to me. We clinked and sipped, enjoying the moment.

We left the restaurant an hour later, relaxed by the wine and sated by the food. It was a five-minute cruise to our motel. Lisa's eyebrows arched when the desk clerk pushed two key cards at us but made no comment. We elevatored to the third floor and found our rooms, side by side as promised. I saw Lisa to her door and waited while she swiped her card and opened the door. "How does eight o'clock local time in the breakfast room sound?" I asked.

"Sounds great, Joe," she said while she gave my arm a gentle squeeze. I said good night and turned back for my room door, sparks sending a tingling sensation through all six-foot-four of me. Lisa waited until I'd opened my door. Then she smiled at me and closed her door. I stood there a moment, still a-tingle from her touch before entering my room and closing the door.

When I showed up at the breakfast room the next morning at five to eight, Lisa was already there, sitting at a table with a coffee cup in her hand. Her warm smile drew me to her. I filled a plate with scrambled eggs, sausage, and a toasted English muffin. She placed a muffin on a plate that was half the size of mine. We returned to the table and disposed of our breakfasts in silence. After, we discussed our strategy for the day.

We would use the GPS to locate Captain Wittingly's ancestral home and drive by it, taking in all its details without causing any suspicion, or so we hoped. Our speed would have to be just right. Not too slow, not too fast. After that, we would drive in every direction from the house for no more than four miles. We figured that any greater distance would trigger Wittingly to drive, not walk. We wanted to catch him on foot for our plan to work.

With our breakfast dishes clean-platter-club winners, we returned to our rooms to check the plumbing and polish our teeth. Done, we strolled to the parking area and climbed into our rented chariot. While I familiarized myself with the car's controls, much easier in daylight, Lisa entered the address of the Wittingly homestead into the GPS. It was already crowding ten. Saturday's morning traffic would be minimal, I figured, so I didn't worry about people in a rush honking us to the side of the road, wanting to pass. I didn't want to cause a scene that brought attention down on us.

The GPS told us to turn right out of the motel parking lot and we were on our way. We drove straight for a couple miles, and then the GPS had us making turns on secondary roads. At length we came to the Wittingly's street, and I slowed down as we approached our destination. The GPS announced that we were arriving at our destination on the left, and there it was: a white, two-story colonial style house set well back from the road, a blacktop driveway leading the way to the garage and entrance. The lots were large here, attested to by the ample space between the neighboring homes. I made note of the white picket fence that ran along the street in front of the house. A line of old maple trees lined the space beyond the fence. Lisa whooped. She'd spotted the fence.

"It's perfect," she said. "I can picture Captain Wittingly draped over that fence, his pants down around his ankles and his offending member tacked to one of the vertical boards."

The image she created made me flinch as my imagination felt the tack being driven home.

I continued by the property at a sedate speed, taking in all the details as we passed it. Once by it, I checked out the houses that followed. They were of a similar style and vintage to Wittingly Manor, and most of them boasted similar picket fences along the road. I moved along, committing what I saw to memory. We passed through four intersections controlled by stop signs before we came to a major road. I did an about-face and drove back towards Wittingly Manor, taking in the homes on the opposite side as we approached it. Once past, I examined the homes on the Wittingly side, figuring that the captain would walk on the side that his home occupied. We passed more picket fences with homes set well back from the road. I pictured Lisa doing her tacking at any of the fences we passed. The imagined pain lingered in my mind.

I drove through three stop signs and came to the road we'd last turned from. While stopping to get my bearings, I asked my copilot, "Where do you think that tavern is from here?"

"Go right for a block, then turn left. It should be on the right," said Lisa, calling on her memory of the maps she studied.

We turned right, then left, and the City Bar and Grille popped into view. The façade was fresh with new paint and a bright sign hung over the entrance. A sizeable parking lot took up the vacant space on one side. We'd located the captain's weekend watering hole.

I drove on by. It looked empty at eleven-thirty in the morning, though two cars sat in the lot. Employees? Maybe. Maybe inveterate drinkers. No doubt the scene would change after five o'clock.

Lisa gave me directions to the strip mall and its restaurant, which turned out to be a short drive from the tavern. I pulled into the strip mall and parked in a space some distance away from the restaurant. It was doing better than the tavern at that time of day. We climbed out, I locked up and we walked together to The Loving Spoonful. It boasted home cooking, offering something for everyone.

Once we were inside, a sign told us to 'Seat Yourself.' I spotted a vacant table for two and steered Lisa to it, checking out the layout as we made our way. There was a section of booths, plus numerous tables arranged for two, four and six occupants. The center of the back wall supported the bar with liquor bottles arranged ahead of a long plate glass mirror. The kitchen access doors were to the right, the rest rooms to the left. Half the tables were already filled. People knew good food when they found it and the memory of it had them coming back for more.

I pulled Lisa's chair out for her, and she rewarded me with a warm smile and a shake of her blond braids. I'd barely sat opposite her when a cute young waitress arrived at our table with two menus. "Welcome to the Spoonful, folks. My name is Alice and I'm here to take care of you. Can I get you something to drink?" she asked, topping it all off with a smile fit to please.

We both asked for iced tea. She hurried off, leaving us to check out the menus. Breakfast was still a vivid memory for me, so I searched out the sandwich menu and found egg salad on wheat with potato chips. Just what the doctor ordered. I sat back and checked out the other diners. Most were chatting away with their table mates, no doubt discussing whether the feds would raise the interest rate or not, or what the Housing Administration planned to do about the homeless situation. Or maybe they were discussing family and friends.

Alice returned with our iced tea, and we recited our lunch choices to her. Lisa chose a sandwich, too. Ham and cheese on rye, hold the chips and double the dill pickles. Sounded good.

She left to tell the kitchen what we'd chosen, we sipped our tea and Lisa asked what was next on the agenda.

"I think we should go back and take every side street on either side of the Wittingly manor for at least a mile in both directions. I hope all we'll find is more houses, which will eliminate surprise traffic on the night we intercept the captain."

"I'm with you there. What we're planning is risky enough. We don't need witnesses driving by while I'm driving my tack home," said Lisa, smiling broadly.

"For sure. If there's going to be a lot of traffic, we need to rethink the plan," I said.

"Any thoughts on an alternative?" asked Lisa.

"I don't know. Maybe I render him unconscious with the chokehold he's so fond of using and I fireman-carry him to a quiet location for your tacking session."

"I like it. That means we need to search out a backup spot where I can do my tack attack without interruption," said Lisa.

We were saved from further conversation by the arrival of our sandwiches. Alice set our plates in front of us with a little flourish she'd perfected and asked if there was anything else we needed. We both said no, and she disappeared to tend other tables. The sandwiches looked as good as her flourish, and Lisa and I launched into them.

With our lunches history, Alice spotted our clean plates and dropped off the check after we declined cherry pie, rice pudding and fresh fruit cup. She informed me that the cashier would handle the payment. She swept a hand in the cashier's direction and left us with her well-rehearsed farewell smile. Lisa and I pushed back and stood up, and we weaved our way through the tables to the cashier. I paid in cash, included a generous tip and we headed for the parking lot to reclaim our rental car.

Once inside, I fired up the engine and turned the air on max to knock down the heat that had taken over the car in our absence. The next step in our recon was to drive down every street along the route from the tavern to the Wittingly manor house, plus a few streets beyond it for good measure. I didn't want to miss a commercial area that could add to traffic on a key road. It could increase the chance that a car passing us might see Lisa upholstering Wittingly's weenie. That could seriously complicate things. With all the cell phones out there, we didn't need a do-gooder calling the cops on us. Neither one of us fancied jailtime in Schenectady, or anywhere else for that matter.

I drove and Lisa created a map of the streets, including their names and what was on them. I drove a minimum of a mile in each direction, not wanting to miss something around the next corner. I followed the speed limit, not wanting to attract any attention. It gave me the opportunity to do my own search as we drove along.

After cruising every cross street for a mile each way, we came back to what we affectionately called Wittingly Way, feeling both relief and confidence. Wittingly Way was the center of a large residential area, and none of the side streets ran into commercial establishments for the mile or more that we traveled. Things were looking up for a successful attack on the captain. I knew we needed to worry about evening strollers and dog walkers. The responsibility of spotting them and warning Lisa of their approach would be my job.

Though we were past the midpoint of the afternoon when we finished our recon, the heat and humidity were still doing serious damage to our comfort level. I suggested a return to the motel and a jump in the outdoor swimming pool, and Lisa seconded the motion with unbounded enthusiasm. I drove while Lisa put the finishing touches on her map.

I pulled into the motel parking lot, and we hurried inside to the elevator, the air conditioning cooling our bodies. At our doors, Lisa said she'd see me in the hall in five, and we key-carded our way inside. With the door closed behind me, I began peeling off shirt and shoes, then pants and skivvies, leaving a trail behind me as I made my way to my suitcase and my bathing suit. Nothing fancy. Dark blue mid-thigh nylon bathing suit. I tugged it on, peeled off my damp socks and drew a fresh T-shirt over my head. I pawed around in my suitcase to find my flip flops, stepped into them, and finished by grabbing a bath towel from the rack in the bathroom. I was ready for the pool in well under five. I flip-flopped out the door and turned to face Lisa's entrance. It opened before my eyes and a gauzy mirage stepped out. Lisa was wearing a thin white wrap over her shoulders and upper body. It struggled and lost at hiding what was underneath. Lisa wore a modest pink bikini that accented every curve and feature of her body. I sensed my mouth dropping open and struggled to close it. She caught my reaction and rewarded me with a warm smile. "You ready?" she asked.

Yes, I'm more than ready. You didn't hear that, Mom.

"Yes, let's go get wet," I said. *And cool off.*

We elevatored to the lobby and out through the entrance to the pool. A glance at my watch told me it was close to four-thirty. I could see that we had the pool to ourselves. When we stepped onto the concrete surrounding it, I saw little wet footprints left behind by kids, or possibly midgets, though I figured midgets were less likely.

Lisa led the way to a pair of chaise lounges. She dropped her wrap and towel on it and stepped out of her flip flops while I shed my T-shirt and flip flops and parked my towel. She turned to the pool and in three bounds she arched her body and dove in, leaving a slight splash in her wake. I followed close behind, my two-hundred-and-forty-pound body causing a much bigger disturbance to the surface.

Ignoring Lisa for the moment, I surfaced and swam with energy. I swam freestyle for a lap, then did the backstroke for a lap, and finished with a breaststroke. I made like a porpoise through the water to the deep end, passing Lisa as she did her own thing, and swam to the side. I held onto the edge with my forearms. Lisa swam up alongside of me and mimicked my position. She was first to speak.

"Two questions, Joe. What do you do to keep your abs in shape? I couldn't help noticing your six packs," she said, a curious expression on her sweet face.

"I've kept up the exercises the army taught me. For a while I neglected them, and I started feeling weaker and had less confidence in myself, so I got back into them. What's your second question?" I asked, feeling shy talking about my body.

"Question two, where did you learn how to swim like that?"

"When I was in college, I applied for a job as a counselor at a summer camp. A lot of camps were looking for college kids to cover the waterfront, so I took a Red Cross course in water safety. I spent a lot of time in the YMCA pool, and by the time I was done I could do all the different strokes, plus rescue swimmers in distress. The big thing I learned was how to rescue someone drowning without having them grab hold of me and drag me under with them. Now tell me how you learned how to swim so well," I said.

"Funny you should ask. When I was ten, a boy pushed me into a pool in a friend's back yard. He just walked up to me and gave me a shove. I landed in the water and struggled to get to the side. I swallowed a lot of water and hung there coughing after I finally grabbed the side. The boy looked down at me and said, 'You better learn how to swim, girl.' I took his taunting to heart."

While Lisa told me her near-tragic tale my eyes roamed across her upper body, filling my mind with thoughts that would draw a severe reaction from Mom. When she finished, I drew in a big breath of air, relaxed my arms, and let my body glide downward, underwater. Once submerged, I swam towards the far end, made a turn, planted my feet on the poolside and pushed off, gliding underwater to the other end. At the halfway point a shadow to my left caught my attention. I glanced that way to find Lisa swimming along next to me, matching me stroke for stroke. We reached the poolside together, and I pulled myself up on my forearms as before. Lisa mimicked my position. We took a moment to blow off the buildup of carbon dioxide in our lungs.

Once my breathing was back under control, I turned to Lisa. "You learned well."

In answer, she grasped my arm and said, "You're not too bad yourself." Predictably, her touch sent a course of warmth flowing through my body. I glanced to see if the water around me was boiling, so intent was the feeling. It wasn't. Close, maybe.

I powered myself out of the water with my arms and stared in surprise as Lisa did the same. We stood next to each other, the water dripping from us. Lisa broke the spell when she said, "That was a great idea to have a swim. Thanks for thinking of it."

We walked side by side to our clothes and towels, our feet leaving wet impressions next to the smaller ones that were rapidly evaporating in the afternoon heat. After we toweled off, I pulled on my T-shirt and Lisa draped herself in her sheer wrap. We slipped into our flip flops and padded our way back to the motel lobby and elevator. When we reached our doors, Lisa asked me what our plan was. My watch told me it was five-thirty.

"Let's shower and change into some casual duds for the evening. We've got plenty of time since dark isn't until eight-thirty or so. Knock on my door when you're ready, okay?"

"Will do," she said, warming me with a smile before she ducked into her room.

I stripped and showered and dried off and splashed some mild bait on my face and climbed into a fresh button-front shirt and jeans. I'd finished pulling on fresh socks and was putting on sneakers when I heard a knock at the door. It was at the connecting door, the door that accessed the room next to mine. Lisa's room. "Are you decent?" I heard her call out in her soft, melodic voice.

In answer, I stepped to the door, unlocked it and swung it open. Lisa stood framed in the doorway, looking like a million bucks in a pale blue loose-fitting blouse and a darker blue skirt that reached to just above her knees. Her only makeup, as far as I could tell, was a faint hint of lipstick. The rest of her face was all Lisa, fresh from the box. She spoke first.

"You look nice, Joe. What's the expression? You clean up good," she said, tossing me her impish smile as she stepped into my room.

"You clean up good, too, Lisa," I said, feeling like the world's biggest jerk for my clumsy duplicate offering.

"Oh, my, Joe. You certainly have a way with words," she said, her eyebrows dancing in time with her comment.

"Some words, maybe. Not those words, sad to say."

Lisa's eyes spotted the mini bar by my bed. "Do you want to share a glass of wine before we go?"

"That's a great idea. You choose the wine while I get the glasses," I said.

While she opened the mini bar I scooted into the bathroom and picked up two of those Sani-sealed plastic cups motels are famous for. A far cry from glasses but they'd have to do. I yanked the plastic covering from them as I made my way back to Lisa. She held a miniature bottle of white wine and twisted off the cap as I neared her. She plopped down on the edge of the bed and patted the area next to her. I sat down and held out the cups while she concentrated on pouring equal amounts in each. Done, she set the empty bottle on the bedside table, and I handed her a cup. She raised it towards me, and we brought the rims together. "Cheers!" we both said. I stared into her liquid black eyes as I sipped the wine, losing myself in their depths. The slurp of chilled wine in my mouth pulled me back.

"What do you think?" she asked. I knew she meant the wine, but to be honest my thoughts were elsewhere.

Thinking fast, I said, "It has a nice bouquet with mild tannins and a faint grape/strawberry aftertaste. What are your thoughts?"

"I couldn't have said it any better," she said, a wolfish grin flooding her features. For emphasis she took another healthy sip.

I joined her, a comfortable silence expanding between us as we fought to picture the wine as anything but average.

Lisa was first to break the silence. "So, my revered recon leader, do we need to review our plans for the evening?"

"I think our plan is pretty straightforward. We dine at the same restaurant, and after we finish and it's near dark we go on an after-dinner stroll, maybe in the moonlight if we're so lucky," I said.

"A stroll that takes us to Captain Wittingly's family homestead, if I'm not mistaken."

"Exactly. We'll leave the car in the restaurant parking lot and walk the two blocks to the tavern, and from there we'll follow the route to Wittingly's, checking out ambush possibilities as we stroll along."

"Sounds like a perfect after-dinner stroll to me," said Lisa.

"Yes, and we can BOLO the other strollers as well," I said.

"BOLO them? That sounds violent, even painful," said Lisa.

"Not at all. BOLO stands for Be on the Lookout for," I said, making my eyebrows dance as I explained.

Lisa rewarded me with a light blow to my upper arm, which caused as much of a warm energy flow as her light touches did to me. Maybe I could become addicted to violence. I discarded the thought. "Ow!" I said as a knee jerk reaction, though ow didn't describe how I was feeling.

"I think I hurt my hand more than I hurt you," she said as she shook her right hand from side to side.

"Well, cheers to both your hand and my arm," I said, raising my plastic cup to hers.

She 'clinked' her cup to mine and we drained them together. I took her empty cup and telescoped it with mine. The waste basket was three feet away. An easy two-pointer. I missed, blaming it on the puffy plastic waste basket liner.

Lisa leaned forward, retrieved the two cups, and leaned back to fire, making a perfect rim shot. Lisa two, Joe nothing. I took heart in knowing the game was a long way from being over.

A glance at my watch told me it was time to go. Drive to the restaurant, have a leisurely dinner and start our stroll at dark minus thirty, say eight-thirty. "You ready to go?" I asked.

"You bet I am," said Lisa as she bounded up from the bed. I joined her, patted my pockets to be sure I had wallet, car keys and room key card, and we left my room behind, elevatored to the lobby and climbed into the rental for the fifteen-minute drive to the restaurant.

Sixteen

SATURDAY EVENING AND traffic overshadowed the daytime traffic. The drive took twenty minutes, and the restaurant parking lot was already filling up. We found a short wait line outside the restaurant entrance, something I hadn't anticipated. I asked a couple waiting in line ahead of us if we needed to go inside and give our names. "They don't take names. It's first come, first served," the man told us, his expression saying *What side of the moon are you from?* I thanked him and Lisa and I moved to the back of the line. We were three couples from getting a table. Our timetable was still on schedule.

Lisa and I chatted about everything and nothing as the line inched forward. When a couple or group came out, the next in line went inside and took the empty table. Our turn came, and we scooted inside and spotted the empty table being attacked by a busboy. He worked quickly, piling dishes and glasses on a tray, and finished up by giving the table surface a quick swipe with a damp cloth that had seen plenty of action. He picked up his laden tray and weaved his way to the kitchen. Lisa sat down and I sat next to her. It put me closer to her than if I sat across from her.

A solidly built female waitress materialized from somewhere in the busy restaurant. "Welcome to the Loving Spoonful, the best restaurant in Schenectady, folks. My name is Mimi and I'll be taking care of you.

Can I get you folks something to drink?" she asked as she set menus in front of Lisa and me.

"Iced tea, please," said Lisa.

"Make that two," I said.

"Is that sweet or plain tea?" asked Mimi sweetly.

Sweet tea in Schenectady? Will wonders never cease. "Regular tea, please. With lemon," added Lisa.

"Make that two," I said again.

Mimi recited the specials du jour and left us to our decisions while she fetched our teas.

Lisa eyed me, smiling, and said, "You're having the meat loaf special, aren't you?"

"How'd you know? Hey, the best restaurant in Schenectady can't afford to screw up the meat loaf, right?"

"Good point. I'm going to take my chances with a cobb salad," she said.

"Another good choice. It's hard to mess up a salad, even a cobbed one."

Mimi wove her way through the tables with our tea on a small tray and set them in front of us. "Have you folks decided?" she asked.

"I'll have the cobb salad," said Lisa.

"Perfect. And you, sir?"

"I'm having the meat loaf special."

"Excellent. You can't go wrong," she said while she picked up the menus and performed her vanishing act.

We sipped our tea, and I searched the restaurant for our lunch waitress, Alice. She was nowhere to be seen. It seemed that she didn't work the dinner crowd. Maybe she had a little one to tend to.

"Are we still okay timewise for our after-dinner stroll?" Lisa asked.

"Yes, we're fine. Twenty minutes, a half hour either way isn't going to make a difference," I said.

"Once more, with feeling, I want to thank you for all you've done, all you're doing and all you're going to do to help me deal with my demons," said Lisa, her warm eyes enveloping my own.

"Oh, pshaw, ma'am, it's nothing," I said, my way of making a molehill out of a mountain.

"Stop it, Joe! I'm serious. Without your help I could never do this."

"All right, Maid Marian, I accept your heartfelt thanks. But know that I am doing this because I want to, and not simply because you're a damsel in distress," I said, making a bowing motion towards her as an exclamation point.

"Oh, Joe, you're so, so chivalrous," she said while she put her supercharged hand on my arm. The flowing warmth was expected, but it still left me breathless. Mercifully, Mimi appeared with our dinners. Lisa removed her hand, breaking the spell.

My meat loaf platter looked as good as the picture on the menu and Lisa gave out with a big 'Oh, yum,' when she settled her eyes on her cobb salad. Mimi and the best restaurant in Schenectady were batting a thousand. We picked up our forks and set to work, an easy silence falling over us as we made inroads into our chosen meals. The meat loaf, mashed potatoes with gravy and whole kernel corn had my full attention. For the moment, anyway.

We both set our forks down at the same time. My plate was wiped clean by a dinner roll and Lisa left a few stray morsels of salad on hers. Her way of saying that she'd had more than enough. My way of saying that I'd enjoyed everything completely. Ever alert and attentive Mimi arrived at our table when she saw that we'd finished. "Can I bring you folks a nice homemade dessert to top everything off? A piece of pie with ice cream? Some nice warm bread pudding?" she asked expectantly.

"I'm sorry to say, Mimi, I didn't leave room for it," said Lisa.

"Look at my plate, Mimi. I didn't leave room, either" I said, pointing at my immaculate plate.

"Very well, then. I'll be right back with your check."

She was. With a little tray that held two mints anchoring the receipt. I scooped up the mints and passed them to Lisa while I picked up the check to eyeball the total. I dropped a generous tip on the table and pushed back. Lisa did likewise, and we made our way to the cashier. I paid and we headed for the entrance. I pushed it open slowly, wary of colliding with the next couple in line, and we stepped out into the lingering humidity. We passed five waiting groups. Business was booming at the best restaurant in Schenectady. The time had come for us to begin our recon.

Lisa and I walked past my parked chariot and turned the corner, heading for the tavern. Foot traffic was light. I walked with an eye out for trouble, a reflex developed and honed to a keen edge in Iraq. I probed every dark nook and cranny as we passed. I missed the weight of my M9.

We arrived at the tavern unscathed. Business was booming there as well. The parking lot was crammed with cars and pickups, and a few vehicles took spaces along the street. No line formed outside. Everyone had found standing or sitting room inside.

The tavern was a landmark, not our destination tonight. We turned and followed the route to Wittingly Way. I checked my watch, so I'd know how long it took us to Wittingly's. I guessed at ten minutes.

As we strolled along, we quickly left the hubbub of the tavern behind. Now we were on quiet suburban streets where Saturday night meant a TV movie for most of the residents, with a drink at home, not in a tavern. The sidewalk was clear as far as I could see. Most dogs didn't need a walk this early.

Lisa surprised me by taking my hand in hers as we strolled along. She completed the picture of a young couple out for an evening walk together. A closer look with the right electronic detection equipment would show a radiant glow coming off the man. It never failed. Lisa's touch suffused me with warmth. I wondered idly if it would diminish, fade even, with the passage of time. I hoped not.

We were approaching ambush site number one and we slowed, checking for other people about. Seeing that we had the street to ourselves, we ducked behind the screening bushes to examine the area more critically. Faint, diffused light filtered through the gloom, helping us with our inspection. Lisa was first to speak. With her hand resting lightly on the wood fence, she turned to me and whispered, "It's perfect, Joe."

I thought so, too. Captain George Wittingly would meet his Waterloo here, if all went well. We stepped back onto the sidewalk and continued. As we passed Wittingly's, I saw lights on in a front room. The flickering light of a TV floated from the window. Ma and Pa Wittingly were enjoying Saturday night in front of their boob tube, perhaps daydreaming about their son's approaching visit.

A check of my watch confirmed my guess. Ten minutes had passed. It included our brief sojourn behind the bushes. We went on to the end of the block before we crossed the street and made our way back on the opposite side. Lisa took my hand again, and the warm flow made me weak in the knees. A solo walker coming towards us diverted my attention from Lisa's energy field to the man's intentions. It was a perfect place for a person with evil intentions to commit a robbery, or worse. I watched him closely. I thought about my M9 pistol left behind in Surprise. If he tried anything violent, I'd need to rely on my self-defense skills.

As the gap between us closed, the man smiled and said, "Good evening, folks. It's a nice night to be out, isn't it?"

The man's words meant nothing to me. They could have been spoken by Ted Bundy. Lisa responded with, "It certainly is." Short and sweet. We passed each other, and I looked over my shoulder to follow his progress, knowing from my Iraq experience that it was a crucial moment. The assailant acts all friendly, passes by, and then turns back with a weapon in hand to rob, maybe kill.

Not this time. The man kept on walking without a glance back. When he was well beyond us, no longer a threat, I turned my attention back to the street ahead. Lisa gave my hand a small squeeze and said, "What?" She had sensed my unease. I told her why I was wary of strangers passing in the night. She gave my hand another squeeze and threw in a smile for good measure as we continued.

Ambush site number two came into view, and we slowed our pace while I checked for other nightwalkers. With the world to ourselves, Lisa released my hand and stepped into the site. Like the first one, bushes grew between the fence and the sidewalk, offering a shield to a potential tack hammer-wielder. I could see that the space between the fence and the shielding bushes was smaller, making it more difficult to swing a hammer. Still, it offered a good second choice. Watery light filtered through to the space, providing some illumination to work by. Lisa summed it up perfectly. "Number two is number two."

We emerged from the hidey hole and continued our way back to the tavern and the additional two blocks to my car. Nobody else was out and about. Nobody else posed a potential threat to us. The tavern continued offering up its usual fare and the restaurant had four late diners waiting patiently outside. Who knows? Maybe it really is the best restaurant in Schenectady.

The parking lot was crowded so my car didn't stand out like a pounded thumb. I unlocked it, held the door for Lisa like the good knight that I am, and came around to climb in the driver's side. She rewarded me with a smile and a squeeze. All I needed. *Right, Mom?* I pulled out of the lot and pointed the headlights at the road leading back to the motel.

"That was a productive walk, Joe. We learned what we needed to know about the two sites, and I enjoyed your company," she said, breaking the brief silence between us.

"Yes, it was. On all counts," I added as I piloted us towards our home away from home.

I parked in the motel lot, and we did our final stroll of the evening into the motel and up to our floor. At my door I asked Lisa if she wanted to split another mini bar wine. "Why not, Sir Galahad. The night is yet young." I opened my door, and we entered my room together.

"You choose the wine while I get two more of those crystal glasses," I said. I plucked two sterile plastic cups from the bathroom counter while Lisa ran through the wine options in the mini bar. She picked up a bottle and closed the mini bar door as I returned, stripping off the wraps.

"Oh, my, what perfect crystal glasses you've found. Are they Waterford?" she asked.

"If they aren't, they're a close second. They're a perfect match for the perfect wine you've chosen," I said.

"How perfect is that?" she said, exhausting the use of *perfect* for the foreseeable future.

Lisa had chosen a red wine to top off the evening. I held out the cups while she unscrewed the cap and poured. When she'd shaken out the last drop, she set the bottle on the bedside table next to the other empty and took one of the cups, holding it up to the light. "Ah, just look at that rich red color. Clearly a wine made in heaven," she mouthed.

"Let's hope it's not vinegar," I said. I took a sip and smacked my lips with enthusiasm. "Nope. It's not half bad."

"My goodness! We have a budding wine critic in our midst," she said, putting on her happy face.

"More like two, I'd say."

Lisa sat close to me on the side of the bed. We weren't touching, but I could feel her warmth through the clothes that separated us.

You tread lightly with her, you hear me, Tojo?

I'm trying, Mom. I really am.

We sipped our wine, a comfortable silence settling between us. Lisa was first to speak.

"We've done all this planning and searched for the best ambush spot, but there's still one great big unknown: Captain Wittingly himself. If he doesn't go to the tavern, and if I can't lure him into taking me home with him, then we've wasted all this time," she said, her expression turned serious.

"True. Every plan has the potential for failure. From what we know he'll go to the tavern on Saturday night, and I think you could coax an ogre from its lair. Together, we can do this," I said.

"Thanks, Joe. I mean that," she said, her soft black eyes capturing mine. She tipped her cup to drain the last of her wine and handed me the empty. I slid it into my drained cup and turned to set them on the bedside table. Lisa stood up and when I turned back to her, she brushed her lips on mine for the briefest second. Fire leaped between us.

You tread lightly with her, you hear me, Tojo.

It gets harder every time, Mom.

"Good night, Joe. Thanks for the lovely evening." She stepped to the connecting door, opened it, and closed it behind her. She took the fire with her. A part of me exited through the connecting door with her.

I dropped the cups and empty bottles into the trash can, distracted from trying a two-point shot with the cups. In the bathroom I went through my pre-bedtime checklist and stripped to a T-shirt and skivvies. When I climbed into bed. I remembered to go through my nightmare checklist, reviewing the adjustments I needed to make to blunt my nightmare's attacks. As I had done many times before, I hoped for uninterrupted sleep. I turned on my side, pounded the pillow into shape and settled in.

Seventeen

A MUFFLED SCREAM woke me from a sound sleep. I sat up, listening. It came again. Lisa! I could hear her words. "Get off me! Stop!" she cried out. Someone had broken into her room and was assaulting her!

I leaped out of bed and raced to the adjoining door. When I turned the knob it swung open. Thank God, she hadn't locked it. I dashed into Lisa's room. She was sitting up in bed, a wild expression on her staring face. She was naked from the waist up. I looked at the outside door. The chain was hooked, undisturbed. Nobody had broken in. The realization of what happened swept through me.

Turning from the door, I hurried to her bedside. Her screams had died to a loud whimper. "No!" she kept saying. "No! No!"

I put a hand on her bare shoulder. It was damp with perspiration. "It's okay, Lisa. I'm here with you. It's okay," I said, keeping my voice soft, soothing as I tried to bring her out of her nightmare. As I spoke, I watched her eyes clear, begin to focus. She turned her face toward me, and recognition flooded her features. She wrapped me in a death grip and held me against her nakedness for a long moment. I hugged her to me with equal ferocity. Sparks flew between us.

As she regained awareness, she realized that she was unclothed. She released her grip on me and pulled the sheet around her, hiding her beautiful, upturned breasts from my view. "It was a nightmare, Joe," she said, her voice hoarse from screaming out.

"I know, Lisa. Thank God you left the connecting door unlocked so I could get to you."

"I did?"

"Yes. I came in, expecting to find someone assaulting you, and when I saw that your outer door was undisturbed, I knew you were having a nightmare."

Lisa lay back down, her head on the pillow, the sheet drawn up. "Do you think they'll ever end?" Her question was meant for me as much as it was for her.

"Yes, I do," I said. I believed it. The alternative could lead to suicide, dependence on drugs or alcohol at the very least.

"I really want to believe you, Joe. Please, stay here with me. You comfort me, make me feel protected."

Without a word I swung my feet up onto the bed and lay down next to her. The warmth coming from her flooded through me.

You tread lightly with her, you hear me, Tojo?

I hear you, Mom, though I have to say, your voice is getting harder and harder to hear.

Daylight was leaking around the window shade when I woke up. Confused by my surroundings, I couldn't figure out where I was until I felt Lisa's warm breath on my neck. I turned slowly to face her, not wanting to waken her. She was under the sheets. I was on top of the sheets. My promise to Mom remained intact.

Lisa stirred and stretched, awakened by my movement. She opened her eyes, saw me, said "Huh," and then a smile broke out across her sweet, round face. "I remember now. Thanks for rescuing me, Sir Galahad," she whispered, her hand reaching for my arm. Knowing what her touch would do to me I bolted upright. "At your service, my dear lady," I said as I stood up.

"I owe you, Sir Knight," she said.

"You owe me nothing," I said.

"Let me be the judge of that."

"Whilst you're judging, might I suggest that we reclaim our clothes and invade the breakfast nook, pillage it for whatever fits our fancy," I said.

"Your brilliant suggestions are exceeded only by your chivalry. I shall knock three times on yon door when I am ready to join you in the attack on the breakfast room," she said, her happy face back in place.

I scooted through to my room and closed the connecting door. Alone, and feeling very much alone, I went through my morning bathroom rituals, double-checking my face for stubble before setting aside my razor. I added a splash of bait to my clean-shaven face and padded to my suitcase to retrieve my final change of clothes. First on was a pale-yellow polo shirt, followed by light brown slacks. I socked my feet and stepped into my loafers, then donned my belt and fed my pockets with all the items I lug about with me every day. My wallet was last aboard. With my shirt tucked, pants buttoned, and belt buckled I was ready to face the day. I sat on the edge of the bed with the TV remote in my hand, prepared to play the waiting game with Lisa.

As I hit the remote's POWER button, I heard three distinct knocks on the connecting door. I hit POWER again, turning the TV off in mid-awakening, stepped to the door and pulled it open. Lisa looked spectacular. She wore a light green chiffon blouse that topped a dark green mid-thigh skirt. Her black hair was tied back in a small ponytail. She had green flats on her feet. If she was wearing makeup it was minimal at best. Her full lips had a natural flush to them. "Perfect timing," I managed to say, my eyes, my senses filled by her presence.

"We time out well together," she said, leaving me and my befuddled mind to figure out if there was a hidden meaning in what she said.

"You hungry?" is the flat-out dumb thing I thought to say.

"I'm ready when you are," she said, leaving me with more questions about what she meant.

Stop jumping to conclusions, Tojo.

You're right, Mom.

At the breakfast bar Lisa picked up a lemon poppyseed muffin and coffee while I found scrambled eggs, sausage, and home fries. I skipped the toast and bagels. My waistline silently thanked me. I grabbed coffee and joined Lisa who was tugging off the paper muffin wrapper. She blessed me with a smile as I set my tray on the table and sat down.

Amen.

Lisa nibbled on her muffin, setting a pace that had us finishing at the same time. We set aside our plates, refilled our coffee cups, and lounged at the table, in no hurry to go. After a sip of her coffee Lisa asked me what was on our agenda for the day.

"Our flight isn't until 5:30 this afternoon so we have the day to explore more, maybe lounge at the pool, whatever you want," I said.

"I saw checkout time is one, so let's do the pool thing this morning and the explore thing after we check out," she said.

"Makes perfect sense. It's good that one of us thinks logically," I said.

"Come on now! You're the most logical person I've ever met."

"I'll attribute that observation to your youth and inexperience," I said.

"See? Your logic spills over into your sarcasm, it's so ingrained in you."

I drained the rest of my coffee and set the cup on my tray. I knew I was losing the argument, so I changed the subject. "Did you bring more than one bathing suit?" I asked Lisa.

"Why? Don't you like the one I wore yesterday?"

Oh, boy! Take your foot out of your mouth, Joe.

"No, I love your bathing suit. You look great in it," I rushed to say.

"That's good to know because it's the only one I own," she said, her eyes searching me for a reaction.

"It's perfect on you. Let's go back to our rooms and suit up. The pool awaits us."

We did, and Lisa looked as stunning in it the second time as she did the first.

By noon we'd had our fill of swimming, diving, and sunbathing in the humid sunshine of Schenectady. Back in our rooms, we showered and dressed, then packed our bags for the trip home. We made it to the lobby and the one o'clock checkout time with ten minutes to spare.

On our cruise to the Wittingly zone I spotted a Chick-fil-A restaurant and pulled into the drive-through lane. "Oh, I love Chick-fil-A!" said Lisa.

"What's not to love? Cluck-cluck!"

Lisa clucked back.

We ordered, picked up our sandwiches and I parked in the shade, the car's air conditioning winning the battle with the high humidity and noonday sun. We devoured our sandwiches in a comfortable silence, using ice water as a chaser.

When we finished, I drove on to the tavern, now looking forlorn in Sunday afternoon's glare, and followed the streets that took us to, and by, Wittingly Manor. All was quiet. We passed one couple being dragged along by a rambunctious rottweiler, their efforts devoted to controlling their pet. They never looked our way when we passed them. We approached and crept past ambush site number one. Both Lisa and I gave it a critical examination, looking for problems we hadn't spotted before. We both gave it a passing grade. At the next block I did a U-turn and cruised back on the other side so we could have a good look at ambush site number two. I slowed as we approached it. Lisa was first to react. "Look at them!" she whispered, shock in her voice.

I saw what she saw. A young couple was lying between the bushes and the fence, fully occupied with their lovemaking. The hedge, though dense, wasn't hiding what they were doing. So much for ambush site number two. It had two obvious flaws. It could already be occupied when we approached it, and the thin hedges could reveal what we were doing there to anyone passing by.

That brought up the point that ambush site number one could be occupied when Lisa came to it with the captain. I decided it was a risk we needed to take, that most lovers would be indoors, not in the bushes on a Saturday night. Lisa agreed.

With ambush site number two crossed off our list, I drove a short distance down the intersecting streets closest to the Wittingly home, searching for a backup site. We found nothing suitable. It became critical that backup site number one worked for us.

After Lisa and I discussed the situation and how thin the plan had become, I hurried to reassure her. "We'll make it work," I said.

"I know," she said, though her tone said that doubt had reared its ugly head.

We drove through Schenectady in a haphazard manner until it was time to head for Albany and the airport. We dropped the rental off and took the shuttle to the airport. We were through check-in and security screening without a hitch and settled into a table for two at a combination bar and restaurant. It was four-thirty. We had an hour to kill. We each ordered a glass of wine and I thought to call Rachel, see how she was getting along.

She picked up on the second ring.

"Hi, Rachel. It's Joe. How's everything?"

"Ohmygod, Joe! I've had the scare of my life!" she shouted into her phone. I put mine on speaker and set it on the table so Lisa could hear.

"What's happened, Rachel?" I asked, fears for the worst.

"I was sitting in the attorney's lounge area on Friday afternoon, waiting to see Mike, when the door burst open and my husband charged inside. He glanced over at me and thank God I had my blond wig on, and he didn't recognize me. He shouted out that he wanted to see my attorney, Mike. A short time after, Mike came into the lounge, very polite and respectful, and asked Bill what he could do for him. Bill shouted, "You can fuckin' stop this divorce case against me! I don't agree to it!" and Mike looked him squarely in the eye and told him he better be hiring his own lawyer because the divorce proceedings would be going forward. Just then two security guards came in and surrounded Bill. Seeing what was happening, Bill yelled, "Keep your hands off me. I'm leaving!" With that he stormed out," said Rachel, her voice trembling with the memory.

"Thank goodness he didn't recognize you, Rachel. I'm sure you'll be fine," I said, doing my best to calm her.

"It was a total shock, seeing him so unexpectedly like that," she said.

"I'm sure it was. Look, Lisa and I are waiting to board our plane. We should land in Phoenix and be back with you by ten, okay?"

"Okay. I'll pack up and take a cab back to the motel."

"No!" Lisa shouted. "You'll do no such thing. There's room in my apartment for both of us. I want you to stay right there."

"Are you sure, Lisa?" asked Rachel, her voice thin, childlike.

"I'm absolutely sure. We can have a woman-to-woman talk, come up with a plan to keep you safe," said Lisa.

"Oh, thank you! Thank you! I'm ever so grateful," said Rachel, clearly relieved.

I told her we'd see her soon and ended the call. "That poor woman. What she's been through," said Lisa.

I compared the two of them and what they had survived. They were both tough women, no question.

Lisa and I enjoyed an in-flight first-class dinner on the way back to Phoenix. The flight went off without a hitch and we made it to Lisa's apartment at a little after ten. Rachel was waiting for us. She hugged Lisa to her and murmured her thanks while I carried Lisa's suitcase to her bedroom door. I started for the door, ready to leave the two women alone to chat and decompress. Lisa broke away from Rachel and intercepted me. I mean, intercepted me. She wrapped her arms around me and gave me a hug I'll never forget. I hugged her back. The next thing I knew she was kissing me. It wasn't a light brush of our lips. It was a kiss, long and deep. I was lost in it. At length she drew back, her eyes searching mine, and said, "That was not a test. I repeat. That was not a test."

I don't remember leaving her apartment and walking back to my car. The fog was so thick in my brain that it obscured all rational thought. It began to shift and fade away when I turned into my apartment parking lot. I had enough foresight to take my suitcase from the back and haul it behind me to my apartment. Once inside, I set my suitcase down and dropped into my lounge chair, my head still spinning. It struck me that I might be in love. I remember asking Mom what love was when I was a teenager. I'll never forget her reply. She said, "Tojo, love is a feeling you feel when you feel that you're having a feeling that you've never felt before." When she said it all those years ago, I laughed. Now it made perfect sense. There was no doubt in my mind that I was having a feeling that I've never felt before. For as long as I'd known her, Lisa's touch had left me both supercharged with boundless energy and weak in the knees. It was an electric current that passed from her to me. I wondered if she felt something pass from me to her. That would be a completion of the connection. I couldn't remember a time when she seemed to share in the connection, but I might have missed it, so preoccupied was I with my own reaction.

A distressing thought swept through me. What if Lisa was playing a game? What if she was toying with me, enjoying watching me squirm and flounder under her spell? First, she kissed me and said, "This is a test. This is only a test," and tonight she kissed me and said, "This is not a test." Which one is the truth?

I decided to call the love expert. My Mom. Perhaps she could help me understand what was happening between Lisa and me.

"Hello?"

"Hi, Dad. It's Joe. Lisa and I just got back from our trip to New York."

"Did you accomplish what you set out to do?"

"Yes, I think we did. The next time we go will be for real," I said.

"You want to talk to your mom, am I right?"

"You know me all too well, Dad."

"Hold on, Son."

I heard him set down the phone and call to Mom, and then she was on the line.

"Did you have a good trip, Tojo?"

"I did, Mom. We did everything we set out to do," I said.

"Are you still treading lightly with Lisa, Tojo?"

"I am, Mom, though it's getting harder and harder," I told her.

"You're a good son, Tojo. How can I help you?"

"Do you remember me asking you what love is, and you said, 'Love is a feeling you feel when you feel that you're having a feeling that you've never felt before'?"

"You've always had a fine memory, Tojo. Yes, I remember."

"I think I understand your explanation now."

"It's Lisa, am I right?"

"Yes, it's Lisa," I said.

"I have to tell you, Tojo, as soon as I saw you two together, I knew in my heart that you two were meant for each other. Call it women's intuition, call it maternal instinct, but I knew. That's why I urged you to tread lightly with her. She has been seriously hurt by an ugly, cruel man, and she doesn't need another man to invade her space until she heals, whether it's an act of love or not," she said.

"I understand, Mom, I do. But Lisa has been sending me messages that suggest that she wants me as much as I want her."

"That's wonderful, Tojo. They are all signs that she is healing, but no matter what she says or does, she is still not fully healed. I know this is hard for you, but I can tell you, you will know when she is healed. Until you know, you need to continue to tread lightly with her, Tojo," she said.

"I will, Mom."

The phone call left me feeling both happy and worried. Happy because Mom had confirmed that my feelings for Lisa were genuine. Worried that I wouldn't be able to tell when she was healed and end up blowing the whole relationship. Mom was right. Tread lightly.

Eighteen

I CALLED LISA the next morning to see how she and Rachel were getting along. "We're doing great, and Rachel is a real trooper. Her attitude has been a wakeup call to me. That husband of hers is the world's biggest jerk. I can't imagine being married to a man like that. She said he was all peaches and cream before they got married, and then he changed into an abusive wife-beater. His attitude is, she's his wife so he can do whatever he wants to her. He's one sick son of a bitch, excuse my French," said Lisa.

"Yeah. Who knows what he might have done to her if he'd recognized her as she sat in the attorney's waiting lounge?"

"That was a brilliant move on her part, buying that blond wig. I think my blond wig is going to be a game-changer for me, too," said Lisa.

"We'll find out in less than two weeks. Let's hope all our planning pays off," I said.

"I have every confidence in you and your planning, Joe."

"I'm a bit player. You're the star of the show, you know. What's the next item on Rachel's agenda?" I asked, changing the subject.

"Mike canceled the meeting last Friday when her jerk husband showed up and threatened him. He figured that Rachel was too shaken up to work on her deposition after that nasty scene, so he rescheduled her for this afternoon at two. I told her I'd drive her there," said Lisa.

"I want to meet her attorney. I've spoken on the phone with Mike, but I've never met him face to face. I'll come there on my own and see you there. A quick how-do and a handshake shouldn't disrupt his day too much," I said.

"I don't see a problem with that. I'm sure Rachel wants to see you, too. After all, you're her knight in shining armor," said Lisa.

"She deserves everything I can do for her."

"I agree. I'll tell Rachel you're coming, and we'll see you at the law office," said Lisa.

"It's a date," I said.

"That has a nice ring to it," said Lisa. She disconnected the call before I could respond.

Her comment left me wondering what she meant. No question, she had a way with words. Did she mean the ring of a bell or a ring for a finger?

When I drove up to the law office there was a fight going on. I saw Lisa, who stood a head taller than Rachel. She was yelling at a man at Rachel's side, her blond wig clutched in his fist. It didn't take a rocket scientist to figure out what happened. Bill Bonner staked out the attorney's office and when Lisa and Rachel arrived, he figured out it was Rachel under the wig and yanked it from her head, confirming his suspicions.

I parked and jumped out, making tracks for the screaming threesome. I approached Bill from behind. He never saw me coming. His attention was totally focused on Rachel. As I closed on him, he drew back his fist, intending to drive it into Rachel's face. I reacted. I reached out and grabbed his fist in my left hand and yanked, spinning him around. As he turned to face me, I launched my right fist at his exposed face. He had no time to focus on me or react. My fist connected squarely with his broad nose and upper jaw. The solid, fleshy splat filled the resulting silence. His nose was flattened, and his front teeth took a beating from my punch. When Bill's head rocked backwards from my punch, I held onto his fist and eased him down onto the sidewalk. I didn't want him falling backwards and whacking his defenseless head on the sidewalk, maybe split his head open. When he dropped into a sitting position, I released my grip. He flopped over on his side, unresponsive. I knew he'd recover. His breathing made a wet, bubbling sound as it fought its way through his wrecked nose. The jerk never knew what hit him. I liked it that way. Bad enough he wanted to beat the crap out of his sweet wife. No need to have him seek to avenge me, too. I plucked Rachel's blond wig from his limp hand.

When I turned away from Bill, Rachel launched herself at me. She wrapped me in her outstretched arms and clung to me. "Oh, my God, Joe! Thank you! Thank you!" she murmured into my chest, the highest point on me she could reach.

"It's over now, Rachel," I said, my voice calm so it would rub off on her.

"He was going to hit me! I saw him pull his fist back and aim for my face. You saved me, Joe," she said, her voice pitched high.

"Everything turned out well," I said, trying to make light of the situation.

"Thanks to you, Joe," said Rachel, her warm eyes directed up at mine.

"Too bad somebody couldn't catch that whole scene on a camera, to add to the other pictures of Bill's abuse," I said.

"Somebody did," said Lisa, holding up her cell phone. I caught the whole thing."

Rachel let go of me and walked over to Bill. She glared at him, then delivered a solid kick to the side of his chest. I swear I could hear ribs crack. She turned back to Lisa and me, a wide smile of satisfaction spreading across her narrow face.

"What's going on here?"

One of the security officers who worked for the law firm, hearing the hubbub, came out to investigate.

I opened my mouth to speak, but Lisa spoke first. "That man on the sidewalk came running at us, yelling wildly, and just before he got to us, he tripped on something, maybe his own feet, and landed on his face. I think he broke his nose," she added, pointing down at Bill's limp form.

The security officer knelt by Bill and checked his injuries. Satisfied that they weren't life-threatening, he stood up and asked if we wanted to press charges against him.

"For what? Yelling at us, running at us?" asked Lisa. She had taken charge and was doing fine.

"Okay. You folks can be on your way. I'll see that this man gets medical attention," said Mister Security.

We took his cue and walked together to the law office entrance. I considered what I'd done. I knew I was justified in punching William Bonner, the asshole husband of Rachel Bonner, and I had no regrets about doing it. The question was, if I continue offering help to men and women who need a boost in their lives, will violence play a part in it? I knew there was no ready answer, but it nagged at me.

Attorney Michael Harbinger was waiting for us in the lounge. Rachel introduced Lisa to him and then turned to me and said, "This is Joe Roberts. He's the man who called to make the appointment with you," she said. She put her hand on my arm, I guess to point me out, though at six-four and 240 I stood out in the group like a bear in an apiary. No electricity flowed from Rachel to me with her touch, I noted.

Attorney Harbinger stepped forward and shook my hand. He was around five-ten, in his early thirties, I guessed. He had the tight physique of a man who exercised regularly. "I remember our phone conversation, Mister Roberts. Thanks for referring Rachel to me. I think we're a perfect match. As attorney and client," he hastened to add, topping it off with a benign smile.

"Please, call me Joe. My father's name is Mister Roberts," I said, releasing his hand.

"Joe it is. And please call me Mike. Let's all go in my office. I think we have chairs for everyone," he said with a gesture towards an open mahogany door.

When we were all seated comfortably, Mike asked about the disturbance outside. Rachel took charge. "It was Bill. He was waiting out there, and when he saw me, he recognized me somehow. He grabbed the wig off my head to confirm it and started screaming at me. He pulled back his fist and I could see he was going to hit me in the face, but out of nowhere Joe grabbed his hand, spun him around and punched him in the face. Bill dropped to the pavement, out cold. Then your security officer showed up. Lisa thought fast and told him the man tripped and landed on his face while running at us," she said, a bright smile breaking out on her face.

"I'm not surprised by that. Your husband is a violent man, Rachel. Do you want to press charges against him?" he asked.

"For what? Simple assault? He never laid a hand on any of us," I said.

"Oh, I could come up with a variety of charges, aside from assault," said Mike, smiling.

"Would it do any good, do you think?" I asked.

"Hard to tell. Sometimes people sober up when charges are brought against them. Then again, some people end up getting more belligerent," said Mike.

"I caught the whole thing on my phone camera," said Lisa. "Maybe you can add it to the other pictures you have."

"You bet I will." Mike called his secretary on his intercom. She came in and took Lisa's phone to copy the video from it.

"I have one request, Mike. Don't show the video to Bill until the trial. I'm featured on it, I'm sure, and I wouldn't want him coming after me, if you get what I mean," I said.

"I get it, Joe. It'll be our clincher at the trial if it goes that far. For now, let's put charges against him on the back burner. We can always charge him in the future if he continues to harass Rachel. Who knows? Maybe he learned his lesson today."

"That's right. Hey, I came to meet you, Mike, and I've done what I came for. I'll leave you with the ladies to proceed with Rachel's deposition," I said, standing up.

Mike reached out and shook my hand again. "You've got a solid right jab, Joe. I'm glad you came along today," he said, smiling at his apt summary.

"Me, too. See you all later," I said.

I closed his office door behind me and made my way to the street entrance. When I stepped outside, Bill was gone, either carried away by an ambulance or on his own two feet. I thought an ambulance ride was more likely. A small patch of drying blood on the sidewalk remained behind as the only evidence of the encounter. I wondered if I'd have another run-in with him. To satisfy myself that he was really gone I walked slowly around the block, searching every parked car and all the hiding spots along the way. No Bill. Good. I climbed into my car and drove home.

My phone trilled nearly three hours later. It was Lisa, calling in to report. Rachel made it through all the questions posed to her by Mike. "She's a trooper, Joe. She had to answer a lot of difficult, personal questions, and she did great."

"What happens next?" I asked.

"It's up to Bill. If he refuses to get a lawyer, he has the option of representing himself in court or rolling over and letting the divorce go through uncontested. Mike is sending him a registered letter explaining his options, so the ball is on its way back to Bill's side of the net."

"Let's hope his broken nose helps persuade him to roll over and accept the divorce," I said.

"Uh huh, and maybe some cracked ribs, too, thanks to Rachel's swift kick. Meanwhile, Rachel and I are going shopping for a new and better disguise. She doesn't want a repeat of the scene outside of Mike's office," said Lisa.

"I can understand that. Do you have something in mind?"

"Yes, but I'm not telling. When Rachel's new disguise is complete, I'll let you know. If you can't recognize her, I doubt Bill will be able to either."

"I like it." I told her.

Shortly before seven I was trying to decide what to put in the microwave for dinner when my doorbell rang. I pushed the intercom button and asked who was there. "Delivery for you, Mister Roberts," said an assertive female voice.

"What kind of delivery?" I asked, my suspicion growing by the second.

"A food delivery from Asian Oasis," said the voice.

"Do you know who sent it?" I asked.

"Yes. A woman named Lisa Goodweather ordered it for you," said the forceful female voice.

"Come on up," I said as I buzzed the door open. I was still puzzled by Lisa sending me dinner when I heard the knock at the door. I swung it open and glanced at the young woman holding food bags. She looked tough, capable of taking care of herself. No doubt a delivery person could be faced with all sorts of aggressive people, made worse if it's a woman making the deliveries.

"Where would you like me to put the bags, sir?" she asked.

"Oh, I'll take them from you." I reached out and she passed the two bags to me. I was surprised at the weight. It was a lot of food. I carried them to the kitchen counter and set them down, then turned back to the delivery woman, taking my wallet from my pants pocket to give her a tip.

"There's no need for that, sir. Miss Goodweather paid me well," she said, holding up her hand.

"Are you sure?"

"Yes, sir." She turned back to the door and pulled it open. When she did so, Lisa burst through the open door, a wide smile splitting her face.

"You didn't recognize her, did you?" Lisa asked me, a sweep of her hand indicating the delivery woman.

I looked closely at the delivery woman, seeing Rachel under her new disguise. "I recognized her right off. I wanted to see how the whole scenario played out," I said, trying to keep a straight face.

"You did?" asked Lisa, disappointment clouding her face.

"No, I didn't. I cannot tell a lie. Rachel and her new look fooled me completely," I said.

"Seriously?"

"Seriously."

"Do you believe him, Rachel?"

"I do. Unless he's the best actor on the planet, he showed no sign that he recognized me," she said, grinning as she spoke.

"Thank God! Okay, let's eat before the food gets cold," said Lisa.

I brought out three dinner plates, serving spoons and forks for everyone. Rachel and Lisa took them from me and set my modest table. I took a bottle of white wine from the fridge, uncorked it and set it on the table with three glasses. The containers of Chinese food were arranged neatly in the center.

We sat down and Lisa reached her left hand to Rachel, her right hand to me. I took Rachel's hand, then the electric hand of Lisa. Joined, Lisa and I recited the familiar grace: *Itadakimasu. Thank you for this meal.*

Rachel hadn't heard it before. "What did you say?"

"It's a Japanese grace. It means 'Thank you for this food,'" Lisa explained.

"I like it. Short and sweet," she said, a happy smile filling her fresh new face.

We passed around the food containers and filled our plates. I poured the wine. Rachel picked up her wine glass and held it aloft. "Chigadoo!" she said, and we clinked glasses.

"Chigadoo?" asked Lisa.

"My turn!" said Rachel, adding a wide grin.

"Where did you learn that?" I asked.

"My mother is French-Canadian. It's a toast she learned as a child watching grownups clinking glasses. I think it means something like 'cheers!' She's always said it whenever she touched her glass to someone else's," said Rachel.

"Well, Chigadoo, then! Let's eat," said Lisa.

I grabbed my fork and set to, casting sidelong glances at Rachel as I tried to decipher her disguise. If she could fool me, chances were good that she could fool her husband. Simple but effective, it was a combination of carefully applied makeup and an intricate new hairdo.

After we'd all had our fill, Lisa and Rachel refused to take their share of the leftovers. I packed up what was left. It would easily feed me both lunch and dinner tomorrow. At the door, Lisa surprised me with a new response. Instead of a kiss, she placed her index finger on my lips, pressing gently. The expected flow of warmth surged through her finger and into me. Watching my expression, she smiled and nodded her head. I knew then that she understood fully what her touch did to me. I only hoped that the feeling was mutual.

Nineteen

I SPENT MOST of the next morning with Dad, discussing my incredible wealth and my plans to use it. He heard me out, holding his tongue until I was done. He thought I had a noble plan, and he said he was proud of me for sharing my wealth with less fortunate people. When I told him of the violent episode with Rachel's husband and what I'd done to him, he sat silent a moment, ruminating on it. At length he said, "I think you can expect that occasional violence comes along with what you're doing, what you plan to do. Somebody wins and somebody loses. Losers can be violent," he said, summing it up perfectly.

"That's true, Dad. I'll need to anticipate possible violent situations in the future, so I don't get caught flat-footed. The last thing I need is someone sticking a knife in me or putting a bullet in me because they take offense at what I'm doing."

"To be forewarned is to be forearmed,' an old wise man once said," opined Dad. I knew that part of his quote included the M9 holstered at my side.

I left wondering whether I needed to consider hiring a bodyguard when things got dicey. I absentmindedly brushed the bulge on my right hip.

Lisa called me the next morning to tell me Mike had heard back from Bill about the divorce trial. "The fool said he's going to represent himself. Mike said his voice had a decidedly nasal sound to it, like he had a bad cold," said Lisa.

"More likely his swollen, broken nose is changing the way his words come out," I commented.

"That sounds right. Mike thinks it's a huge advantage for Rachel to have Bill pleading his own case. He hasn't a clue about what those pictures of her old injuries will do for Rachel's case, and he doesn't know that I made a video of his assault on Rachel two days ago." Said Lisa.

"What happens next?"

"Bill has to go through the deposition process, like Rachel did. Since he's representing himself, he'll have to be deposed by one of the law clerks in Mike's office, someone not associated with Mike," said Lisa.

"That should be interesting."

"It should be. Mike doesn't think he can come up with anything substantial in his rebuttal, considering the circumstances, and Rachel will find out how much he's worth. That will help her decide how much of a settlement to ask for," said Lisa.

"Does Mike smell a rat?" I asked.

"You mean about Bill representing himself? He said it's unusual for one side in a divorce case to choose to represent him or herself. He thinks it's Bill's way of saving legal fees because he thinks he can win," said Lisa.

"Did he say when the trial might take place?"

"No. He has to send a petition for trial to the court. He said it depends on how busy the judge is. He'll let Rachel know as soon as he knows," said Lisa.

"So, we're back to a waiting game."

"Uh huh. Meanwhile, you and I have a date with destiny in Schenectady."

"Right you are. We agreed that the second Saturday night he's home with his parents is a better bet for his solo outing to the tavern. He may take them out to dinner on the first Saturday he's home," I said.

"I stand by that choice," said Lisa.

"Okay. I'll take care of the reservations. Let's hope the judge doesn't set a date for Rachel's case that conflicts with our plans," I said.

"It shouldn't be a problem since we're going on a weekend," said Lisa.

"True. Friday is the only chance for a conflict. By the way, the Asian Oasis leftovers were a perfect dinner last night. Thanks again for the treat," I said.

"You're welcome. It was worth every cent of it, watching the surprise on your face when you found out the delivery lady was Rachel," said Lisa.

"I'm curious. Who did the makeover on Rachel?"

"A beautician friend of mine. She did her hair as well as the makeup work."

"Will it be easy keeping her looking that way?" I asked.

"Yes. She showed me what I needed to do to maintain the disguise," said Lisa.

"Outstanding. You and Rachel are a great team," I said.

"I really like her. She's been through so much and she has a great attitude. I'm so glad you introduced her to me," said Lisa.

"You've been a big help to her, and I'm sure she appreciates it."

"You know something? Since she's been staying with me, I haven't had one bad nightmare. I guess I'm too busy," she joked.

"Let's hope that continues," I said.

Two hours later Lisa called me with terrible, near-fatal news. When she called Mike to tell him we'd be out of town over the weekend, Mike's secretary told Lisa that when Bill walked into Mike's law offices to do his deposition, he spotted Mike and pulled out a handgun. Seeing the gun, Mike's secretary hit a button to alert security. Bill pointed the gun at Mike and demanded to know where Rachel was staying. Mike told him he didn't know, and all he had was her phone number. Bill shouted that he didn't believe him and if he didn't tell him, he'd shoot him. Mike swore that he didn't know, and Bill shot him. The firm's security guards burst in with their guns drawn, and they yelled at Bill to put down the gun. Bill turned to shoot at them, but they were faster. One of them shot Bill in his right thigh. They kicked away his gun, handcuffed him, and went to help Mike who was lying on the floor, bleeding from a bullet wound in his right upper chest. The injury, though serious, wasn't life-threatening. The bullet missed his lung and major blood vessels, it turned out.

The secretary said that two ambulances arrived. Mike was treated and put in one while Bill was treated and put in the other. The big difference was, Bill was handcuffed to the stretcher and had two burly policemen ride with him to the hospital.

Lisa told me that Rachel blamed herself when she heard the news. She told Lisa that if she hadn't gone to Mike to get a divorce this would never have happened to him. Lisa said it was crazy to blame herself for Bill shooting Mike. There was no way Rachel could have known that Bill would do something like that. Rachel said she wasn't surprised, considering the threats and violence Bill brought down on her.

Lisa went on. "I asked Rachel if she knew Bill had a gun, and she said no, but maybe he kept one at the garage, for self-defense. I told her she should be thankful that he never pointed a gun at her when he blew his top at her, that she might not be here today if he did. I told her that Bill has demonstrated over and over that he's a violent man, and there's nothing she could have done to control it, so she had to stop trying to blame herself for him shooting Mike. When I finished speaking to her, I wrapped Rachel in my arms and gave her a big hug. I could feel the tension drain out of her."

"She pulled back, looked up at me and said she knew I was right, but it was sad and pointless, what happened to Mike. I agreed with her."

"Good Lord, Lisa! That's terrible news. Is Mike going to, is he going to survive?"

"Yes, Joe. His injury isn't life-threatening. Neither is Bill's, for that matter, though I think Bill's in a world of hurt with the police over what he's done to Mike. I wouldn't be surprised if he gets jail time out of it. Hell, he should get jail time for everything that he's done to Rachel," Lisa added.

"What happened next?" I asked, guessing that Lisa's story wasn't complete.

"Rachel insisted on going to see Mike in the hospital, so I drove her. The nurse on duty told us we had five minutes with Mike since he was fresh from surgery. She led the way to Mike's room and pushed the door open. Rachel and I filed in. Mike smiled when he saw Rachel and me standing there. The nurse left and Rachel rushed to his bedside. I could see his bandaged right shoulder. A small spot of blood oozed through, showing where the bullet hit him.

"Rachel told Mike she was sorry, and he made light of it, saying that it gave him an excuse for taking time off from work. He said he was long overdue for a vacation. Rachel laughed at that, and said she hoped Bill would be locked up forever. Mike said he didn't know about that, but he guaranteed that Bill's actions would get her the divorce she deserved. Rachel said it couldn't come soon enough for her.

"Mike went on to say that he'd get the papers ready and send them to the judge as soon as he got out of the hospital, which he guessed would be in four or five days. He predicted that the judge would issue a divorce decree in record time, after he read and saw the pictures of what Rachel went through. Mike was interrupted when the nurse came back to tell us our time was up. Mike told Rachel he'd call her when he was back in the office, and we left. When we got back to my car I called you, and that's where we are right now."

"That's one hell of a story, Lisa. Thank God Mike's going to be all right," I said.

"I know. I hope this lands Bill in jail for a long time. He deserves whatever's coming to him, I say."

"Unintended consequences."

"What?"

"Unintended consequences. Would any of this have happened if I kept my nose out of it and I didn't meet up with Rachel on that park bench?"

"Oh, so now you're going to blame yourself for what happened?" asked Lisa.

"I did start it all, if you think of it," I said.

"Sure, and everything you did along the way was carefully planned, orchestrated really, so Rachel could get out of the violent relationship she found herself in. There's no way you could have known how violent Bill would turn out to be. By the way, did you make the reservations for Schenectady?" she asked me, adroitly changing the subject.

"Not much gets by you," I said.

"You'll have to tell me what does get by me when you come over," she said. I could feel her sly grin coming through to me.

I hung up, my mind reeling over the shooting. I felt responsible in a way for what happened, but Lisa was right. There was no way I could have known, anticipated the violence in Bill. I chalked it up to my new learning curve as a rescuer.

My computer sat patiently waiting for my return, the reservation page open and ready for my keystrokes. I tapped and typed, filling in the blanks to make the flight, motel, and car reservations. When I finished, it looked like a duplicate of the reservation I'd made the first time around. Same flight and motel. Same car? Doubtful, but time would tell. I printed everything out and headed off to Lisa's apartment.

When Lisa opened the door for me. I saw Rachel hanging back, wary, until she saw it was me. I couldn't blame her, considering everything she'd been through. "Okay, tell me, Mister Roberts. What gets by me?" asked Lisa, her eyebrows lifting with the question.

"I thought about that all the way over here, and I need to amend my previous, impulsive statement. Nothing gets by you," I said while I struggled to suppress the smile trying to take control of my face.

"I humbly accept your amendment, kind sir. Were you able to procure the reservations?"

"Yes. They are an eerie duplicate of the ones for our first trip. Same flight, same motel. Time will tell if we get the same car with the parking lot dent in the passenger side door, or if our rooms are the same," I said.

"You're right. That's eerie," said Lisa.

"If it's the only eerie part of the trip, I'll be happy."

"I second the motion," said Lisa.

I thought of all the things that could go wrong. My army team leader might have scrapped the mission, faced with so many unknowns.

Michael Harbinger's prediction turned out to be right. He was released from the hospital in four days and was back in the saddle in five, his right arm in a sling to take the strain off his shoulder. "Thank goodness I'm left-handed," he told us when the three of us went together to his office.

I watched as Rachel made a big fuss over his bandaged shoulder and added a meaningless apology for Bill having shot him.

"You can't take any blame for what happened, Rachel. I'm just happy that Bill's marksmanship left something to be desired," said Mike, a wide grin bisecting his face.

"I am, too. I'd hate to have to hire another lawyer," she said, her grin matching Mike's. We all laughed at that.

"You know, don't you, that this has become the easiest divorce proceeding I'll ever handle. Between the selfies of your injuries that Bill gave you, Lisa's video of his attack on you and his attempt on my life, the judge will grant you a divorce without hearing a word from Bill. I'll be keeping track of him and the charges he faces. Jail time is a certainty, though how much is yet to be determined. When I know, you'll know. Do you think Bill could try and track you down after he serves his time?" asked Mike.

Rachel shuddered at the thought. "I wouldn't put it past him," she said.

"We have to do something to guarantee your safety when your soon-to-be ex-husband is a free man. Do you have friends or relatives who Bill doesn't know about, maybe out of town or out of state?" asked Mike.

Lisa and I watched Rachel consider the question for a moment, then shake her head. "I can't think of anyone who Bill doesn't know about."

"What about the witness protection program?" asked Mike.

"You mean, where I get a new name and identity and move somewhere miles from all my friends?"

"That's it," said Mike.

"I couldn't do that. I'd rather risk being killed by Bill than leave all my friends and family behind," said Rachel, her voice loud and clear.

"Okay. For now, let's think about your options. We have time. I think Bill will be tied up in the legal system for the foreseeable future," said Mike.

"That works for me. Do you need me to say or do anything more about my divorce?" asked Rachel.

"No, not a thing. I'm going to put together a document containing all the evidence you have against Bill and send it to the judge. He has the authority to make decisions when the evidence is incontrovertible. It might take him a few days to get to it and weigh all the evidence, but it's my guess that you'll be a free woman within two or three weeks, maybe even sooner," said Mike, his left hand absentmindedly exploring the dressing on his right shoulder.

"That would give me relief from my nightmares. They're bad, but they're nothing like the ones Lisa and Joe have," said Rachel.

"Why do you two have nightmares?" he asked, looking first at Lisa, and then at me.

"We were both in the army and we had stuff happen to us that gave us nightmares," I said, speaking for both of us.

"Is that what they call PTSD?" asked Mike.

"Yes. The symptoms of PTSD can include nightmares, night terrors and flashbacks," I said. I felt a shiver pass through me as I spoke. I hoped nobody noticed. If Mike did, he ignored it.

"Are you getting any help for it?" he asked.

"Yes. We both go to the VA hospital for a PTSD clinic every week. That's where we met. Now we help each other, too," said Lisa, speaking up.

"I wouldn't wish that on anyone. PTSD, I mean. My occasional nightmares don't come close to that," said Mike.

"When you have nightmares do you cry out?" asked Rachel.

"I don't know. Maybe."

"Your wife has never commented on you crying out at night?"

"I don't have a wife," said Mike.

"Oh. I just assumed you were married."

"I'm still looking for that special woman," said Mike, his eyes searching Rachel for a reaction.

"I hope you find her. I think you have a lot of nice qualities," said Rachel. I could see that she was aware of Mike's eyes on her.

"Thanks, Rachel. I'll get that document off to the judge by the end of the day, and I'll call you when I hear anything. Meanwhile, stay safe," said Mike.

"You, too," she said, her eyes lingering on Mike. Shortly after, we all filed out.

Lisa kept me up to date on Rachel's divorce progress. If all went well, she could be a free woman before we flew off to Schenectady. She told me that Mike continued to voice concerns that Bill might come after her when he was released from jail. It was a sobering thought. I considered what I could do to stop him from doing that. It was worth thinking about. I considered checking the want ads for vigilantes for hire. How would it read? *Someone after you? We'll make them think twice.* Or maybe *Someone threatening you? We'll convince them to leave you alone.* To hell with that. I decided that I could save all that money by taking on Bill myself. If I had to.

Four days later I had a phone call, and when I answered it, the speaker was filled with shouts and squeals of joy. "Hello? What's going on?" I fairly shouted to be heard over the din.

"I'm a free woman! I'm a free woman!" It was Rachel.

"Tell me!"

"Mike just called! The judge looked over all the evidence we had against Bill, and he declared in my favor on the petition for divorce. I'm free of the sonofabitch! I mean, I'm free of the bastard! I mean, I'm free of Bill," said Rachel, barely able to contain herself.

"That's wonderful news, Rachel. I'm so happy for you! And by the way, I agree with you. Bill fits all of those descriptions you gave him." A sense of accomplishment, of deep satisfaction settled over me. All my efforts had paid off. Rachel was my first successful rescue. The first of many, I hoped.

"And that's not all! Mike said that he wanted to take me out to dinner, to celebrate my divorce," she said.

"That makes two celebratory dinners. Lisa and I want to take you out, too," I said.

"Oh, my! It looks like I'll have to start watching my waistline, what with all these dinners out."

"I'm sure you can handle it, Rachel."

"I want you to know, Joe, I'll always be indebted to you for all you've done for me. I could never make you enough clothes to repay you," said Rachel, her voice gone serious.

"You owe me nothing, Rachel. Your happiness is all the payment I need," I hastened to tell her.

"My words stand, Joe. I'll never forget you," she said.

I knew in that moment that I'd chosen the right path, a path that led to helping those in dire need.

Twenty

I PULLED LISA's and my suitcase from the back of the car and locked the doors. My clothing selection was a close match to the ones I'd taken on our first trip to Schenectady, and I wondered if Lisa's wardrobe matched her original one, too. The addition of her upholstery hammer and tacks might be the only difference. I crossed my fingers and hoped that security wouldn't open her checked bag and think of them as lethal weapons. If they only knew! The August heat and humidity brought on by monsoon rains wilted us as we made our way to the terminal, but once we were inside the air conditioning brought us back. We breezed through check-in and dropped off our suitcases, and then we shed our shoes and got wanded by security without a hitch. Unhindered by baggage, we made our way to the same café we'd visited on our first trip. I opted for a glass of red wine and Lisa seconded the motion. I put a twenty on the table so we wouldn't have to wait for a check when our flight was called.

"Are you ready for whatever adventure lies ahead?" I asked her after I took a sip of my wine.

"As ready as I'll ever be," she replied. She held up her wine glass. "To a successful Schenectady caper."

I touched my glass to hers. We sipped our wine. With all the possible challenges we faced, I hoped that Lisa would come away happy. I knew I would do everything in my power to help her realize her dream of tacking Wittingly to that white picket fence. Despite my best efforts, I winced at the thought.

The flight was smooth and uneventful, and the drinks and snacks helped pass the time. I pitied the passengers in cattle class. They had the option of purchasing an uneventful meal for an outrageous price. I recalled my own time in cattle class. I was oblivious to the decadence occurring beyond the closed curtain ahead of me. Just as well. Uprisings on passenger liners are frowned upon.

The rental car we picked up outside the Albany airport was different than the earlier one, or maybe they had the dent taken care of. Same make, same model, though. I didn't have to go through the hassle of learning where all the controls were. We dumped our bags in the trunk, climbed in, and took the exit route. "Schenectady, here we come," I said.

"Captain George Wittingly, here I come," said Lisa. She snuggled up against me, flooding me with that warm feeling I'd come to know. And Love. Life was good.

We made the same stop at the same Italian restaurant on the way. They remembered us and gave us a gratis carafe of wine. We ate heartily and they told us to hurry back when we left. Neither Lisa nor I shared their wish.

Same motel, different rooms, but eerily similar. We were one floor above our previous rooms, but when we opened the doors and walked in everything was the same. Lacking imagination, the designers had duplicated everything, right down to the floral prints on the wall. The connecting door was there, too. After parking my suitcase on the caddy, I opened my side of the door and tapped on Lisa's door. "The mini bar is open," I said to the closed door.

"I'll be right there," I heard Lisa say.

I glanced at my watch. It was seven-thirty Phoenix time, but already ten-thirty Schenectady time. Three hours different. Arizona skips daylight savings time, putting them on Pacific time during the summer months. I was tired from the travel, but I was a long way from bed ready. A drink with Lisa made a perfect way to end the day.

I heard her door click open and she stepped through the gap, leading the way with her warm smile. "So, kind sir, what is your drink preference for this special occasion?" she asked.

"Is this a special occasion?"

"You know it is. Any occasion shared with you is a special occasion. The man who singlehandedly rescued Rachel Hartack Bonner from a life of abuse is undeniably special," said Lisa.

"Oh, that," I said, struggling to minimize Lisa's praise.

"Yes, that. And more. But I won't get into that. What can I get you?" she asked as she brushed a strand of silky black hair away from her right eye.

"I think the red wine we enjoyed on our last trip would be a perfect fit for this evening," I offered.

"I'll have a looksee," she said as she stepped over to the mini bar fridge and pulled open the door.

"And what to my wondering eyes should appear," I said as she reached inside.

"But a bottle of red, waiting patiently here," Lisa finished my intro as she drew it out with a flourish.

"I'm off to secure our fine crystal goblets," I said, leaping from the bed and dashing into the bathroom. I wasn't disappointed. A supply of stacked and sterile plastic cups sat waiting. I pulled out two and returned to Lisa. She'd negotiated her way past the screw cap in my absence. I handed her one of the cups and we peeled away the plastic film, unmindful of the bacteria we were planting on them in our haste. I held the cups and she poured. She parked the empty bottle on the bedside table and I passed her the cup that seemed slightly greater, gentleman that I am. She said "Cheers!" and I said "Chigadoo!" We bumped our cups together and sipped our wine, making a big show over its bouquet and balance.

"Ah," I said, at a loss for words.

"Double ah," said Lisa.

We sat side by side, her left hip making the barest contact with my right one, energy flowing. At length words came to me. "It doesn't get any better than this, does it?" I asked by way of filling the void.

"I disagree. I think it does. When I have bestowed upon Captain Wittingly his just reward, I'll be able to move on."

"What makes you so sure?"

"His sneak attack on me took control and power from me, leaving me feeling vulnerable and weak. I want that control back. My tack attack on him will help me regain what he's taken from me," said Lisa. She stared at the far wall, her eyes unfocused as she spoke.

"I'll do everything I can to help you."

"I appreciate you, Joe. If it wasn't for you, I would have abandoned my dream of evening the score."

We chatted on, and Lisa ducked into her room to grab a matching red wine from her mini bar. She split it between us, and we sipped on, making small talk. The main event loomed over us, and we had our own thoughts about how it would go down. Me, I hoped everything would go according to plan and Lisa could be free of her nightmares, her painful burden. I knew what she was going through.

At length we drained our cups. Lisa bounced up and handed me her empty cup. As I took it, she leaned in and brushed her lips on mine, sending a cascade of energy flowing through me. "Good night, sweet prince. Parting is such sweet sorrow," she said.

"Shakespeare," I said, recovering. I watched her scoot into her room and close the door.

I made a big mistake, which I regretted later. I failed to review the defenses against my recurring nightmare, and it blasted through my neglected defenses like a tornado through an Oklahoma town. I found myself crying out as I sat upright in bed, my T-shirt drenched in sweat. I came to my senses to find Lisa beside me, hugging me to her and murmuring in my ear.

"It's all right, Joe. It was just a bad dream. It's over now. I'm here with you," she murmured in my ear.

I shuddered as the last tendrils of my nightmare faded away, leaving me drained, disoriented. *How did Lisa get here with me?* Then I remembered the connecting door. "You heard me through the door?" I said as the fog lifted.

"It was impossible not to. Let's hope the police aren't on the way," she said. I couldn't see her smile in the gloom of my unlighted bedroom, but I knew it was there on her sweet face.

I put my arm around her and hugged her to me, thankful for her presence. Unlike the scene at her own nightmare, she wore a T-shirt that covered her and provided some separation, a minor barrier between us. The energy surged through me and then Lisa was kissing me. I knew I had to stop it. I pulled back from her and put my hands on both her shoulders, fending her off. At length she relaxed, her black eyes searching mine. "Is there something wrong?" she asked.

"No. There's nothing I'd rather do than make love to you right now," I said. I took deep breaths to calm myself

"Then why?" asked Lisa.

"You remember me telling you what my mother said? After she met you, she told me to tread lightly with you. She sensed what you had suffered, and she told me you didn't need me adding to your confusion and pain."

Lisa lay silent a moment. "I remember, Joe. Like I said, you have a very wise mother. Thank you for respecting her words. She's right. This could have been a disaster for me. But I'm not going anywhere. You stayed with me after my nightmare, and I'm staying right here next to you." she leaned in and kissed my cheek. We fell asleep together, side by side, me under the sheets, she on top of them, barely touching.

I woke up to daylight leaking in around the window shade and was startled to find Lisa lying next to me until I remembered what had happened. Thankfully, my nightmare didn't pay me a second visit despite my neglect of the defenses I'd built. I wondered if Lisa's presence had something to do with that. Food for thought.

Lisa stirred and stretched next to me. Her right hand bumped into me, and her eyes flew open, startled. She pushed herself up to see who the stranger was and gave out with a deep, throaty laugh when memories flooded back. She collapsed next to me, a contented smile warming her face. "Good morning, Joe," she whispered while she hugged my arm.

"Good morning to you, fair lady. Thank you for staying with me and keeping my nightmare at bay."

She appeared deep in thought a moment, and then she said, "I didn't have another nightmare when you stayed with me. Do you suppose our being together works to fend off the demons?"

"I look forward to testing that theory," I said.

"You!" she responded, punching me lightly on my chest for emphasis, breaking the spell.

We rolled out of bed and Lisa ducked back into her room while I padded into my bathroom. I heard her shower running so I fired mine up, too, happy to wash away the remnants of my sweaty nightmare.

Dressed, I turned on the TV to see if the world as I knew it was still out there. It was. Albany reported a fatal shooting, the rape of a seventy-year-old woman, and a carjacking. The world kept right on turning. Lisa stepped into the room. She looked fresh and bright, beaming at me. Now here was a world I could embrace. On impulse I stepped up to her and gave her a big hug. When I stepped back, she said, "What did I do to deserve that?"

"You know damned well what you did. You saved me last night," I said, my voice husky with emotion.

"It was payback time," she said, her way of minimizing what she'd done to help me.

"Whatever it was, it worked. Thank you, fair lady," I said, sidestepping the emotion bubbling up in me

"I don't know about you, but this fair lady could use a cup of coffee," she said, a broad smile taking charge of her face.

A glance at my watch told me it was seven-thirty. Phoenix time. I'd forgotten to change the time to Schenectady's time, now ten-thirty. "Let's go. As I recall, they serve breakfast until eleven."

They did, though the breakfast room was deserted and forlorn, with our options seriously depleted. We secured coffee and Lisa rescued a muffin while I scraped the remnants of scrambled eggs and a single sausage link from the heated chafing dish. We sat together and chomped on our choices.

Lisa finished her muffin and wiped her fingers on her napkin. "What's the plan, Mister Man?"

I chuckled at her way with words. "Let's drive by Wittingly Manor to see if there's any sign of increased activity."

"It'd be a bummer if the captain made other plans for his furlough," said Lisa.

"More than a bummer," I agreed.

I drove to the tavern on autopilot and turned to follow the street to the Manor, going slow and steady, blending in. The heat and humidity were already climbing, adding another reason for the neighbors to stay inside. The sidewalks were bare. As we passed the Wittingly homestead, looking for signs of the captain's presence, we spotted it at once. A second car was parked in the long driveway. Unless Ma and Pa Wittingly were entertaining at eleven-thirty in the A.M., the captain was in residence. A collective sigh of relief escaped us. "It appears that we're in luck," breathed Lisa.

"It does. Now we need to cross our fingers and hope that this is his night on the town," I said.

"What time are you thinking that I should go into the tavern?" she asked.

"I doubt he'll show up any earlier than eight. He'll have dinner with his parents and say 'see you later' as he heads out the door. If you get there by eight-thirty he'll be into his first, maybe second drink and searching the room for female prospects. Your blond wig will snag his attention in a hurry," I said.

"What about you?"

"I'll go in twenty minutes after you and grab a stool at the bar, order a drink, keep an eye on you and your progress. When you and the captain leave together, I'll pay my tab and follow at a safe distance behind. When we reach the ambush site I'll rush behind the captain and put him in a headlock. When he goes limp, I'll continue the squeeze for another ten seconds to put him out for a good long time. Squeezing his neck any longer than that could leave us with a dead guy to dispose of. Not part of the plan," I said.

"Definitely not. I want to nail him, not knock him off," nodded Lisa.

I drove the streets surrounding the Wittingly residence to reassure me that nothing had changed. A newly opened mini mall or a detour could make a big difference in the traffic flow, and we didn't need cars driving by while Lisa performed her upholstery work on the captain. Happily, everything was as before. We found nothing that could bring more cars to our ambush site. All was well. Or so it seemed.

It was just past noon and lunch was in order. "How's your appetite?" I asked Lisa.

"For what?" she asked, an impish smile tracing its way across her face.

I ignored the implication and said, "For a bite of something."

"I like it when you talk dirty, Joe," she said, with the right amount of sexiness in her soft voice.

You tread lightly with her. You hear me, Joe?

What was that you said, Mom? You need to speak up.

"I was thinking more like soup and sandwich," I said, forcing improper thoughts to the back of my churning brain.

"Come to think of it, a little nourishment would hit the spot," she said. I could feel her eyes on me as I drove. I squelched the thought of asking her which spot she was referring to.

Since we'd be going to the best restaurant in Schenectady for dinner, I searched as I drove for an alternate lunch stop. I breezed by two fast food restaurants and a pizzeria, and there it was, just ahead of us. A large sign over a sixties diner announced MAZIE'S HOMESTYLE. Nothing more, nothing less. The full parking area said it all. I pulled in and took a space when the previous occupant drove out.

We joined one other couple waiting outside. We made small talk with them while we waited for a table. The weather, of course. The traffic, sure. They didn't ask and we didn't say that we were there to tack a rapist's pecker to a picket fence.

The couple moved inside to take the next free table and we stood together, waiting our turn. "I think we've discovered the second-best restaurant in Schenectady," I said to Lisa.

"If the wait is any indication, I think you're right. Bottom line is, the proof is in the pudding, she said."

"You're having pudding?"

At that moment the door opened to disgorge a sated couple and we moved inside, saving Lisa from having to answer my dumb question. A waitress met us and led the way to a vacant table for two. Murmured conversations floated from the other lunch-goers seated around us as we sat down. The waitress passed us menus and asked us for drink orders. We ordered iced tea, naturally. "Be right back," she said, and she hurried off to get our drinks.

The menu offered everything from salads and sandwiches to liver and onions. I opted for a BLT and a side of fries while Lisa settled on a garden salad. The waitress returned with our tea, and we told her our choices. "Excellent," she said, and left us to pass on to the kitchen staff the excellent choices of the attractive couple at table nine.

Lisa and I picked up our iced tea and sipped, my eyes searching hers over the rim of my glass. "What?" she asked, setting her tea down.

"Full speed ahead, I say."

"I think Admiral Farragut said that at the battle of Mobile Bay, only he started with 'Damn the torpedoes!', right?" said Lisa.

"Right." She confirmed what I already knew. I was in the presence of one sharp lady.

Our lunches arrived and we dove in. Lisa's salad bowl was bigger than she expected, and my order of fries was super-sized, dwarfing my BLT. They were the kind of fries that had the skins left on, which I've always loved. A little extra roughage never hurts, right?

The waitress reappeared when she saw we were done, and I had to ask. "Are you the second-best restaurant in Schenectady?"

"No, sir. We're the best," she countered.

"Is there a poll or a judging contest that makes the decision?" I asked.

"Yes. Our satisfied customers. When they check out, they often tell us we're the best," she said, adding her smile to the statement.

"I have to agree. My lunch was perfect," I said.

"See? How was your salad, Miss?"

It was both scrumptious and abundant," said Lisa.

"I will add your accolades to the growing list of praise. It will help us maintain our position as the best restaurant in Schenectady. Can I get you anything else?" she asked.

We both declined, she gave us the check and wished us a pleasant afternoon.

When we stepped outside, the heat and humidity enveloped us in an oppressive, tight-fitting blanket. I figured we had three options and the first two didn't count. Drive around in our air-conditioned car, sit in the motel with the air going, or go to the motel pool. Lisa agreed with my third choice. Done.

I changed into the same bathing suit I'd worn before, and Lisa looked fantastic in the same one she'd had on before. Another woman might have thought she needed a change. I was glad Lisa didn't think that way. She looked stunning. Eye candy. The whole package.

At that hour the pool was free of urchins, and if they'd been there earlier, their tracks had evaporated away. A young couple sat together on chaise lounges, their noses buried in books. They glanced at us as we closed the gate behind us and gave us a smile and a wave before returning to their books. They were a testimony to total concentration.

Lisa chose two lounge chairs well away from the bookworm couple and we plopped down. I peeled off my T-shirt and Lisa shed her diaphanous wrap. I checked my watch. "Ten minutes to go," I said to Lisa.

"What happens in ten minutes?" she asked, a quizzical expression on her face.

"You know. The thirty-minute rule," I said.

"Explain, please."

"I'm sure you grew up knowing that you shouldn't swim for thirty minutes after eating," I said.

"Oh, that old wives' tale. I think it originally applied to competition swimmers after many of them barfed in the pool after eating and swimming right after," said Lisa.

"You paint a very credible picture. In other words, we can frolic, but avoid vigorous swimming?"

Lisa answered my question by bounding from her lounger and leaping into the pool. Her cannonball sprayed the poolside. My cannonball drenched the poolside. When I surfaced, I glanced at the readers. They simultaneously looked our way, frowned, and dove back into their books without a ripple.

The cool pool water washed away the heat and humidity that we were wearing. I began swimming a slow, easy breaststroke. Lisa swam to meet me. With her hands holding onto my shoulders, she relaxed her body and let me do the swimming for both of us as she trailed along above me. Her touch did its magic. A surge of warmth and well-being flowed into me. I knew for a fact that, linked together, we could swim the English Channel. And back again. Maybe twice. Who knew?

When I pulled us to the end of the pool and reached for the edge, Lisa circled my neck with her arms and hugged me to her, setting off a full-blown fireworks display in my brain. I gasped and sucked in a huge breath.

"Are you okay? Think you're going to barf?" she asked in a whisper as she eased her grip on me.

"No. I'm good. Ready for the trip back?" I asked after the last rocket exploded in a riot of color.

"I'm ready when you are," she said.

I turned and we paddled back to the other end of the pool.

Did you hear her, Mom? She's ready when I am.

A simple figure of speech, Tojo. Stop trying to read something into it.

You're probably right, Mom.

When we reached the end of the pool Lisa volunteered to be the breaststroker and pull me along behind her. "It's only fair," she said. I clasped her shoulders and we set off for the deep end. She surprised me with her strong strokes. Not once did she falter or struggle to take a breath. She was an accomplished swimmer.

She grabbed the pool edge and pivoted us around, and we were on our way back to the shallow end without a hitch. Reaching it, I put both hands on the edge and bounded out, then held my hand out to Lisa. She smiled, grabbed my hand and I lifted her out. She settled gracefully on her feet at my side. "Tarzan strong," she said in a low voice, not wanting to disturb the readers.

"Jane light as a feather," I countered.

We moved back to our loungers and settled in, the sun warm on our cool, wet bodies. I glanced at the bookworm couple. They hadn't moved. I wondered what they had to say to each other when the books were set aside. Maybe they were literary critics and discussed plots and turns of phrases.

I closed my eyes and let the sun warm me. I thought of what lay ahead and of all the things that could wreck Lisa's plans. First and foremost, the captain doesn't go to the tavern. Next on the list has the captain resisting Lisa's advances, though I couldn't imagine that happening. Still. And next was the possibility that passing cars or night strollers could show up at the critical moment when I was poised to put the captain in a knockout headlock. Oh, and showing up while I held the captain's limp body over the fence while Lisa at-tacked his manhood. Any one of those possibilities meant failure. I didn't share my thoughts with the reclining Lisa.

We baked in the afternoon sun for an hour. Neither of us needed to worry about getting a bad sunburn. We share a common light brown skin, a gift from our Japanese mothers. At length Lisa reached over to me and brushed her hand along my arm. Sparks flew with the casual contact. I turned to look at her.

"This is blissful, Joe, but I have a small problem. The tea I had for lunch is trying to make its exit," she whispered.

I glanced at my watch and was surprised to see it was crowding five. Time to go. "I could do with a tea break, too," I whispered back. We gathered our stuff, slipped into our flip flops, and made our way to the pool entry gate. The bookworms were oblivious to our departure.

Back in the motel we separated, Lisa to her room, me to mine. I disposed of my processed tea and stripped out of my now-dry bathing suit. The chlorine odor from the pool clung to me. A shower was in order. As I reached to turn it on, I heard a surge of water coming through the wall from Lisa's room. She had the same idea. I formed an image in my mind of her standing naked under the cascading water.

You tread lightly with her, you hear me, Tojo?

I'm all thought and no action, Mom.

I swear I heard Mom's voice saying, "Yeah, sure, Tojo."

I was all dressed and ready to go by five-thirty. Five minutes later Lisa tapped on the communicating door. "Are you decent, Joe?" she said.

"As decent as I'll ever be," I said, and she opened the door and stepped through. When I saw her, I was thankful I was sitting down. I rocked backward, momentarily stunned by her appearance. She had her blond wig on, each braid circled by a bright pink ribbon and tied in a bow. A filmy, clingy pale blue blouse revealed a tantalizing portion of her breasts, and a tight-fitting dark blue skirt came within inches of being X-rated. R-rated at the very least. Her feet were clad in sensible sandals. I expelled a breath I didn't know I held and said, "The captain won't know what hit him."

Lisa smiled at my comment, obviously pleased with the effect she had on me. "I hope you're right, Joe. Since he's about my height,

I thought it wouldn't do to wear heels," she said while she lifted her sandaled foot for emphasis.

"Flats will help with your balance when you go to work, too," I said.

"That, too. Shall we toast the evening with a beverage from your mini bar?"

"An excellent thought. You fetch the beverage while I fetch the stemware."

I snagged two plastic cups while Lisa procured our favorite red wine, the supply replenished by the visiting maid service. I held and she poured. We clunked cups together.

"To success," I said as our cups met.

"Success," she seconded.

We sipped our wine, our eyes joined together.

"I had a thought. I think we should have dinner at Schenectady's second-best restaurant. If the captain happens to go to the best restaurant for dinner and sees us there, he might be suspicious when you show up at the tavern, especially if he spots me sitting away from you."

"You're right. Why didn't I think of that?" said Lisa with a shake of her head that set her braids in motion.

"You thought of everything else. I had to come up with at least one thing," I said, making light of it.

"I'm glad you did," she said, her warm black eyes caressing mine.

"Do you have all your equipment?" I asked her.

Lisa picked up her large black purse and opened the clasp. She reached inside and pulled out her tack hammer. I saw an upholstery nail held to the magnetic head of it. "Locked and loaded," she said, holding it aloft.

"Locked and loaded, indeed. I declare you ready for action. One more 'cheers' and we're off."

We clunked cups and drained them. It was time for a casual dinner before the main event.

Twenty-One

THE DRIVE TO the second-best restaurant in Schenectady was uneventful, marked only by a noticeable increase in traffic. Saturday night. Schenectadians were out and about. I found a space in the restaurant parking lot, and we walked together to the entrance. It was already obscured by three waiting groups. We moved to the end of the line. The couple in front of us turned to see us. When they identified us as strangers they smiled and faced forward again. I didn't take affront. If they'd struck up a conversation, what would we tell them? That we were on our way to nail a rapist's pecker to a picket fence? Hell, they'd probably laugh and say that was a good one.

One more couple showed up to stand behind us, and then it was our turn to be seated. We walked into a scene eerily like the lunch crowd, only now half the diners wore dresses and long sleeve shirts. Lisa and I fit right in. Our table sat alongside the right wall, giving me a view of two-thirds of the diners. I watched Lisa run her eyes over the other tables. "Checking to see if he's here?" I asked in a low voice.

"Force of habit," she said while she toyed with her right-side braid.

"I'm guessing you came up empty."

"Thankfully, yes."

Our waitress brought us menus and recited the dinner specials, ending by telling us that her favorite was the meat loaf platter. That settled it for me. I'd order the meat loaf and compare it to the one

I had at the other best restaurant in Schenectady. Time to find out which one deserved top honors.

"Can I get you folks something to drink from the bar?" she asked us, her heavily mascaraed eyebrows lifting with the question. We disappointed her by ordering iced tea. No question about it. Our drink orders lacked imagination. Tea for two, though, had a nice ring to it.

"Very good. I'll leave you to check out the menu and make your choices, and I'll be right back with your drink orders," she said on autopilot. She departed and Lisa and I checked out the menu, though I'd already made up my mind.

"Do you know what you're having? Wait a minute. Let me guess. Meat loaf, right?" said Lisa.

"You got it. I'll compare it to the other meat loaf I had, maybe stand up after and announce which of the two restaurants is the winner," I said, topping my remarks with a lopsided grin.

"Finally, the truth shall be told," said Lisa.

"Have you made a choice?" I asked her.

"Since I might have to toss back a couple drinks with the captain, I've decided to order a chicken Caesar salad with extra croutons," she said.

"The extra croutons are to soak up the drinks?"

"Exactly. What do you think?"

"Good choice. Light enough so you don't get logy, and croutoney enough so you don't get tipsy."

Our waitress returned with our tea, took our orders, mumbled 'an excellent choice' and 'you can't go wrong with that' and hurried off to tell the kitchen staff our choices.

We picked up our iced tea glasses and took test sips. I swallowed and said, "It seems that we spend a lot of our time sipping iced tea."

"We're tea connoisseurs. You judge the meat loaf and I'll compare the teas. With luck we'll choose the same establishment. If we don't, the winner will have to be chosen by other critics," said Lisa. She took another sip and said "Aah."

"Did that mean you've made a decision?" I asked.

"Oh, no. And even if I had I wouldn't say. I don't want to influence your decision in any way," she said while twirling her right braid between thumb and forefinger.

Our meals came. Lisa's salad was top-heavy with croutons, as ordered, and my meat loaf platter was well-presented, with the right amount of meat loaf, mashed potatoes and gravy, and fresh garden peas. We armed ourselves with knives and forks and dove in.

Halfway through my platter I decided that meat loaf is meat loaf, and I suspected that both restaurants used identical ingredients in their preparation. I couldn't honestly tell the difference. They were both delicious. If forced to choose one over the other, I'd be forced to flip a coin. I chewed happily until I could see the surface of my plate shining through. I set my knife and fork down and watched Lisa polish off her chicken Caesar and all those extra croutons. "Good?" I asked her when she parked her utensils.

"Better than good. Positively yummy," she said.

"Have you made a decision on the tea?" I asked.

"Yes. First, tell me which restaurant won the meat loaf contest."

"It was a tough choice. So tough that I declare both restaurants to be winners," I said.

"Funny you should say that. The teas were a tie, too," she said.

"The teas were a tie, too. Wow. Say that five times, fast," I said with a grin.

"Not on your life. I'm still struggling with rubber baby buggy bumpers," she said, grinning back at me.

Lisa was tempted to order the homemade bread pudding for dessert, thus adding another absorptive layer in her stomach, but she opted out. I passed on dessert, too, and our waitress fetched our check while we tossed back the dregs of our iced tea.

Check in hand, I dropped a generous tip on the table, and we shuffled our way to the cashier who sat waiting for us, hand outstretched, permanent smile in place. I paid and we made our way out through the entrance. We passed a much longer line of waiting patrons. I wondered idly how many of the men would choose meat loaf, how many women a salad. We wove our way past them and back to the car.

Once we were settled inside, I turned toward Lisa and said, "One last checkup. Are you feeling up for this?"

She reached over and placed her hand on my arm, sending a charge of warm energy through me. "Don't worry about me, Joe. I've been up for this for a very long time," she said.

"Okay. Just making sure," I said.

"As you said, 'Full speed ahead,' if I recall correctly."

"Full speed ahead, it is." I fired up the engine and backed out, taking extra care. Now was not the time for a fender bender. Back on the highway, I pointed the car in the direction of the tavern. Though we'd never ventured inside, the road that led to it was as familiar as any I've traveled.

I pulled into the tavern parking lot and found a space, one of a few still available. I killed the engine and turned to face Lisa. She seemed relaxed, at ease. I wished I felt the same. I mentally reviewed all the potential scenarios we faced and considered solutions for each one. I gave up, realizing that an unexpected scenario could pop up. On-the-spot creativity could make us or break us. Everything depended on our quick wits.

"Are you ready to rock and roll, my pretty upholsterer?"

"As ready as I can be. What about you, my Sumo wrestler?" She was referring to my role as the stranglehold man, the man who needed to put the captain to sleep with an arm around his neck.

"Ready, willing and able," I said while uncontrolled scenes tumbled about in my head.

Lisa pulled down her visor, exposing a lighted mirror, and checked her reflection. She made a minor adjustment to her blond wig, pushed back the visor, and looked my way. "With that, I'll weave my way inside and scout for the unwitting captain. See you in about fifteen."

Lisa opened the passenger side door and made her way to the tavern entrance, leaving me alone with my thoughts. I checked my watch. Eight o'clock. The plan was to head inside at eight-fifteen and grab a seat at the bar.

That fifteen minutes crept along like the loser in a snail race. I must have glanced at my watch a hundred times. It was time. I climbed out of the car and headed for the tavern, trying to look and act casual to the handful of people who ignored me as I stepped purposefully along.

When I pulled the door open, the sounds of laughter and idle chatter assaulted me, a sharp contrast to the silence in my car. I stood a moment, absorbing the scene. The long bar sat along the wall to my right. It looked like something out of the wild west, not native to Schenectady. A large full-length mirror covered the wall above it, and three huge lines of liquor bottles came close to obscuring it. The bar itself was a slab of dark wood, heavily sealed against the inevitable spills. Approximately twenty barstools were placed so the occupants could dismount without falling. I expected to see spittoons set at convenient distances from the barstools. A little over half of them were occupied. I spotted Lisa close to the middle of the pack. There was an empty barstool next to her. She glanced at me, and I saw a subtle shake of her head. The captain was not in the house. Uh-oh!

I ambled up to the bar on the side away from Lisa and climbed aboard a vacant stool, then pivoted around to scan the rest of the tavern. Most of the space was taken up by round and square tables with comfortable-looking padded chairs for patrons who wanted to chat it up with friends while they drank and ate. Two-thirds of the tables were occupied. The doors in and out of the kitchen were spring hinged, another reminder of the wild west. The rest rooms sat to the left of them. I couldn't see the doors, but imagined signs on them saying Bucks and Does, or Pointers and Setters.

I turned to face the bar. A smiling young female barkeep met my eyes and said, "Welcome to Saturday night madness, sir! I'm Marie. What can I get you?" It sounded like 'Wut kin I gitcha?'

"I'll have a draft beer," I said.

"Which one?"

"Surprise me," I said.

"I like your attitude. Comin' right up!" She turned away to draw my surprise brew.

While waiting for my beer, I glanced around the big room. Most of the seated groups were busy yakking it up, oblivious to everything and everyone else around them. Beer glasses dominated the tables, and there was already a line for the ladies' room.

"Here you go, sir! Bottoms up," said Marie as she set my surprise down on a coaster. I turned back to the bar to see a pint glass of dark beer, its creamy head threatening to escape its bonds and slide down the side. I leaned forward and slurped, ending the escape attempt. It was rich and thick. A porter, with a hint of chocolate, or was it peanut butter? I'm no beer critic. I liked the taste. I'd be nursing it anyway. If the captain stayed with the script and made an appearance, I needed to be clear-headed to play my part.

I leaned back and glanced towards Lisa's seat at the bar. She was chatting with a woman sitting next to her, but after a moment she looked my way. When she saw me, she did a subtle negative headshake and turned back to her companion.

So, what was our Plan B if the captain was a no-show? Fly back to Phoenix and come back next Friday, or hang out in Schenectady and hit the tavern every night in hopes that the captain ventured there other nights beside Saturday? Lisa might come up with another suggestion. I didn't like the idea of spending every night at the tavern. Too many people, including the cute barmaid, might start wondering what we were up to. I turned back to the bar and sipped at my beer just as Marie came up to me.

"What Cha think?" she asked, offering up a well-rehearsed smile.

"I like it. Good choice. Is it chocolate porter?" I asked.

"Porter, yeah. But peanut butter," she said with a subtle toss of her head.

"Hey, I got half of it right."

She reached forward and rested her hand on my arm a second before saying, "I like a man who admits when he's wrong."

Dammit! That was stupid of me. She'll remember me now.

"I think that's the second time I've been wrong," I said, trying to save my ass.

"When was the first time?" she asked, batting her eyes at me.

"I thought the Red Sox were going to win the pennant in 2003. I missed it by a year," I improvised.

"Barkeep! Another round, if you please!" came a shout from somewhere east of me, bringing to an abrupt end the inane conversation with the young Lady Marie.

I sipped at my porter and glanced towards Lisa. She gave me her subtle headshake. I fell into a routine, alternating between sips and glances.

A clock over the bar told me it was quarter of nine. Getting late. If the captain didn't show up by nine-thirty I figured we'd have to call it a night.

The porter in my glass was at the two-thirds level when I checked on Lisa. She surprised me with a subtle nod of her head. Was I reading her wrong? I watched her turn towards the entrance and follow the progress of a young man. He strode towards the bar like a man on a mission, his eyes searching for a vacant barstool. Self-confidence radiated from him. The army had taught him well. He saw the empty seat next to Lisa and closed on it. He was too far from me to hear his words, but I surmised that he asked if the seat was taken, Lisa said no, and he sat down next to her. The rest, I knew, was up to her.

I said a silent prayer. One, that he didn't recognize her in her blond wig, and two, that he'd offer her a nightcap at his home, a short walk away. So much to pray for. I sipped my porter and mouthed *amen*.

My barmaid buddy carried a boilermaker towards Lisa and the captain. I hoped it was for him. Two or three of those would make my part in the plan much easier. As she came back. I glanced towards Lisa to see the captain taking long draughts from his glass. I couldn't see if the shot glass was dropped into the beer glass, or if he'd tossed back the shot and then drank from his beer. Either way, he was off to a good start. Our hopes for a successful evening went up astronomically. Now it became a waiting game for me.

Fifteen minutes and another half inch of my porter disappeared when Marie carried another boilermaker to the captain. I watched her return with the drained beer glass. The empty shot glass tinkled inside it. He drank it army-style. A bomb shot. The beer pushed the alcohol into the bloodstream faster that way. I took a fat sip of my porter to celebrate. I wondered if Lisa was keeping pace with him. More likely she was putting on a show, pretending to be well on her way. Or so I hoped. If she was tipsy, her hammer swing might be off the mark. Not good.

I'd sipped my porter down to the one-third level when Marie walked past with boilermaker number three. The captain was a drinking man, no doubt about it. How well he held it was still a big question. I turned to see Lisa excuse herself from the captain and sashay towards the ladies' room. Sashay was the only term I could think of that described the way she manipulated her hips seductively as she made her way.

The captain, I saw, had his eyes locked on her the whole way. When Lisa emerged from the ladies' room a short time later, he followed her progress all the way back to her stool. He held out his hand to assist her up. I felt a pang of jealousy, but it dissipated quickly when I remembered what was in store for the hapless rapist.

Marie stopped to ask me if I was ready for another round. "I'm good for now," I told her as I eyed the two inches of porter remaining.

"Okey dokey," she said as she turned away.

Now, who says that in today's world? Oh, yeah. Someone who says 'Wut kin I gitcha?'

The unwitting Captain Wittingly was well into his third boilermaker, but I had no idea if he'd include Lisa when he made his way uncertainly for the door. For all I knew, he didn't like blondes. That would be a huge game-changer, but not a game-ender. Lisa and I could still shadow him when he left for home and ambush him at our chosen site. Without Lisa at his side to distract him, my job of rushing forward and putting him in a chokehold would be more difficult, but not impossible. I thought back to my first patrol in Iraq when the would-be assassin sneaked up behind me and rushed me with his knife. I'd sensed his approach and took the right action. Captain Wittingly could do the same when I rush him. My edge? Wittingly has three boilermakers on board. I have an incomplete porter, sipped slowly.

When Marie passed by with Wittingly's empty boilermaker glass on her tray and she hadn't delivered a refill, I figured it was getting close to showtime. I took out my wallet and slipped a twenty under my glass, figuring it paid for my porter and gave Marie a fat tip she could put in her diction lesson jar. I slid my stool back from the bar so I could see Lisa and the captain if they got up to leave and picked up my glass for one last sip of my porter. My mouth felt dry. A splash of chocolate porter would help.

I set my glass back down on my twenty and glanced down the row of barstools in time to see the captain stand up and back away from his stool. For a disappointing moment I thought he was leaving alone but it was short-lived. Lisa climbed from her stool, with Wittingly's hand on her back to assist her. She appeared to be unsteady on her feet. I hoped it was for show. The tipsy twosome wove their way to the entrance and disappeared outside. It was my cue to follow behind them at a discreet distance.

Marie stopped in front of me, saw the twenty and said, "Thankya, sir! Ya hurry back, okay?"

"I'll do my best," I said, thinking that chances of a return were slim to none. But then again, who knew?

I bailed from my stool and made my way to the door. A table of three young women eyed me as I passed, and one whispered something to her companions, but other than that I made it out without attracting any attention. The parking lot was full, and I panicked for a moment, thinking that Wittingly had driven there, not walked. If so, Lisa would be on her own. My eyes swept the parked cars for any sign of a departing vehicle. No headlights or taillights shone back at me. Once I made it through the parked cars, I headed for the route the walking couple would be taking.

I turned the corner and relief flooded through me. A hundred yards ahead of me Lisa and the captain weaved their way through unseen obstacles as they meandered along the sidewalk. The streetlights were on, pushing back the gloom of early night, but they were spaced far enough apart so there were poorly illuminated sections of sidewalk. I used that to my advantage, holding back in the bright areas and moving forward quickly in the dimly lit areas. So far, the tipsy twosome and I were the only sidewalk occupants, but I knew that could change in a heartbeat.

On our recon mission Lisa and I had covered the distance from the tavern to our chosen ambush site in a little over ten minutes, but she and the captain were cruising along at a much slower pace. I guessed that they'd take twice that time to get there. My memory of the landmarks we passed told me we were halfway there. It would be another ten minutes, give or take, until we reached the chosen ambush site.

As the couple passed through a brightly lit area, I saw that Wittingly had his right arm looped around Lisa's waist. It was unclear whether it was to steady Lisa or to steady himself. I hoped it wasn't mutual.

We were maybe three minutes away from the ambush site when a man walking a small white dog approached the tipsy twosome. I turned and hurried back a few paces, using darkness as a shield. I didn't want to give the approaching dog walker the impression that I was following the couple. As he drew near to me, I walked casually towards him and gave him a quiet 'Good evening' as I passed him.. His dog paid me no attention. If he'd barked at me, it might have alerted the captain to my presence.

Once he and his dog were well past me, another worry settled over me. What if he turns around and retraces his steps in time to witness our ambush of the captain? Not a good thought. I hurried forward on my silent running shoes, closing the gap on the unsteady couple once again.

I peered ahead in the gloom. Lisa and the captain were maybe twenty paces from the ambush site. Time for me to close the distance, the watery light helping to conceal my movement. I crept silently forward, my eyes locked on the captain's back, alert for any sign that he was aware of my presence.

The couple was two steps from the ambush site when the unexpected happened. The captain stepped behind Lisa and circled her neck with his forearm, clearly intending to render her unconscious. The son of a bitch had a well-rehearsed routine he used on every one of his victims!

Two can play that game, captain.

I closed on the would-be rapist and wrapped my right arm around his neck, drawing his body back against me while pushing his head forward into the vee of my elbow with my left hand. He released his grip on Lisa and she ducked down and away from him. She turned to face him, peeling the blond wig from her head. Her dark eyes glared daggers at him, her face contorted by hate.

For a nanosecond the captain stared at her. Then he groped his hands towards me, flailing the air near my head as he struggled to reach a vulnerable spot. I turned my face away from his groping hands and maintained my squeezing grip around his neck. At length his efforts grew weaker, and then he went limp. I maintained my grip and counted silently to ten. It would keep him unconscious long enough for Lisa to drive her point home. Maintaining the pressure longer could kill him. That wasn't part of the plan.

I dragged the captain's limp body behind the bushes and rolled his upper torso over the white wood fence, his knees resting on the ground. Lisa tugged her blond wig back over her black tresses and set to work. She dragged his pants down around his knees. I glanced down and saw the thin light washing over his pale, skinny butt.

I watched Lisa open her purse and take out her penlight and tack hammer, then pull on a pair of latex gloves. She switched on the penlight with her left hand and picked up the hammer in her right. I made out the upholstery tack magnetically held to the business end of the hammer. Lisa was ready to avenge the pitiless rapist who used the same tactics to rape many women, not just her. I drew in a breath, waiting for the thunk of her hammer as she drove the tack home. Waiting, I searched the sidewalk for any approaching walkers.

And waited.

And waited.

After what seemed like an eternity, soft, bubbling laughter rolled out of Lisa.

I glanced down at her. "What's funny?" I whispered.

Her laugh continued a moment longer, and then she drew in a breath and whispered, "There's nothing here to tack. I don't know how he even pees out of this pathetic little stump."

"What are you going to do?" Worry that her revenge would go unfulfilled flooded my thoughts.

"I have an idea," she whispered. I watched her reach up to her right-side braid, untie the pink ribbon and pull it loose. She turned back to the slumbering captain and wound the ribbon around his mini penis, snugging it as tightly as she could before retying the bow. Satisfied with her handiwork, she dropped the unused hammer and penlight back into her handbag, stripped off her gloves, turning them inside out in the process, and stuffed them into a zip lock bag she'd thought to bring along. The bag went into her purse, and she regained her feet, a satisfied smile on her face.

"Are we done here?" I asked in a whisper.

"Yes. Stretch him out on the ground, face up. I want to check my handiwork."

I lifted the limp captain off the fence and positioned him on the ground, belly up. I could make out the pink ribbon tied around his pathetic penis, the bow making it look even more insignificant. As I recall, the medical condition plaguing the captain was called micropenis, or, in layman's terms, teeny weenie. "Move him so anyone walking by can see him," whispered Lisa.

I dragged him from behind the bushes to an open area along the sidewalk. Anyone passing by couldn't help but spot him there.

"Perfect, Joe. Let's get out of here," said Lisa as she linked her arm in mine.

We hadn't gone fifty paces when two girls approached us. They gave us a cheerful hello as we passed them, and we returned the greeting. Lisa squeezed my arm and whispered, "Let's backtrack." She wanted to see the reaction they'd have when they spotted the reclining captain. We turned and moved silently along behind the two women, using the bushes for cover. We were within earshot when they spotted the napping captain.

"Oh, look, Rita! That man has a pink bow tied around his winkie-dinkie. What do you suppose it means?"

"Maybe he's trolling, Sasha," said Rita.

"Trolling?" said her friend Sasha.

"Yeah. Hoping a stupid woman comes along and wants to untie the bow."

"It doesn't look like there's enough under the bow to get excited about," said Sasha.

"Yeah. Poor guy must be desperate, maybe lies out here every night, hoping," said Rita.

"Maybe he's like Sleeping Beauty. He lies out here all tied up in a bow waiting for a fair maiden to come along and plant a kiss on it and untie it," said Sasha.

"Oh, gross! That's disgusting, Rita," said Sasha.

"Yeah, it is. I'm grossed out just thinking about it," said Rita.

The captain chose that moment to return to consciousness. He sat up, clearly struggling to get his bearings.

"Yipes, Sasha! He's awake. Let's get out of here!"

Sasha's response was to race off down the sidewalk, with Rita hard on her heels.

Lisa struggled to contain her pent-up laughter. I held her tightly to my chest, my back facing the captain in hopes he wouldn't hear her. I could feel her laughter bubbling out and washing over my chest. When she was able to control herself, I steered her back along the way we'd come. For all the world, we were one of many romantic couples out for a Saturday night stroll. If the passers-by we met knew what we'd been up to, they might have joined Lisa's laughter.

Twenty-Two

W E REACHED THE tavern parking lot and searched for my rental car. The lot was still full of vehicles. The tavern door opened to disgorge a homebound couple, and the sounds of the happy patrons inside followed them out like a breaking wave on the beach. I located our car and opened Lisa's door for her before circling around, checking for door dings, an occupational hazard when parking at a bar. Everything checked out. I climbed in and closed the door. Lisa was perched sideways on her side, watching me. I turned to face her.

"What happened back there?" I asked her, my voice soft, non-judgmental.

She responded by doubling over in laughter. Tears rolled down her cheeks. I rested my hand on her shoulder and waited.

At length her laughter subsided. She wiped her tears away with the back of a hand and turned to me. "I should start at the beginning," she said.

"By all means," I said, wondering where that might be.

"When the captain finally showed up at the tavern, he spotted me and the barstool I'd been saving for him and came over. He looked me up and down, undressed me with his eyes if truth be told, and asked if the seat was taken. I said it was now, and he parked his butt. He said he was George, and I told him my name was Puddin' Tane, ask me again and I'll tell you the same. He laughed at that, and we were off to a good start. Anyway, halfway through his second drink he looked at me funny and asked if we'd met before, that I looked familiar. I returned his stare and said I didn't think so, not in this life, anyway. He laughed and said I was probably right, so we should get better acquainted. I fluttered my eyes at him and asked him what he had in mind, and he told me he lived nearby, and we should go there for a nightcap. I said that sounded nice, but let's have one more drink for the road.

"He said I sure had a way with words, and he ordered us another round. Oh, did I say that I'd arranged with the barkeeper to make me Manhattans without the whiskey because I had a drinking problem? Anyway, she brought us our drinks, we clinked glasses and drank up. I slurred my words a little for effect.

"When you saw us leave you followed us, just like we planned it. You can imagine my fear and surprise when he wrapped his arm around my neck and started to squeeze. All I could think was, here we go again. Then you were there, wrapping him in your arm, and he let go of me. When I was free, I turned around to face him and pulled off my wig. I saw surprise and recognition on his face when he saw who I was. I can't tell you how good that felt. When he stopped struggling and went limp, I charged ahead with my plan.

"After you draped him over the fence, I pulled his pants down and got everything ready. When I switched on my penlight and shone it on his privates, I couldn't believe my eyes. I mean, I'm not that knowledgeable about the size of men's equipment, my previous experience was a couple porn movies in college, so I wasn't prepared for what I saw. Truth to tell, I almost missed it, it was so small.

"All at once I had a picture in my mind of a pathetic excuse for a man, a man so inadequate that the only way he could have a woman was by knocking her out and raping her, raping her with a silly little penis that couldn't penetrate. You heard my laugh. I couldn't help myself. The monster who raped me, who haunted my dreams after, was a pathetic excuse for a man. So, I tied my pink ribbon as tightly around the thing as I could, made a knot and retied the bow. Those two girls who came along and saw him lying there put the finishing touches on him with their comments. I'm free, Joe. For the first time since that terrible evening in Baghdad I feel free again! That creep didn't rape me. He was physically incapable of doing that. My virginity is intact." Tears of relief, joy rolled down her cheeks as she spoke.

"I love a happy ending," was the best I could come up with at that moment. My eyes began leaking, too.

Lisa raised her head and saw my wet face. She launched herself into me, her arms encircling me, her face against my face. "Oh my God, Joe. I love you so much," she murmured into my ear.

Her words released a flood of emotion in me. The words I'd held in check for what seemed like an eternity rushed out of me, freed by the change that took place in Lisa. "I've loved you since the first day we met, Lisa. You sent a warm flow of energy through me when we first touched, and it grows stronger with each passing day. I can't imagine a life without you," I said.

Hearing my words, Lisa drew back, her dark eyes searching mine, and then she brought her sweet lips to mine. Our kiss began slowly, tentatively, and gained in passion and abandon as we explored each other. At length, breathless, Lisa broke the contact. She drew in a breath and whispered, "This is not a test. This is the real thing. I repeat. This is the real thing."

I sealed her statement with another kiss, which was interrupted by a couple who looked in on us as they passed by. "Get a room," they said in unison. I looked up to see them smiling, waving at us. I waved back. Lisa threw them the finger, tempered by her own smile.

"They have a point, you know," said Lisa, her warm eyes on mine.

I kissed the end of her nose and started the car. I was out of the tavern parking lot and on our way to our motel before I could say rubber baby buggy bumpers. Lisa snuggled against me all the way, her contact sending rivulets of fire through me.

Back in our rooms, Lisa suggested a celebratory drink to top off the evening. Wine, or something stronger?" I asked.

"Let me check," she said. She opened the mini bar and peered inside, taking in the offerings.

I sat on the edge of the bed, watching her every move, loving her every move.

"Oh, look, Joe. This is perfect!" she said. She held up a mini bottle of champagne.

"You're right. I'll go get the champagne flutes," I said. That meant a trip to my bathroom and two more of the sterilized plastic cups. I peeled off the wraps on my way back.

"Here, Mister Strong Hands, you can do the honors." I took the bottle and passed her the two cups. It was dressed the same as any other champagne bottle, only in miniature. I peeled away a foil metal cover that held the plastic cork in place and twisted the cork out of the bottle. The resultant pop was well below the decibel level of a full-sized bottle, but Lisa uttered an enthusiastic YAY! anyway. She held, I poured, and the sparkling liquid foamed up appropriately. When I finished pouring, we had maybe three ounces in each cup. I set down the empty and she passed me a cup.

I raised my cup and said, "To a shared lifetime of pops and yays."

"Hear! Hear! and to a shared lifetime of love and joy."

With eyes linked together we raised our cups, touched their rims together and drained them in a single fizzy swallow.

Lisa's next words came as a surprise. "It's been a long, stressful day, Joe. My energy level is way down. I'm going to my room and get a good night's sleep, okay?"

She was right. It had been a long day, and she'd had plenty to stress her out. "You're right, Lisa. We've both had more than our share of stress."

She handed me her empty cup and stood, turning to face me, her hands on my shoulders. "I love you, Joe. You mean the world to me." She punctuated her sweet words with a warm, lingering kiss that dissipated all the stress and fatigue I'd been feeling. She brushed my cheek with her hand and made her way to our shared doorway. I heard the latch click as she closed the door behind her.

I sat there, thinking of everything Lisa had said earlier, and suddenly it hit me. She said that her only experience with men was watching porn movies in college. My sweet Lisa is virginal, interrupted only by the captain's fumbling attempt at rape. Now, after she saw how absurdly small his equipment was, she thinks herself a virgin once again.

You tread lightly with her, you hear me, Tojo?

I don't know where Mom got her insight, but she'd been right all along. Treading lightly was the name of the game.

After washing and brushing and stripping down to a T-shirt and skivvies, I came out of the bathroom to find Lisa standing inside our connecting door. She was wearing one item: a warm smile. I lost myself in her full, upturned breasts, her narrow waist, her round hips, her long legs.

"I couldn't sleep, Joe. All I could think of was making love to you, holding you close and never letting you go. Do you think we could do this?" she said, her voice thick with emotion.

Mom's words echoed in my head. *You'll know when the moment is right, Joe.*

"I've wanted you forever. My mother's warning message held me back. Until now," I said. I could feel my own rising passion as I stood there.

Lisa's eyes fell on my bulging boxers, and she rushed forward to meet me. Her hands swept my boxers to the floor, and I stepped out of them. She leaped on me, her arms encircling my neck, her legs encircling my waist, and I carried her the short steps to the bed. I lowered her onto the bed and rested my weight on her. "Are you absolutely sure about this? We still have time to stop," I whispered in her ear, though I had serious doubts that I spoke the truth.

"Please, Joe. Make love to me. I need you. I want you. I can't think of anything else. You are my everything. Be gentle, my love," she whispered while her strong hands pulled me down to her.

I did everything she asked me to do, and when at last we were joined as one everything else in the world slipped away, leaving me awash in a hurricane of passion.

My nightmare was closing in on me. I neglected my defenses, my thoughts elsewhere. I felt someone shaking me. I opened my eyes. Lisa hovered over me, concern written on her face. Seeing my eyes opened she asked, "Are you okay, Joe? You kept saying 'No! No!' I was frightened."

I circled her in my arms and hugged her to me. "You saved me from my nightmare, Lisa. It was starting its horrible attack on me when you woke me up. Thank you. Thank you," I murmured into the softness of her neck.

"You see? The benefit of sharing one bed has already reaped its rewards," she said.

"That's two rewards already," I said. She couldn't see my smile.

"You're smiling, aren't you? Yes, you're so right. That's two. From now on, when I hear you say no in your sleep, I'll wake you up. We'll send your nightmare to hell where it belongs," she said.

"You're full of delightful surprises, my love. Should we make it three?"

"Did you think I shook you awake because you were saying no?" she whispered.

We took our time, enjoying every innuendo of it, and together we made it three.

As we lay entwined in the damp sheets, basking in the afterglow, as some wise man described it, a realization came to me. Lisa was my second success, my second rescue. Without thinking, I had invested my time and resources into paving the path for her to exact her revenge. Rachel ended up freed of her abusive husband, making her my first success. As I slid down the slippery slope to sleep, I thought how satisfying it would be for Lisa and me to reach out together to help those in need.

I became aware of two things at the same time. Thin rays of daylight seeped around the window blinds, and Lisa was tracing a finger along my neck. What could I do? I joined my body with Lisa's, and we rode the roller coaster. We made it a fantastic four.

After, I remembered my long-overdue gift for her. "Stay right here. I've got something for you," I said. I climbed from our tousled bed, opened my suitcase, and found the jewelry box with the crucifix inside, then carried it back to Lisa. I placed the box in her right hand.

"What's this?" she asked, puzzled.

"Open it. I had it made for you," I said.

She lifted the lid and peered inside. "Oh, my God, Joe. It's beautiful!" she murmured, seeing the crucifix.

"Here, I'll put it on you," I said. I lifted it from the box, undid the clasp and placed it around her neck. The cross dropped perfectly into the upper reaches of her cleavage. Lisa clasped it with her hand, feeling how it rested there.

"I love it, Joe. It fits me perfectly. How did you know?"

"I had one made for Mom and Kim, too. All three of them are alike."

"That makes it even more special. Oh, and it's my first gift with diamonds," she said.

"Does that mean we're engaged?" I asked her, making my eyebrows dance as I spoke.

"Are you proposing to me?" she asked, her eyelashes batting.

"I can't imagine living without you, so yes, I am" I said.

After Lisa accepted my proposal, we made it five, the cross fitting perfectly between us.

We lay together after, the air conditioning wicking away our moisture, my body tingling in the wake of our lovemaking. "I love you, Lisa," I murmured in her ear.

"I think I've always loved you, Joe," she murmured back.

"How is that possible?" I asked.

"From the moment I was old enough to conjure up a picture in my mind of my perfect mate I've had an image in my mind. You fit my image to a tee," she said, her hand resting on my side.

"I like that. I wish I could say the same, but I never had an image to go by. I think the electric charge you send through me every time we touch is my way of knowing that you're my special one. I'm looking forward to feeling that surge from you for the rest of my life," I said.

"I'm more than happy to oblige. You've taught me more in our five, ah, coming togethers than I ever expected. You've opened up a depth of emotions that I never knew existed."

"If I opened doors for you, Lisa, you opened even more for me. I've never experienced the level of emotion you triggered in me," I whispered. I moved a strand of her damp black hair aside, offering me an uninterrupted view of her face.

Additional comments were interrupted by a loud growl from my stomach. "Was that your stomach or mine?" asked Lisa.

"Mine, I think."

"Well, it could've been mine. Let's go see if there's anything left in the breakfast room," she said.

We showered together, which delayed us more.

Dressed, we elevatored to the lobby and found the breakfast room empty. There was still coffee available, and Lisa found two muffins that had been passed over by the hungry hordes that came before us. We enjoyed the surviving spoils. There must have been something special in the muffin. It was the most delicious one I've ever eaten. Lisa confirmed my observation with her sounds of pleasure as she munched away on hers.

Since checkout time was eleven, we hurried to pack and leave. As we walked to the rental car Lisa turned back and murmured, "Goodbye, little love nest."

"Let's come back on our anniversaries," I suggested.

"I'd love that," said Lisa. She took my arm, sending undiminished warmth flowing through me.

Twenty-Three

THE REST OF the day was a blur. I remember driving around Schenectady and having lunch at the second-best restaurant, and then it was back to Albany and the airport and our flight back to Phoenix. We sat in our first-class seats, leaned together, heads touching, and fell fast asleep. The stewardess woke us as we approached Chicago, and we repeated our stop at the bar while waiting for our flight to Phoenix.

Both flights were uneventful. We touched down in Phoenix ten minutes ahead of schedule, and we made it to Lisa's apartment a little after ten. Rachel was waiting for us.

We sat together in Lisa's living area and Rachel filled us in on her latest news. Not much had changed in the three days that we'd been gone. Her husband was tucked away in jail, awaiting his time before the judge the next day, so she'd felt free to go wherever she pleased without fear of seeing him. We asked her if she'd made any new plans, and she surprised us.

"My mother lives in Topeka, Kansas. I've been estranged from her since before I met Bill, and I've never talked to him about her. It struck me that he doesn't know she exists. More important, he doesn't know she lives in Topeka. I'm going back to her, see if we can patch things up, make a life for myself there," she said.

"That's wonderful, made even better if you can patch things up with your mother," said Lisa.

"I hope it works out," said Rachel. Her voice said she meant it.

"Knowing you, I'm betting on it," said Lisa. She placed a comforting hand on Rachel's shoulder.

"Thank you both for all you've done for me. If it hadn't been for you, Joe, I'd still be homeless, still looking over my shoulder for Bill coming to get me," she said.

"I'm glad I found you when I did, and we loved every minute of helping you escape from your horrible marriage," I said.

"I'll never forget either one of you. Oh, and I'll need your measurements so I can make those clothes for you, Joe. And by the way, has something happened between the two of you? I sense a change," said Rachel, her eyes moving between us.

"You don't miss a thing, Rachel. What happened was, Joe and I realized that we were in love. With each other," Lisa added, a shy smile on her face.

"Oh, I knew it! I mean, I knew it before, and now you've confirmed it. I'm so happy for you. You're a perfect match," she said, her smile overspreading her narrow face.

"On that positive note, I'm heading off to my own digs," I said as I got to my feet.

"I'm going with you, Joe. Rachel, you can have my apartment all to yourself. You deserve it," said Lisa.

After hugs all round, Lisa and I left together. I was surprised and pleased with her decision to come with me.

Once you have found her, never let her go.

The words of that song from the movie SOUTH PACIFIC came to mind.

Twenty-Four

LISA AND I arranged a dinner between our two families at my apartment. While everyone mingled and sipped their drinks, I planned to buttonhole Lisa's dad and ask his permission to marry Lisa. If he gave his consent, Lisa and I would declare our intention to marry during dinner, with the hopes that everyone would be surprised and thrilled.

It didn't come out that way.

I buttonholed Lisa's dad and asked his permission to marry Lisa, and as soon as I'd spoken, he yelled, "Hey, everyone! Joe and Lisa are engaged!" Bedlam broke out. Lisa's mom and brother swarmed me, and my family surrounded Lisa, everyone congratulating us. Mom asked me what took me so long, and I heard Lisa's mom ask her what took me so long to ask her. Seems that the moms shared common opinions.

When the hubbub died down, Lisa's mom got serious. "The wedding is going to take time to prepare. We want everything to be perfect. Have you thought of a date yet?" she asked Lisa and me.

"Tomorrow," I said. Lisa smiled and nodded her head.

"Oh, that's out of the question. We'll need at least two months to get everything planned," said Mrs. Goodweather. My mom nodded in agreement.

"Okay. That gives me time to get an engagement ring for Lisa," I said.

"You mean you want to get married tomorrow and Lisa doesn't have an engagement ring yet?" asked Mom.

"I needed to ask Lisa's dad permission to marry her first. I think he gave his permission when he yelled out the news," I said.

"Yes, Joe, you have my permission. Now go get the poor girl an engagement ring," he said, a broad smile filling his craggy face.

"Thank you, sir. Let's eat," I said.

"From now on I want you to call me by my first name, Joe," said Mister Goodweather.

"All right, Charles."

"Not Charles. Charlie."

"Charlie. I stand corrected."

Dinner and the evening were a great success, and everyone left bubbling with happiness for Lisa and me. I now officially called Lisa's parents Eleanor and Charlie, and Eleanor couldn't stop talking about what a wonderful wedding she would plan for us. We told her we couldn't wait. We meant it.

"You're not planning to elope and ruin all my plans, are you?" she asked us, worry creeping into her voice.

"No, we wouldn't do that to you, would we, Joe?" said Lisa. I joined her in saying no. I don't think anyone saw my crossed fingers.

The next day I took Lisa to meet Harold Whiteman. His face broke out in a warm smile, seeing me.

"Welcome back, Mister Roberts. And who is this stunning woman at your side?" he asked.

"This is Lisa Goodweather, Harold. She's accepted my marriage proposal," I said.

"It's a pleasure to meet you, Miss Goodweather," he said.

"If you call me Miss Goodweather, I'll leave at once," she said, adding a frown to her threat.

"Lisa, then. And you must call me Harold," he said.

"Thank you, Harold," said Lisa, offering him a smile that I'd come to know and love.

"Somehow I don't think you came here to exchange pleasantries. What can I do for you?"

"Since we're engaged, it's only fitting that I should provide Lisa with an engagement ring," I said.

"But of course! Let me get you a display of my settings. If Lisa finds one that she likes, I can find suitable diamonds to fill it from your collection, I'm sure." He ducked into his back room and returned with a three-ring binder. He opened it in front of Lisa. I watched as her eyes took in the possibilities.

At length she spoke, turning to meet my eyes. "I know you could give me a huge ring with tons of diamonds in it, but that's not who I am. I've always liked simple things, things that carried more sentimental value. I'll leave ostentatious to others," she said, punctuating her words with a heartfelt smile.

"Harold, the woman has spoken. Simplicity it is," I said.

"Are you thinking of a ring with a single diamond, then?" he asked.

"A single diamond with maybe a small one on either side of it," said Lisa.

"Yes, yes! I can picture it," said Harold. He turned the three-ring binder around to face him and flipped through the pages. He found the page he was looking for and turned the binder back to Lisa. Pointing at a setting, he asked, "Is this what you mean?"

Lisa looked where Harold was pointing, saw the setting, and closed her eyes for a moment. She opened her eyes and said, "It's perfect, Harold. I love it."

"You have excellent taste, young lady. Another in your place would have chosen to be gaudy," said Harold. He made note of the item number.

Lisa smiled, acknowledging Harold's words.

He went on. "That setting is made of the finest platinum from South Africa. It is designed to hold a round cut diamond up to three carats in size, with two baguette diamonds flanking it."

"I don't want to worry about losing it or having somebody steal it. Let's go with a two-carat diamond. I won't love Joe any less, wearing a two-carat stone instead of a three-carat one," said Lisa.

I gave her a big hug. I couldn't help myself. She was special.

"I love your choice, Lisa. I shall have your ring ready for you in one week's time, perhaps even sooner. I will call you, Joe, when it's ready."

Harold measured Lisa's ring finger for the correct size, and we left him to work his magic.

Back in my, or I should say our apartment, I scanned the online version of the Schenectady newspaper called the Daily Gazette for any news about the captain. I was surprised when I came across a small article hidden within its pages.

Local Man Meets with Foul Play, read the headline.

"A local man, a captain in the army, met with foul play while home on leave. Wishing to remain anonymous, the captain said he was ambushed on his way home Saturday evening and awoke to find a ribbon tied tightly around his male appendage. After repeated attempts at untying it, he drove to the hospital ER. The triage nurse questioned him and assigned his case as non-life threatening. With the emergency room crowded with both stabbing and shooting victims as well as traffic accident patients, the captain was left unattended for six hours. When the ribbon was finally removed, the injury was noted to be serious. The doctor stated that he could possibly lose a portion of his appendage."

I showed the article to Lisa. When she read it, she said that she never intended anything like that to happen. After a pause, she added, "But it looks like he got what he deserved." I was relieved by her comment. The last thing she needed was to blame herself.

Twenty-Five

FOUR DAYS LATER Harold called me to say that Lisa's ring was ready. We drove together to the store and found Harold waiting for us, a velvet pad resting on his display counter. Seeing us come in, he retrieved a small velvet-covered box from behind the counter and set it on the pad. "Welcome back, Lisa and Joe. I hope you like it."

I rushed to the counter and picked up the box before Lisa could get to it. Holding it above her line of sight, I opened it and peered in at the ring. To my eyes it was exactly what she wanted. I lifted it from the box and knelt before her. "Will you marry me, Lisa?" I asked her, my eyes holding hers.

"Um, let me think about that. Okay, I've thought about it. Yes! Yes!" she said, her emotion capturing both Harold and me.

I grasped her left hand and slipped the ring on her finger. As I stood up, she turned her hand to see the finished ring for the first time. The central round diamond caught the light, sending dazzling rays that reflected in her eyes. "It's perfect, Joe. Like you," she said as she moved her hand about to examine the ring from every angle.

"No, Lisa. It's perfect, like you," I said.

Lisa rushed to me, her arms encircling my neck, her lips pressed to mine. When at last she drew back, Harold was quick to remark. "This is the first time I've witnessed a marriage proposal in my humble store. Congratulations, you two. You make a perfect couple," he said with sincerity.

"And you, Harold. You made a perfect engagement ring," said Lisa.

While she feasted her eyes on her engagement ring, Harold approached me and whispered, "The diamonds are flawless. You might want to insure the ring. For fifty thousand dollars."

I stared at him, absorbing what he'd said, my eyebrows lifting in surprise.

"You heard me right, Joe," was all he said.

I knew that if I told Lisa the value of the ring, she would be afraid to wear it. It would be a secret shared with Harold.

We stopped by Lisa's parent's home to show off her ring and ask how the wedding plans were coming along. Eleanor held Lisa's hand and had a long, searching look at her ring before saying, "It's you, Lisa." Fine praise coming from her mother. Lisa rewarded her with a big hug.

The conversation turned to wedding plans. Eleanor smiled and said she was making good progress. "If all goes well, we can set a date in October, sometime before Halloween. How does that sound?" she asked us.

"That's six weeks away, Mom. Do you think you could cut it down a little?" said Lisa.

"I'm doing the best I can, dear. You don't want a botched-up wedding with something important forgotten or left out now, do you?" Eleanor knew how to employ the guilt trip thing. I stayed out of it.

"No, of course not, Mom. You know I'm available to help you. You don't have to try and do everything by yourself. Delegate. Isn't that what you've always taught me to do?" Lisa had a few tricks up her sleeve, too.

"I'd be happy to have your help, Lisa. I don't want to take you away from your upholstery work. It wouldn't be fair to your customers," said Eleanor.

Kaboom. More guilt trips.

"I can rearrange my work schedule and have a couple hours every day to help you with the planning, Mom. My customers will understand," said Lisa.

Stalemate.

"All right, Lisa. What two hours of the day are good for you?" asked Eleanor.

Concession.

"You tell me, Mom, and I'll adjust my work schedule accordingly," said Lisa.

"Mornings work best for me, dear. Can you do eight to ten?" asked Eleanor.

"I'll be here tomorrow morning at eight, Mom."

Game, set, match.

Conversation turned to the usual small talk amongst family members.

Two weeks passed and Lisa managed to shorten the date for our wedding to October fifth. A victory of sorts. I was left with the happy chore of deciding where we'd go on our honeymoon. Between us we narrowed the choice down to Hawaii or Japan. Both of us wanted to search out the birthplaces of our mothers in Japan, but Hawaii won out. We agreed that the trip to Japan could wait until we had more time to devote to the search. Hawaii offered us the chance to kick back and relax, eat great food, snorkel off the shore, and share our intimacy, not necessarily in that order. I explored all the different travel sites, searching for the perfect retreat, and found a small hotel right on the beach of Maui. I scheduled a flight out on October Sixth I didn't think Lisa would want to consummate our marriage in a plane.

I continued my casual reading of the Daily Gazette and was shocked at an obituary I found.

We note the passing of Captain George Lawrence Wittingly, US Army. Born February 20, 1972. Wittingly grew up in Schenectady. He entered the army in 1991 at the age of nineteen, and quickly rose through the ranks, becoming a captain while serving his country in Iraq. Home on leave with his parents, he was driving south on Interstate 890 when his vehicle left the roadway and struck an underpass abutment. Captain Wittingly was declared dead at the scene. He was the only occupant of the vehicle. He is survived by his parents, Barton and Olivia Wittingly of Schenectady. Funeral arrangements are pending.

I'll be damned! He took his own life.

I sat there, weighing whether to show it to Lisa. Would she blame herself for his death? I decided to hold off showing her the obituary until I had a sense of how she'd react to it.

My thoughts turned to finding our next rescue person. With Lisa doing great and Rachel on the brink of relocating to Topeka, we needed to find a third deserving person. With four weeks to go before our wedding, we had time to make a start at rescuing someone.

I shared my thoughts with Lisa when she came home from work.

"You're right, Joe. The sooner we find the next unfortunate, the sooner we can begin to help," she was quick to say.

"Can we go for a search on Saturday? I know it's only two days away," I said.

"Yes. When I get done at Mom's at ten, I'll come home and we can head right out," she said in a rush.

"That's solved. Hey, I have a question. How would you feel if you found out that Captain Wittingly died?" I asked her.

Lisa examined my face for a clue as to why I asked such a pointed question. I could see the wheels turning. At length she said, "I'd say, good riddance. He's raped his last female victim. Why do you ask?"

Her response seemed appropriate, genuine. I led her to my laptop and brought up the obituary. She sat down in the chair and read it. When she finished, she turned to me and said, "It sounds like the asshole committed suicide. I say, good riddance. The world is a better place without him."

I believed her. She showed no signs of remorse.

Twenty-Six

SATURDAY CAME, AND Lisa returned home from her mother's planning session at ten-thirty. We climbed in the car and headed for the parks of Phoenix to search for our next rescue. I shared the experiences I had from my search for Rachel so Lisa would have an inkling of what we were up against. She nodded, understanding and said, "Nothing that's worth doing is ever easy."

I was pleased to see that she was fully prepared to share in the search for our next rescue.

We'd earmarked five parks to search. They were scattered through Phoenix and offered a cross section of the city where the unfortunates of the city could find shelter, maybe find a moment of peace. I pulled over and parked outside the first park on our list, and Lisa and I climbed out. We strolled into the park hand in hand, not wanting to pose a threat to anyone watching us. We'd decided to concentrate our search on recumbents. If someone was sitting, either on a bench or on the ground, we figured that they were awake, alert and needed no help.

We found two clusters of benches in the park. The first cluster had two reclined figures. We approached the first of them and Lisa took the lead, asking if everything was right with him. Or her. Filthy, bulky clothing hid the person's sexual identity.

No response.

Lisa asked again, her voice forceful now.

"Fuck off. This is my bench!" came a mumbled reply.

We didn't need to be told twice. We moved on.

The second occupied bench was my turn. "Hey, there. Is there anything I can do for you?" I asked the huddled body.

A head raised up, turned my way. "I'll give you a blow job for a fix," a male voice said.

Message received, loud and clear.

We moved on to the second cluster of benches where three bodies lay stretched out. Lisa's turn. She took my approach.

"Hey, there. Is there anything we can do to help you?" Smart. She wasn't offering something by herself. We were together.

No response.

While Lisa spoke, I glanced around. Under and beside the bench I saw several discarded hypodermic syringes. Druggie. I pointed them out to Lisa. She nodded her head. We moved on to huddled mass number four.

My turn. "Hey, there. Is there anything we can do to help you?"

A dirty male head lifted, turned a bleary eye towards us. "You from mental health?" he asked, fear in his voice.

"No. We're a couple who'd like to offer you help," I said.

"I'm not taking any more of those pills! I'm getting along just fine with those voices in my head, thank you very much," he said.

Mental patient, off his meds. Strike four. On to the next huddled mass. Lisa's turn.

A smaller huddled mass tightly collected. Lisa asked our well-rehearsed question. At first there was no response. Lisa was about to ask again in a more forceful voice when the mass moved, rolled on its side to face us. The face belonged to a young, terrified girl, if her expression said anything. She looked at Lisa and then at me. "Did they send you to get me?" she asked, panic filling her voice.

"Nobody sent us. We're two people offering you our help," said Lisa as her eyes took in the frightened girl.

"There's nothing you can do. They own me," she said, conviction in her words.

"Who owns you?" asked Lisa, her voice soft, non-threatening.

"The people who got me across the border," said the young girl.

"Where are you from?" Lisa asked her.

"El Salvador. My parents lived in the capital, San Salvador," she said.

"You speak very good English. I thought El Salvador was Spanish-speaking," said Lisa.

"It is. My parents sent me to a private school where I was taught English," she said.

"Where are your parents?" Lisa probed.

"Somewhere in the United States," she said.

"You don't know where?"

"I had their address and was going to join them after I crossed the border with a coyote, but before that happened, I was robbed."

"Who robbed you?" asked Lisa.

"A stranger who forced himself on me and took everything I had, including the paper with my parents' address on it," she said, her voice matter of fact.

"Oh, my God! Where did that happen?"

"In Mexico somewhere. I was traveling with a group of eight other El Salvadoreans. We were being led by a Mexican coyote," she said.

"So, your parents left you alone in San Salvador and made the journey to the United States without you?" asked Lisa.

"Yes. They told me the journey was dangerous and they wanted to go ahead of me. When they were safely here, they sent word to me. I had a large sum of American dollars to pay the coyote, and I had the paper with my parents' new address on it. The stranger raped me and took it all," said the girl.

"What happened when you reached the border?" asked Lisa.

"When the coyote found out that I had no money, he said that he owned me. He placed me in the hands of some bad people here in Phoenix who make me have sex as payment for what I owe them."

"What's your name?"

"Gina."

"How old are you?"

"Thirteen."

"Why don't you leave the bad people? They let you come here to the park without them," said Lisa.

"They give me drugs when I need them. I resisted at first, but now I need the drugs. I think I would die if I stopped taking them. The drugs help me forget the bad things men make me do. For a while," she said.

Listening, I couldn't help thinking how calm and flat she sounded. She was a child, forced into being a sex slave, and she was controlled by men whose only interest was seeing how much they could charge other men for the privilege of having their way with her. Were they keeping a tally of the tricks she performed, and when she'd done enough to pay off the coyote, they'd cut her loose? Do pigs fly? Is the pope Jewish? I figured that they'd keep her captive and performing until she lost her girlish charm, and then toss her out in the gutter, an addict without access to the drugs her body cries out for.

I turned to Lisa, and we made eye contact. She slowly nodded her head at me. We had found our next rescue.

Little did we know what was in store for the two of us.

But that's another story.

Author's Note

The idea for Rescue Man came from musings about the marriages of American GIs and Japanese women in the years following World War Two. The Japanese from Hokkaido, the largest of their islands, are larger, taller than the Japanese of the southern islands, and it seemed fitting to pass those genes on to Tojo. It helps to bolster his image as a man to be reckoned with, too. I'm already working on the second novel in the series so you can continue to enjoy the adventures of Joe and Lisa.

Acknowledgements

I wish to thank my wife Janet for getting me back on track after my derailments, and for offering me her strong words of encouragement.

I also wish to thank Teddi Black for her wonderful cover design and Megan McCullough for her insightful interior formatting work, all of which has elevated my novel to a position well above the competition.

About the Author

After his wild ride through life, going to places and experiencing things that many dream of doing, Charles M. DuPuy now spends much of his time at his keyboard, creating stories he hopes are pleasing to his readers and drawing on a lifetime of memories that add humor, romance, suspense, adventure and realism to his words.

He shares his home in Arizona with his beloved wife, Janet, an aging and devoted Westie named Jack, and two rescue cats, one well-adjusted and the other neurotic.